SHATTER

nikki trionfo

SWEETWATER
BOOKS

An Imprint of Cedar Fort, Inc.
Springville, Utah

This is a work of fiction. The characters, names, incidents, places, and dialogue are products of the author's imagination and are not to be construed as real. The opinions and views expressed herein belong solely to the author and do not necessarily represent the opinions or views of Cedar Fort, Inc. Permission for the use of sources, graphics, and photos is also solely the responsibility of the author.

ISBN 13: 978-1-4621-2013-0

Published by Sweetwater Books, an imprint of Cedar Fort, Inc.
2373 W. 700 S., Springville, UT 84663
Distributed by Cedar Fort, Inc., www.cedarfort.com

LIBRARY OF CONGRESS CATALOGING-IN-PUBLICATION DATA

Names: Trionfo, Nikki– author.
Title: Shatter / Nikki Trionfo.
Description: Springville, Utah : Sweet Water Books, an imprint of Cedar Fort, Inc., [2017]
Identifiers: LCCN 2017006044 (print)
    ISBN 9781462120130 (pbk : alk. paper)
Subjects: LCSH: Mystery and detective stories; murder--fiction; sisters--fiction; conspiracies--
    fiction; high schools--fiction | LCGFT: schools--fiction
Classification: PZ7.1.T754 Sh 2017 (print) | fic--dc23
LC record available at https://lccn.loc.gov/2017006044

Cover design by Priscilla Chaves
Cover design © 2017 by Cedar Fort, Inc.
Edited and typeset by Hali Bird, Casey Nealon, and Jessica Romrell

Printed in the United States of America

10 9 8 7 6 5 4 3 2 1

Printed on acid-free paper

Dedicated to Mike, Janice,
and the not-so-little ones.

"Straddling the line between a coming of age heartbreak and a thriller murder mystery—Trionfo crafts a stunning debut that'll keep you turning pages 'til the end."

—Jolene Perry, author of *All the Forever Things*, AW Teen

"Is her sister's violent death an accident or murder? Salem's hunt for the killer thrusts her into a community endangered by gangs, a high school tainted by betrayals, and finally to a mock trial and the bittersweet truth. Trionfo dazzles the reader with pitch-perfect characterization and a gripping portrayal of impending doom."

—Kathleen Dougherty, author of *Moth to the Flame*, Penguin Books.

"*Shatter* is a riveting debut novel that takes the reader on a roller coaster ride of danger and intrigue as a young woman tries to learn who killed her sister. An absolutely terrific read."

—Kathi Oram Peterson, author of *Breach of Trust*, Covenant Books.

"A tense, multi-layered mystery that kept me reading late into the night."

—E. B. Wheeler, award-winning author of *The Haunting of Springett Hall* and *Born to Treason*

CHAPTER ONE

Day One. A Day like No Other. Ever.

Kiss a guy?

I'd had sushi once, which felt like eating a pair of lips. I assumed kissing would be similar, only without the ginger and wasabi sauce.

Did I want to kiss a guy? Ginger and wasabi sauce were the only good parts of sushi.

Still, I didn't interrupt my sister when she told me I needed to talk to more guys so I could eventually kiss one of them. Instead, I pressed the cell phone to my ear so I could hear better. Nearby, teammates jogged the final yards of the four-mile cross-country summer conditioning my coach insisted on, despite the rumbles of a rare thunderstorm.

"Salem, you cannot get rid of those virgin lips if you never talk," she continued, probably alone in the kitchen, winding her hair on her finger. Dad had decided we were old enough at sixteen and seventeen to stay home while he drove to Reno for business.

"Yes, I can," I said.

I was joking. When Carrie told me how to live my life, I listened, even though she was only a year older than me. Mom left when I was nine and Carrie became my advisor. She got me entrance to fundraisers sponsored by rock stars, preached against the villainy of littering, and convinced me with a triple dare to run around the barn in just our bras because it never occurred to us that there could be people in the orchard.

Dangerous people.

"That will be amusing," she said drily. "You're going to grab a guy and plant one on him? Have you picked your f—?"

Those were the last words I ever heard my sister say.

PRESENT DAY

"Conspiracy theories!" Mr. White announces after the opening bell rings on the first day of my junior year of high school. "Much as we might mock them, psychologically, we need them."

I don't look up from the *XII* tagged onto the corner of my desk as my Verona High political science teacher speaks. The lettering is carved into the fake wood veneer, probably with a knife. Black ink has been driven deep into the cutting, making the Roman numeral twelve look like a scar. I've seen graffiti like this a thousand times and somehow I've never really registered it before.

Not like now.

My gaze jumps away from it and back. What *is* a gang symbol exactly? A warning? A calling card announcing brutality already committed? I hate how I'm afraid of it now. A two-inch symbol etched with a knife, and I'm afraid of it.

It's safe to say that none of the Advanced Placement students here defaced the desk. Not these juniors and seniors gearing up for what Carrie called the hardest AP class at Verona High. Every year, it includes a mock trial competition that makes up half the grade.

"The idea that Kennedy, JFK, President of the United States, could be killed on his own soil seemed preposterous. It had to be . . . a con-*spir*-acy." Mr. White has a high-pitched voice.

I keep my head down, paying more attention to my thoughts than my environment. It's my twelfth day without Carrie. I have one goal—to not cry in public. I dodged Carrie's two best friends when they tried to hug me a few minutes ago. Now they're sitting in the front row and sending me questioning glances. My own closest friends are on the cross-country team, and none of them are in this class of mostly seniors. With one of the highest grades last year, Carrie and her partner were supposed to be the teacher's assistants this year.

I can't help but glance at one of the chairs facing the class next to the teacher's desk. Empty.

Moisture invades my nasal passages and eyes. I run my finger along the black lines on the desk. I push harder and harder until my skin is red and sore. The graffiti seems so anonymous and detached, like it etched itself. Power.

Violence. Death. These gangs leave their mark like it's no more than a brand logo on Abercrombie and Fitch jeans.

"Nothing," Mr. White says. "*Nothing* is more impossible to accept than random events with large consequences. So, people talk. Witnesses come forward. And soon . . . John F. Kennedy wasn't shot by a lone gunman. No! The mobs are involved, the USSR deeply implicated, a *conspiracy* is born and *that*—" Mr. White slaps something against the chalkboard, probably a ruler. I can't tell without looking up, which I don't. I wipe my nose with the base of my thumb. I keep my eyes wide, so the tears won't pool.

"*That* is what we are putting on trial. A notion. Yes, a conspiracy. Is it true, beyond a reasonable doubt? Or will it be found guilty, false, and fallacious?"

A fly lands on my elbow. A fat, lazy summer fly escaping the oppressive California heat outside. I watch it crawl, partially blocking my view of the lower half of the graffiti. The letters are harsh and thin. Nothing like the sprawling *XII* Carrie found all over her car that morning. Black spray paint, soft rounded edges over buckled metal. A tire iron had been involved, the police decided.

Do some things just happen? Or is there always a reason?

"*That will be amusing.*" Carrie's voice from twelve days ago plays in my head. Carrie did not say things. She announced them. After the police had come and gone, she called me to rehash the details of her car vandalism. *"You're going to grab a guy and plant one on him? So have you picked your f—?"*

Was she about to say fellow? Fall guy? First victim? I stay awake for hours at night wondering.

One tear falls.

Mr. White's oration continues to intrude on my thoughts.

"This year's trial is scheduled at the state courthouse in Sacramento," he announces. "You must dress like you're a lawyer or a witness from 1963. No exceptions. That means tweed jackets or beehive hair or whatever you come up with in your research, or you won't participate. And mark your calendars. The mock trial is in three weeks."

A girl next to me gasps. I sniff and try to focus on her. She's a senior and has lived only half a mile from me for the past few years ever since her mom married the mayor, who owns half of the growing acreage in Verona.

"But last year's team got four weeks," she says.

Mr. White zeroes in on her, approaching through the desks. "Name?"

"AddyDay Knockwurst."

His face breaks into a smile. "I know your stepfather. But I suppose most of us know Verona's mayor. We have less time to prepare this year because scheduling is tight at the courthouse. Addy, nice to meet you."

"It's not Addy. It's all one word. AddyDay."

Someone snickers. AddyDay doesn't seem to notice. She just smiles away, mounds of brown hair swaying around her face.

I hardly know AddyDay. I would venture that she doesn't think I'm part of her crowd. Carrie's Students for Strike club was good enough for her, however—she's a member. Over a hundred students are. Ever since Carrie was a kid, she had supported a string of causes. For six months in middle school, she ate only whole, raw foods. She learned to grind make-up out of pure minerals. But when she supported the Farm Workers Union's idea to go on strike, Dad got pissed. That was the ignition she needed to go all out.

Fundraisers, a Verona High rally emceed by the mayor of San Francisco, dozens of trips to crop fields to photograph violations of the Migrant and Seasonal Agricultural Worker Protection Act. The union wanted higher wages for the field workers, many of whom earned less than McDonald's employees. Their employers—people like Dad, who owns an orchard—said the market couldn't pay more or the fruit would be grown overseas. As the tensions increased between pickers and growers, so did the tension between Carrie and Dad. It had been getting out of hand. She and Dad would argue for hours about the amount of money he paid his peach pickers.

The more deeply Carrie got involved, the more extreme her views became. Slapping the hand that kept us down protected the weakest members of society, she'd say. She said the growers were getting violent and hiring thugs. She was a true believer.

I watched mostly from the sidelines, rooting for Carrie but always worried that her passion to fight back could get her in over her head.

AddyDay is still talking to Mr. White. "I'm cold. Will you always have the air conditioning on so high?"

"Yes, bring a sweater."

She pretends to shiver. "But I'm f-f-freezing," she complains.

F-f-freezing. The letter *f*. A voiceless consonant produced by blowing air past a constricted bottom lip.

Carrie's last sound.

I heard the house explode around her. Right before the line went dead, I heard it.

My memories of the past twelve days are like photographs—some sharply focused, some not. I remember coming home from cross-country conditioning and seeing the whirling lights of emergency vehicles in front of the soggy, burnt remains of the house and Carrie's car. It had been re-parked in the garage to protect it from further vandalism. I remember the police showing Dad and me pictures of Primeros gang members—men trapped in the bodies of teenagers dressed in blue—pictures of their green-clad enemies, the Últimos. Dad was as confused as me. Carrie hadn't been involved with any of them, we kept telling the police. Those guys in ropes of gold, in muscle shirts, in tattooed skin. Their faces didn't matter. I knew she hadn't been involved with any of them.

I really thought I knew it.

When Mr. White starts handing out a packet of information to each desk, my attention refocuses on the class.

"You'll work in partners, which I've assigned to you. All the partnerships are listed in this packet." As he goes around the room, the door slams shut like someone is arriving. Several students in the room turn to look at the new arrival and stay looking. Must be someone interesting. No one says hello, however. Strange.

When I get my packet, I scan for my name. An uneven number of people are in the class. I'm in a group of three. I don't recognize either of my partners' names.

"Let's get right to it," Mr. White says when he finishes. "Break into partnerships and start your first assignment."

A voice near the door calls out to the teacher, halting the sounds of shuffling class members.

"My name is not on that page. What should I do for a partner?" It must be the new arrival talking. He has a subtle, attractive accent.

Mr. White glances up and steps back slightly. "You're in the wrong class."

"I'm Cordero. I requested this class last year. They didn't give it to me. I spoke to the office. Now I am on the role."

The class is dead silent. Mr. White's lips tighten. He swallows. There's something dangerous about the new guy. The teacher leans over AddyDay's desk and spins her packet so he can read the list of partnerships. "Fine. We'll break up the threesome. You'll pair with . . . Salem Jefferson."

At the sound of my name, I turn to look at my new partner.

The guy near the door is tall. He has the kind of incredibly good looks that invite stares, but that's not the only reason he's getting them now. The cursive lettering of a tattoo rises from the opening of the guy's worn flannel shirt. Two gold chains hang from his brown neck. A guy accessorized in gang paraphernalia, not caked with it. His only completely visible marking is an upside down *V* inked onto his right cheekbone, black and distinct. The tattoo calls my attention for some reason, even though I'm sure I've never seen a symbol like that before. An upside down *V*. . . it seems so familiar.

His expressionless, dark eyes dart to meet my gaze from under a stiff, backward-facing ball cap. My classmates watch him stare at me.

"Salem Jefferson," he says slowly, putting a slight emphasis on my last name. He waits for my response.

I realize he knows exactly who Salem Jefferson is. Exactly who I am. I'm Carrie's sister.

Terrified, I whirl back around to face forward. Gang members targeted Carrie, made her frightened. Was he one of them? The skin between my shoulder blades tightens. Why were gang guys after Carrie? Does he really know Carrie, or am I crazy? How can I possibly think someone like him is hot? What is wrong with me?

The thought of Carrie is so vivid, I wish I could tell her to shut up. *". . . get out there more. Talk. Kiss a guy,"* she had said.

Stop *thinking*.

Mr. White leans closer to the packet on AddyDay's desk to re-read it. "Salem *Jefferson*?" Intrigued, he looks up, scanning the room.

Students whisper. I duck my head. Strands of blond hair hide me, but it doesn't help. I'm not Carrie—I'm not assertive. I wish I could be.

"You don't know who Salem is?" AddyDay asks Mr. White.

"She's Carrie's sister," another girl says.

Jeremy Novo is seated to my left. He rolls his eyes. He's been a jerk since first grade. "So what about Carrie? Hello, people. Cops unearthed a freaking corpse on Salem's property yesterday."

Mr. White smiles at me sympathetically. "Yes, Carrie's sister and Brian's daughter," he says, reminding me what a small town Verona really is. "Mm, tough stuff your family is dealing with. Well. Carrie was one of my favorite students. What a legacy to live up to, huh?"

Whispered conversations burst around me like scattered drops of rain.

"Legacy?" Jeremy Novo asks in a stage whisper. "You think he wants another murdered guy to show up in her orchard?"

"Shut up, Jeremy," AddyDay tells him.

The new guy strides confidently to the seat behind me.

Mr. White nods to him. "Well, Cordero, you and Salem get to work. Got to score well on these first assignments. Got to show you want to be here."

Mr. White probably only said that because Cordero has gang accessories that make him look different than the other AP students. Everyone in Verona acts tough about gangs, but most of us are afraid of them. I'm terrified. My memories swirl.

YESTERDAY

I was jogging far out in my family's orchard in the dead heat of the afternoon because physical punishment left no room for emotion.

"Stop! Miss, stop! This is a crime scene!" an officer called to me. Dad was with him. A Hispanic woman was at his side.

I slowed from my conditioning pace. The rows of trees around me had ended abruptly, opening to a wide vista. The bare field was full of trucks, workers, and piles of nitrogen fertilizer like it had been when I left to go on a run. Dad was in the process of planting new trees. With the peach strike going on, no farm laborers would have come to pick peaches for us, but the workers who planted trees were part of a whole different industry.

Unlike when I left to go on a run, the field now was also full of cameras and cop cars, as if something were terribly wrong. Like Carrie was going to die all over again.

"Dad?" I looked to him, his light hair and round glasses.

He turned from the officer he'd been speaking with and pulled me into a hug. "It's okay, Salem."

"What happened? Are you hurt?" I asked.

"It's okay," Dad repeated. He was an inventor. Not the crackpot kind; the double PhD kind who also owned an orchard and worked at a university. All the growers had day-jobs. Growers on a small-time orchard can't support themselves on ranching alone.

"The workers found a body on our property," he explained. He ended our hug. Ever since Carrie died, he'd been more aloof than usual. "It's no one we know."

"No, no, no, no," the Hispanic woman agreed. I found out later she was a journalist for one of the newspapers. "No one you know."

She was short with crisp, black hair. She put her hand on my arm and inadvertently brushed the inside of Dad's wrist. Pausing, she tried on his touch like it was a dress in a shop window. She glanced at him and moved her hand away, though he didn't appear to notice. I wondered how Dad knew her.

A body? Like a *dead* body?

"The police released a preliminary statement," the journalist lady continued. "The corpse is in the morgue now, already identified. Hispanic, male. Maybe one of the laborers working here last spring. Or a gang member killed by a rival."

"The crew found some gang symbols around the site," Dad explained.

"Carrie's car was tagged by gangs." I glance again at the crew of workers. The union and growers and peach strike got all the press, but gangs sure seemed to be up to all kind of things around here lately.

The officer who had called to me when I arrived in the field stepped closer to me. He had red hair and a boyish face. "Salem, I have a few questions about Carrie and her car, actually. Not now. Tomorrow. Could you answer some questions?"

I looked at him. He was the same officer who had investigated Carrie's death. He wore a nametag. J. B. Haynes.

The encouragement of his phrasing didn't mask the scrutiny he was giving me.

"After Carrie died, you mentioned she'd had a secret," Officer Haynes continued. "Could it have been tied to a crime she may have had information about? A murder?"

PRESENT DAY

Someone trips on the cord of a portable fan in the front of the classroom and it face-plants into the carpet, pulling me from my thoughts. I don't know if minutes have passed or seconds. I only know reliving the scene from yesterday is awful.

Murder.

What does it mean to have information about a murder?

Mr. White heads back to the front of the room while students and their partners pull their desks together. Cordero and I are the only ones who don't. While the class digs into the assignment, Carrie's two best friends, Envy and Kimi, stand and speak with the teacher for a moment. They come over and kneel next to me.

"Girl, I'ma open Jeremy's backpack and dump it over his head if he talks to you again," Envy says, her lower lip trembling. Her pearl earrings dazzle against her dark skin.

Kimi shakes her head, her almond-shaped eyes red from crying. Her cheerleader-ponytail sways, black, shiny, and straight. She's a captain this year. "We tried to get Mr. White to let one of us work with Cordero instead of you. He won't let us."

"Oh . . . thanks . . ."

Kimi drops her voice. "I've never met him before, but that guy's hardcore. This morning I heard him straight up tell the vice principal there's nothing she can do about him being in a gang because it's not illegal. He said it's racist not to let bangers wear their numbers at school. He's a senior.

Transferred in from another school. I heard he got kicked out. Carrie would be furious at Mr. White for making you work with a guy like that."

How can I explain to them that Envy with her tears and Kimi rattling off Carrie's name is worse than anything Cordero could do to me now? My chest aches. I can't look up from the graffiti on the desk.

"I . . . please, I . . . I'll just work with him. It's . . . just a few weeks." My voice cracks, and I can't get to *Thank you*, and *I know you're hurting too*, and *Forgive me*.

Envy squeezes my hand. She exchanges a look with Kimi, who motions for her to leave. They return to their desks.

Leaving me alone with my sorrow.

I make my mind focus on the black lettering of Cordero's *V* tattoo, the one that seems so familiar to me. Other details won't come. I don't even know which gang he claims. The only things I know to look for are the Roman numerals and the colors. *XII* for the Primeros gang. *XI* for the Últimos. Blue. Green. Dumb as dead cats in a dryer, each of them. Violent as live ones in the same place.

Stealthily wiping away a tear, I make myself as small as possible in my chair, hyperaware of air movement at the curve of my shoulders. My lower back is tense. I focus so I won't cry.

How did Cordero know my name?

You can't be Carrie Jefferson's little sister without certain people knowing your name. Kids on the A-list like Envy and Kimi, for sure. A gang banger rockin' colors, though— why? I think of his baseball cap, a sissy hat that no athlete

14

on earth would use for sporting equipment. I can't remember what color it is. He's a gang member, but which color does he claim? Blue for *XII*, like the Primeros who targeted Carrie? All I can picture are his dark eyes blinking lazily, as if advertising his indifference to the world. All I can picture is a tire iron clenched in his fingers, his gold chains swinging as he windmills the weapon down onto the hood of Carrie's yellow VW bug. I see Carrie terrified.

I tell myself not to be fooled by his beautiful accent and physical confidence. Cordero might know exactly why my preppy sister was a beep on the radar of a hardcore gang. He might even have clues that suggest her death was more than an accident.

Yesterday, nobody let themselves think such wild thoughts. Yesterday, nobody said a word about how a corpse had shown up not a quarter mile from where Carrie got toasted to charcoal. Just what kind of coincidence was that?

It's like Mr. White said. Nothing is more impossible to accept than a random event with large consequences.

"Assignments are due tomorrow." With Mr. White's reminder comes an awareness of the classroom around me.

The bell rings.

In a swish of noise, I whirl to look behind me, determined to find out which gang he claims.

The cap on top of Cordero's tall frame has a stiff bill pointing just askew of straight backward.

Blue. Primero *XII* blue. So he *is* in the gang that targeted Carrie.

Salem Jefferson, he'd said earlier.

My scattered thoughts solidify into a question. A question I know I have to answer.

What if everything I've been told for twelve days about Carrie, everything I've been told about the day she died, everything I've been told about her supposedly accidental death in our supposedly empty orchard . . . was wrong?

CHAPTER TWO

Day One, Morning

Whats going on?" I begged Carrie. My track bag was open at my feet inside our bedroom. Carrie was supposed to take me to the summer conditioning cross-country practice. Dad had left for his business trip that morning.

Seated on my bed, Carrie stared in my direction as if she saw nothing at all. Brown hair fell in heavy curls past her shoulders, wispy at her temples. I didn't know what had come over her this summer. Nervous fidgeting and long, whispered conversations with her boyfriend over the phone—Carrie had been keeping something hush-hush for months.

I felt a chill. "Carrie?"

She startled and looked at me. "What?"

"Something's wrong," I said.

She walked to her closet. "You've been saying that all summer," she said in a harsh tone, maybe because she hated lying. She dealt in capital letter Truth. She stared at clothes hanging on the rod, but didn't rifle through any.

Leaving them, she came across the room to me.

"Salem, the Farm Workers Union is on strike. It's not like the other times. If they keep the media's sympathy, they're going to win. A full one dollar-an-hour increase in wages. Do you understand?"

"You're freaking me out." Before this summer, I'd never seen Carrie frightened before. I didn't even think she could *be* frightened.

She sat on the bed. "I'm going to talk to someone important today . . . about righting a terrible wrong." She looked like she might cry.

"Who? What terrible wrong?" I asked gently, sitting next to her.

She shook her head.

I put my hand on her arm. "Do you mean when the growers hired someone to beat up those union guys?"

The incident was months ago, but Carrie still mentioned it often. Three union members were sent to the hospital with knife wounds after carrying a pro-strike sign in a vegetable field. I wondered if Carrie would break the law to fight back. A plan like that could be why she was so worried. For her sake, I should tell Dad on her. For her sake, I could never tell Dad on her. Carrie had to trust me. I needed her. She *knew* I needed her.

I bit my lip. "Are you planning to do something that's . . . I don't know . . . illegal? I won't tell Dad. I promise."

"Hurting people is wrong, but not everybody believes that," she whispered. She was always saying stuff like that.

"I told you I wouldn't tell Dad," I begged. "Why does everything have to be secret?"

"Salem, just stop asking me questions. Please?" She stood and walked to the bedroom door, motioning for me to follow. "We need to get you to practice anyway."

Present Day

"Ever had a friend betray you? Happened to me once. A girl told everyone my secrets," Coach Johnny says.

I hear his question and reality rushes at me, replacing my memories. I'm not at home with Carrie. Home is uninhabitable, half-burned to the ground. Carrie is dead. Seventh period ended fifteen minutes ago, bringing the first day of classes to a close.

I'm standing in bright green shoes on Verona High's track alongside my closest cross-country friends and the rest of the team. The shoes are new. So are my shorts and shirt. After searching the smoke-blackened house for treasures like Carrie's nearly undamaged jewelry box, Dad and I shopped for essentials—clothes, a men's electric razor, office supplies—until literal exhaustion set in.

At practice, everyone has been really nice—offering to grab me a water bottle or politely smiling. The whole team is doing stuff like that, all without talking much to me, like maybe Envy and Kimi spoke personally to every student at Verona High with instructions that I be given space or else.

I want to show that I'm grateful, but I want more to disappear into my team, the way I used to.

My cross-country coach's white hair nearly glows, reflecting sunlight. In this type of weather, your mouth is dry one minute after you polish off a water bottle.

"That's what a six-mile run is for," he continues as we stretch. The green of Verona High's gym glares in the distance, and the campus looks like a heat-shimmer behind it. "You're about to get that pain out of your system. Time to shut that girl up for good, huh?"

I wince and turn away. Whatever—or *whoever*—killed Carrie obliterated her secret right along with her. What if it was just like Coach Johnny said? What if someone thought it was time to shut that girl up for good?

"Today, we're going to do a nice long run at a target heart rate of 140. Salem." Coach Johnny tosses me a wristwatch with a heart rate monitor on it.

I catch it in one hand. He's got a whole box of them at his feet.

"Veterans, help show the newbies how they work," he instructs, waving me toward two sets of pigtails.

I walk over to the girls, showing them the watch. "See, you just, um, program in a target rate of 140."

"Oh, I get it," one of the girls says. She pushes the buttons and then turns to the other. "You want to hit the mall after practice?"

The second girl shakes her head. "You know I have to pick peaches until dark."

"Why don't your parents just hire workers who are willing to break the strike?"

"We can't find any."

The girls glance at me out of the corners of their eyes. They seem cool. I could talk to them if I were sure they wouldn't bring up the issue of the corpse found in our orchard. Or how the peach strike is all because of Carrie and her Students for Strike club.

Carrie put together a fundraiser with the Portland rock band *Pawnbrokers* that raised thirty thousand dollars for the Farm Workers Union. She was quoted in local newspapers saying that peach pickers needed higher wages. As the higher wages mantra went viral, a union worker named Juan Herrera went missing. Some say he returned to his native Mexico. Some say he was murdered. The union blamed his disappearance on the growers, but the growers said the union accused them with no evidence. Within a month, the union voted to go on strike.

Today, the earliest crops are already rotten and gone. California peaches start ripening in late June. It's still mid-August—Verona High is on a semester system—but every day, more of the two hundred million dollar crop falls to the ground and decays.

Coach Johnny comes back from the other group. "Salem, I've got a challenge for you."

A guy stands next to Coach Johnny. Black hair swept sideways over deep blue eyes. A smirky mouth. He has the olive skin and high cheekbones of an Eastern European.

Slate Panakhov.

At the sight of him, a memory of Carrie's voice plays inside my head. *"Slate Panakhov, that's who. We're going out Friday night, can you believe it?"*

I don't remember when the conversation took place exactly. Sometime last year when they started dating, I guess. By summer, I'm pretty sure they shared Carrie's secret—a weight they frowned over and wouldn't tell.

"Salem." Slate runs his hand over his bangs to keep them back. He watches me, like maybe he'll see some sign that I'm okay.

"Hi," I say, fidgeting.

So far I haven't been able to talk about Carrie without crying, so I say nothing at all to the people who knew her. Slate doesn't like that, I know it.

"You two are going to do a stress test to find your max heart rate," Coach Johnny says to Slate and me. "You're my best athletes, so your max could be higher than average."

Slate catches my eye and gives me a cautious smile. His skin is darker than mine, but it looks medium-toned compared to his black hair and the traces of dense stubble that would only need a few days to become a full beard.

I step back, and my running shoes catch on each other. I feel guilty because I need to beat that smile off his face. Why did she tell him her secret when she wouldn't tell me?

"Okay, get ready," Coach says.

I head to my track bag while Slate talks to a few girls. Does he think about Carrie when those girls throw their hair over their shoulders and meet his gaze?

Slate hadn't been Carrie's first kiss. He'd been her first love.

I'm angry and emotional and feel stupid for feeling anything at all. I grab a water bottle. Spilled liquid traces down my neck as I gulp. Heat like this can never be beaten.

I throw the bottle into my bag and head for the track.

Our teammates cheer as we line up, separated by six empty lanes. Slate will have to travel considerably more distance than me, being so far from the center lane. He runs cross-country to stay in shape, but he's a sprinter at heart—Verona High's best. No way can I stay with him. He bounces on his toes to get his blood pumping.

I lean over my watch and set it to a rate of 180. Carrie's secret is gone now.

Or is it?

CHAPTER THREE

DAY ONE, MORNING

My memories of the day Carrie died center on the thunderstorm. I was just finishing a four-mile run, watching Slate Panakhov stretch his quad while clouds churned above him. Coach planned to have us record our goals for the season and then sprint five sets of one hundred meters as a final hurrah. That's when Carrie called and told me a gang had spray painted her car after she got back from dropping me off.

"What?" I asked her. "A *gang*?"

"Everything is under control." She didn't sound in control. She sounded terrified and breathless. "Hold on, the police are here."

The call ended.

Frantic, I dialed Dad, but didn't leave a voicemail. He was on his way to Reno for work and there's no cell coverage during much of the drive. Coach started us on our goals, which included me taking first in every meet. As soon as we finished, I called Carrie back.

"Carrie?"

"The officers just left. I'm fine," she said, still sounding otherwise.

"Did you call Dad?" I asked. "What's going on?"

"I texted Slate."

I looked for Slate. His friends were hanging out near the long-jump pit. He was nearby, gazing unsmiling at the horizon. His black hair looked darker in the shadow of the gathering clouds. I wondered what Carrie had told him.

"I don't know. They went after my car," Carrie continued, her statements scattered.

On Carrie's end of the phone line, a door shut with a whoosh. I could hear her sniffing.

"That smell is getting worse," she said under her breath.

"The manure?" I asked. All the growers fertilize with manure.

"No, I'm in the kitchen. I have to talk to the police again. I have to. I have to tell them. Only . . . I just don't know if I can."

"Are you okay? Carrie?"

"Salem?" she asked, as if confused I was still on the line. It's like she was in shock or something.

"Carrie, I'm skipping the sprints and coming home. I'll hitch a ride with someone right now."

"No."

"Yes. I can be home in ten minutes."

She paused. I could hear her breathing, like collecting herself. "Whatever. There you go again. Always trying to prove you're the strong one."

"You're such a liar," I said, smiling despite my worry. Carrie was the strong one. But I loved her for letting me see moments when she wasn't so confident. When she wasn't announcing her thoughts like they were speeches for posterity.

Carrie's voice became more coherent. "You *are* strong. But you need to get out there more. Talk. Kiss a guy. Salem, you cannot get rid of those virgin lips if you never talk." This was one of her favorite subjects.

I didn't see Carrie as we spoke. I didn't smell the odor she'd noticed—the natural gas.

Instead, I paced under the darkening clouds. Carrie was scared, but she was okay. And if Carrie was okay, everything was okay. I actually had that exact thought.

"Yes, I can," I said.

"That'll be amusing," she deadpanned. "You're going to grab a guy and plant one on him?"

The memory rolls on with me powerless. I can't yell for her to understand the danger she's in. I can't shake her or drag her from her death. I can only imagine. Does she turn on the coffee pot? The hallway light? Does she pause for a moment to joke with me, her fingers on the switch that will kill her?

Or maybe I've pictured the scene wrong from the beginning.

Maybe the gas never leaked by accident. Maybe the same person who cut the line also threw a switch outside.

"So," she asked. "Have you picked your f—?"

I never saw the flash that ignited the natural gas, killing her and taking away everything that mattered.

I had suspected the wrong thing. I didn't know Carrie was in danger—not *that* kind of danger. It was all there, though, right in front of me. She wasn't fearful about a plan she was hatching to attack the growers. She had a secret that someone didn't want her to spill—a secret she didn't tell me in order to protect me. All summer she had that secret. I should have run to Dad, to the police, to her union friends, and demanded that they help her.

Instead, I did nothing.

. . .

The memories of Carrie fade, but not the anguish.

"What are you stalling for?" Slate calls across the lanes of track separating us. His good-natured words carry a trace of an accent, just enough to be intriguing. "Trying to psych me out?"

At his questions, I'm back in the stifling summer air. My teammates have lined up along the edge of the track to get better views.

Without answering, I plant my foot at the starting line.

"Ready?" Coach Johnny asks.

"Yup," I say.

I tense for the start of the race. I think about it—what Slate knows of Carrie's secret. Nothing, maybe. Everything. More than me.

I want to beat him for knowing more than me.

"Set?" Coach Johnny raises his hand. "Go!"

He brings his hand down.

I sprint into the first curve, making sure Slate stays behind me.

I settle in, kicking up dry dust on the well-trod track. Slate nods as he comes level with me during the straight-away. He doesn't push me to go faster, comfortable with his pace. I don't dare accelerate to make him work. I look at my watch. I'm winded at a heart rate of 106.

"I'm at 84," he calls. "I'm going to maintain for this stretch and see how much it climbs."

I nod. Sweat pours down my face. We hit the second curve and Slate stays with me, running faster since his distance is greater than mine. My heart pounds and my lungs burn.

"138," I call.

"110," he answers.

We get to the straightaway and he goes all out. Or maybe it's not all out for him, but it is for me. I won't let him take the lead, though I'll hit a wall soon.

At the end of the first lap we pass our teammates in a blur of faces. They're shouting.

"Get him, Salem!" Coach Johnny calls.

I explode into the curve of lap two, staying on my toes. I'll mess up the stress test I'm supposed to be doing. I don't care. Slate pulls ahead of me. Halfway down the next straightaway, my monitor beeps. My heart rate has climbed to 180 too early.

This is it. My max. I'm going to die right here on the track and Slate's keeping a reserve. His feet don't touch the ground for yards at a time. We enter the final curve and I gain on him, going so much less distance than him. We come out of the curve at the same time.

The final straightaway. My vision tunnels. Dust, sunlight, track, blue sky.

I lift my knees. I drive my feet into the dirt. A quarter of the way to the finish, he's three feet ahead of me. Halfway there, he's five feet ahead.

Three-quarters of the way there, his strides slow. I can't breathe. I can't control my thoughts. Why is he slowing? What did Officer Haynes mean yesterday that Carrie may have had information about a murder?

I shoot past the finish line, stumbling. I'm surrounded by teammates who cheer for me, telling me I've won.

"Way to go, Salem!" Coach Johnny yells. "Everyone, take a practice lap and then we'll head off-campus."

I catch my breath, trembling all over. Officer Haynes asked yesterday if Carrie had information about a murder. Did she? The students clear out, heading around the track. I try to follow.

Slate comes up beside me, out of breath. "I think . . . *that* . . . was our practice lap."

I lean over, chest heaving. I straighten to look at him, his black hair and his olive skin, touched red at his cheeks.

"You let me win," I accuse. My throat is raw from sucking in oxygen.

He shakes his head. "You were . . . just faster, yeah?"

"It's cheating." I hold my side, too angry to make sense. "Letting someone win."

He holds my gaze until I look away, flushing.

"Well, just . . . please just don't do it again," I demand finally.

A smile slowly spreads across his face. "Do what?"

I step away, too embarrassed to laugh with him. I want to ask what he knows about Carrie's secret, but can't think how to start the subject. *Do you think Carrie was murdered?* seems a little blunt.

"Hey, Salem? Let's call that a day," Coach Johnny yells to me.

Confused, I turn, catching the glare of sunlight off silver buttons—the snap-kind that ornament the pockets of a police officer's uniform. Officer Haynes stands near the bleachers with Coach Johnny and Dad, who motions for me to come.

I gasp, startled into moving forward. I need my bag, though. I hesitate, muscles shaking.

"You okay?" Slate asks in a serious tone. He looks at the policeman. "That's Officer Haynes, isn't it?"

I nod. "He has questions about Carrie."

Slate's expression shifts, once, twice. It can't settle. Horror, fear, guilt, shock. It cycles through them all. Our teammates finish their lap, arriving in a surge around us.

Sorrow. His face settles on sorrow.

Nodding good-bye, I grab my bag and run on exhausted legs toward Dad.

CHAPTER FOUR

A Year Prior

When authority figures betray good morals, we have no choice but to strip them of their powers," Carrie declared.

We were at a Students for Strike club activity. Somehow Carrie had convinced me and forty other Verona High students to pay twenty dollars each to bus up to wine country and clip grapes. You know, get the real experience of field labor.

Sunrays pounded into my hair and made my eyes squint as we walked along a country road. It was the summer before my sophomore year. In every direction, enormous mounds of purple grapes cascaded over full, dark leaves that came up to shoulder height.

"Carrie, quit lecturing," I whined.

"That wasn't my lecture voice." Carrie swiped her face to keep her curls out of her mouth.

"We've walked too far," I said. "This is the neighbor's field."

Carrie and I were trying to locate the remaining club members so we could go home early because we'd run out of water. The grower said he hadn't expected so many students.

"This is why safety laws need to be enforced," Carrie repeated for the tenth time. "I don't care if I'm *lecturing* again. No water?"

"Let's go back," I said, just as I spotted a girl and two other teens up the road and a few yards into the grape rows. "Wait, is that Envy?"

"Where? Oh, I think she's yelling at us."

Envy motioned for us to hurry, shouting, ". . . a girl all by herself."

"What?" Carrie yelled back.

"A kid! Alone in the orchard!" Envy shouted.

"*What?*" Carrie exchanged glances with me. "Salem, make sure the kid's okay," she instructed as I passed her.

We both knew I would get there first. I was faster.

I arrived to find Envy, Kimi, and a guy I didn't know all smiling at a Hispanic girl. She had braids and a small crate of grapes attached to her front via wide straps that went over her shoulders. The teens wore similar crates.

"She doesn't speak English," Envy told me.

"Look." Kimi pointed down the row.

A tiny Hispanic lady walked toward us with her own crate secured in front of her waist. She was barely taller than the grape leaves.

"*Mi mamá*," the girl said proudly.

Carrie arrived beside me, out of breath.

"The girl's okay," I said, dutifully reporting my now unnecessary info.

The girl spoke in Spanish, pointing at a pair of shears she held. I recognized one of the words.

"She's working," I translated. "But not for the grower we worked for."

"A five-year-old working in these conditions?" Carrie straightened her shoulders, looking around as well. The forecast had called for 103-degree weather. "Where are the shade pavilions? The water?"

Carrie's posture meant we were about to be hit with the full measure of her lecturing capabilities. I didn't care right then, but where *was* the shade and water? Didn't anyone here speak Spanish? Half the Students for Strike club was Hispanic.

I glanced at the dark-haired guy next to Envy with his new-in-town charm. More Eastern European than Hispanic, though.

The girl's mother began beckoning frantically.

"*Adiós.*" The girl's hat bounced on her back as she ran. When she reached the mother, both of them ran away from us. Literally ran.

"They're afraid," the new guy said with a slight accent. He nodded.

I looked behind me. A policewoman in a wide hat had pulled off the road to the shoulder. She was getting out of her car.

"Do you have permission to be here?" she called, walking toward us.

"Say nothing. They're probably illegal," Carrie cautioned us in a low voice.

"That's why there was no water," I said.

Undocumented workers got the worst treatment—everyone knew that. The grower who owned this property would have to pay a fine if he was caught having hired the woman, but her situation was much worse. Deportation was on the line for her. That was why some growers cheated undocumented workers out of their wages—because the workers couldn't go to the police.

Envy and Kimi looked at each other with wide, serious eyes. The new guy nodded.

If we moved, the policewoman would see the fleeing figures. The rows were dead straight. The Hispanic lady hadn't ditched her crate of grapes, which meant she probably desperately needed the cash they'd bring.

"I asked if you had permission to be in this vineyard," the cop said, advancing into our row.

"Be nice," I warned Carrie quietly.

"Yes," Carrie answered the lady.

"From who?"

"God."

The policewoman's face went red. Carrie stared her down from the lofty height of moral certainty. The new guy grinned at her.

The policewoman folded her arms. "Leave or I'll arrest you."

"Do you enforce all the laws?" Carrie demanded. "The Migrant and Seasonal Agricultural Worker Protection Act?

Those whom you fail to protect will one day rise to tear down your authority."

Cuffs appeared in the woman's hands.

"Carrie, don't," I begged.

I wasn't so frightened of a ridiculous threat of arrest, but for Carrie herself. Who would save her when she did something that got her in trouble for real?

Carrie caught my eye and sighed. She turned to the officer. "Fine, Thomas Richetta gave us permission to be in his field. All of us."

The policewoman lectured as well as Carrie ever had. When she paused for air, the new guy made eye contact with Carrie.

"I'm Slate, by the way," he said.

"Carrie Jefferson."

His eyes crinkled with a grin. "Oh, I know who you are."

At his appreciative glance, my sister blushed.

"Also, you win." Winking, he looked significantly toward the rows of grapes. Carrie and I followed his gaze.

The grape rows were empty. The Hispanic girl and her mother had escaped.

PRESENT DAY

Twenty minutes after leaving cross-country practice, I sit down at a desk inside Verona's police station.

"Can you see the computer screen?" Officer Haynes asks.

Nervous, I nod.

"I'd like to see the monitor too." Dad props a hand on the back of my chair.

The screen blinks. The image of an open file folder is replaced by a picture. A brown hand with double-jointed fingers is flashing a gang sign, taking up nearly the entire photo. The profile of a face shows up out-of-focus in the background.

"I don't recognize him." Dad's voice is efficient.

I shake my head at my own lack of familiarity with the face.

"I've got three more." Officer Haynes leans over to navigate with the mouse.

The files load slowly. We're looking at new pictures. The police still hope we'll recognize any gang-members who might have tagged Carrie's car.

"How about this one?" he asks.

Dad answers for us. "No."

Two more photos. Two more faces we don't recognize.

The officer opens a new folder on the computer. "I want you to see this. It's from the corpse we found in your orchard, a man we've now identified. He went missing on May 24."

"When school was ending," I whisper. Carrie died on August 10, but I think she acquired her secret around late May.

No one answers as an image opens on the screen. It's a picture of a shoe. The decaying sole is blackened with earth and something darker. Blood. I make out cuts on the shoes—not a pattern inherent to the manufacturer's design, but a carving in the shape of letters. *XII* crossed by an upside down *V*.

Memories and waves of nausea rush at me. Twelve days ago, Officer Haynes told us a Roman numeral twelve crossed by an upside down *V* had been painted on the hood of Carrie's car.

"You okay?" the officer asks. My hands are over my stomach. "We think the killer carved this symbol into the victim's shoe after he died. The workers who discovered the body in your orchard saw the symbol or else we'd have kept it confidential."

"Close that image," Dad snaps at him.

The officer doesn't comply. "The identical symbol was on Carrie's car. Do you recognize it? Do you remember anything more about what was bothering her in the weeks leading up to her death?"

I can't answer. Did Carrie know the symbol left on her car had been carved into the shoe of a murder victim? Why would a gang even be after her?

"Carrie was very upset when we got to the house," the officer continues. "She didn't seem to want to identify any suspects—"

"What are you really after?" Dad interrupts, suspicious.

"—or prosecute anyone for the crime. Do you know why?"

"You could've copied this symbol on a piece of paper for Salem to see," Dad says. "It's not difficult to reproduce."

"What about the victim's name, Juan Herrera?" the officer asks me, ignoring Dad. "Ring a bell? Salem?"

I gasp, and Dad stiffens. I feel it through his hand on my shoulder.

"Juan Herrera, the missing union guy?" I ask. "Carrie helped the union."

"Did Carrie ever mention Juan?"

"We watched the news of him, that he was missing. Carrie cried. I don't know." I can't think. Carrie sobbed on the couch, curled in a ball without letting me hug her. It scared me sometimes, how much she loved the union.

The officer nods. "Any reason why Juan Herrera would be on your property?"

Does he mean while Juan was alive or after he was dead? Everything feels surreal, impossible.

"No," I say.

"Then I'm taking you home." Dad nudges my shoulder as if to get me to stand. "I'm not putting you through any more of this."

My mental picture of the symbol on the decaying shoe morphs into a single upside down *V*, black and bold. The way it looked inked onto the cheekbone of the guy seated behind me in class. *That's* why it looked familiar. Half of the marking left on Carrie's car is printed on his face. But that's not all. He's a Primero. The other part of the marking—the *XII* part—is the symbol claimed by his gang.

"Cordero," I whisper.

The noises in the police station lower, as if the name itself has power. The officer nods. Dad watches me, worried.

"He's a senior, I heard." I force the words through a throat that keeps tightening. "He has an upside down *V* tattoo. I've never seen him before, but he knew me, so maybe he knew Carrie. He wore a blue cap."

"We're looking into that," Officer Haynes says. "Cordero Vasquez lives across town. An upside down *V* tattoo is actually somewhat common, though—lots of Hispanics get them, even ones not in gangs. It's a community solidarity thing."

Cordero Vasquez. I file away a goal to talk to him about Carrie somehow. Maybe Slate's not the only one who knows something about her secret.

Dad turns to the officer. "Salem has had a hard time with her sister's death. If you have more questions, they'll have to wait." Dad fists his thumb, lets it go, and then fists it again. It's strange to see. Dad never gets nervous. But he's never dealt with the death of his own daughter before either. Maybe he fidgets when he's trying not to cry, the way I do.

"I'll see you at school," the officer tells me. He's Verona High's campus officer. "Talk to me any time if you remember anything."

Frowning, Dad glances at me. "No. If you talk to an officer, I want to be there."

The officer looks only at me, boring a hole into my head. "But your dad doesn't *have* to be there."

I glance between the two of them. In the orchard yesterday, they were allies. Now they seem like enemies.

"You guys are arguing? What's really going on?" I demand.

Dad and the officer exchange a look.

The officer turns away grimly. "The apple doesn't fall too far from the tree, does it?"

"She has her moments," Dad responds, pushing me toward the door by the small of my back.

I resist him and address Officer Haynes. "Was Carrie doing something with that guy? Juan Herrera?"

"I don't know. Was she?" The officer's expression is unreadable.

"What's going on?" I demand again.

The officer looks away, his gaze landing on a manila folder labeled *Victim—Juan Herrera*. Under it is a second folder labeled *Victim—Carrie Jefferson*. I point at them. "Juan was a murder victim. Was Carrie?"

Dad goes white. "The explosion was an accident."

The officer separates the folders like he wishes he'd never placed them together. "That's correct. Verona firemen ruled the explosion an accident. However, the *V* symbol being on her car after it was on a murder victim's shoe is troubling. We've considered hiring a forensic expert to check for signs the explosion at your house was rigged."

"It was an accident," Dad says louder this time.

The officer turns to him. "We—"

Dad stands, yelling, pointing his finger even. "Don't you do this. Don't you drag my dead daughter into this. I should have had a carbon monoxide warning in the house. I should have checked the maintenance. It's my fault. It's—" His voice hitches. He drags me up by the elbow. I've never seen him so upset in public. "Salem, we're leaving."

Scared and still confused, I grab my track bag. Dad pulls open the police station door for me, and I go outside into a wave of heat.

Dad thinks Carrie's death was his fault.

Tears run down my face. I can't see where I'm going. The sunlight is vicious.

Dad walks me to our Prius. I don't get in. I fight for control on my breathing. "What's—what's going on? Officer Haynes was mad at you. Why?"

Dad glances to make sure no one in the parking lot is looking. He presses his lips together. "The victim, Juan Herrera—well, you know he worked for the union before he went missing."

I nod, swallowing hard.

"There's a peach strike going on. Some people—among them Officer Haynes, I suspect—think peach growers have reason to kill union officials and stop the strike that's losing them money. One peach grower owns the property the body was buried in, making him a prime suspect."

My tears stop flowing, leaving moisture to dry at the corner of my eyes. I stare at the rays of sunlight twisting through Dad's round spectacles.

"Officer Haynes thinks *you* killed Juan," I say.

CHAPTER FIVE

THREE MONTHS PRIOR

Dad and Carrie enjoyed arguing and offering different viewpoints. But their debates about the peach strike had become bitter. I remember one time while we were in the car, Carrie watched Dad withdraw a bundle of cash from an ATM.

"Whoa, what's that for?" I asked from the backseat.

"The labor company I hired to plant the trees," Dad replied.

Carrie put her feet on the dash, suddenly angry. "Take out twice that much and pay them an honest amount. You at least hired within the union, right?"

I couldn't see Dad's face because he was in the driver's seat in front of me, but I knew he was rolling his eyes.

"I'm under contract. I have to hire within the union," he said. "If you want laborers to earn more money, don't allow the union to take so much of their wages."

"Are you kidding me?" She swung her feet down so she could face Dad. "The union saves that money for disability and early death caused by poor working conditions."

Dad drove away from the bank. "The union saves part of it, sure. What they're given is never what actually shows up on the books. I've given to the union myself, and not all of the money was reported."

Carrie and I glanced at each other. We'd both seen him slip extra money to pregnant women, but give to the union? Dad hated the union.

"You're serious?" Carrie asked. "You *actually* gave to the Farm Workers Union?"

"Back when they tracked every donation," Dad said dismissively. "My donation never showed up. Carrie, you need to face what your beloved union is really like."

"If the funds aren't showing up, write a check next time. A union worker might forget who gives him cash."

"A check can be traced."

"Exactly," Carrie said, confused.

Dad glanced at her. "So has it ever occurred to you that things might go better for a grower if he sometimes gives to the union in cash?"

Carrie's jaw dropped. "That's bribery! You're knowingly bribing them!"

"Carrie, wake up. Unions are shady."

"We're doing everything we can to expose corruption and you're supporting it!"

"*I* don't support the union—*you* support the union."

"You support corruption."

"I don't strong-arm my own members. I don't skim off the top, like a crook. I provide wages. What does the union provide? Promises that reality cannot support."

I tried to think of a response to Dad's argument. I always sided with Carrie even though Dad seemed to win more often.

"At least the union's goals are good," Carrie said. "Your Peach Growers Association pays low wages for greed—even you."

"We pay the going rate."

"The going rate is robbery! Plus, some growers are hiring people to intimidate workers into voting against the strike." She was referencing a media story about three men who said they'd been attacked for carting pro-strike signs.

"Police never found evidence linking any growers to that incident," Dad said.

"The union president himself—oh, like the police-hand that keeps people down can be trusted," Carrie interrupted herself to snap at dad. "Anyway, President Benicio said—"

"Exactly what you want to hear?"

"—that he was at Kelly farm personally," she continued louder. "He saw them. Dad, he saw them. Hired gang members with pocketknives. There were injuries—you know that. And fires start fires. Growers had better pray that the violence doesn't start happening to them."

PRESENT DAY

"Officer Haynes can't prove anything against you," I tell Dad in the sunlight outside the police station. I'm still in shock that he might be a murder suspect. Carrie talked about growers getting hurt, but she never seemed to consider the idea of a grower being falsely accused. "You're smarter than him."

Dad's face softens. "I've trained you so badly. I'm not smarter than everyone."

"Well, they can't arrest you without evidence." I take a breath. I pause, trying to broach the subject of Carrie gently. "If they investigate Carrie's death, they might find out she was killed and then they'll know the killer isn't you."

Dad's face darkens, reverting back to the mask of guilt it was inside the station. "Carrie died in an accident."

I shut up. I don't share his confidence, but I'm not cruel.

Once home, I settle into grandma's couch. With our real house uninhabitable from fire damage, we moved into my grandma's. Dad had held onto her old farmhouse next door to keep the acreage. Grandma had died of leukemia when I was seven. Dad pulled the plug on her, according to Mom. After she said that I was afraid of Dad for a few months. Now, settled on the couch, I can't help but think of Officer Haynes' accusation. He thinks Dad is a murderer. Mom thought he was a euthanizer. For years, I've suspected stray kittens didn't make it to the animal shelter unless Carrie or I found them before Dad did.

I become aware of my thoughts. A muddy litter of kittens under the barn floorboards, and Dad takes care of the problem. A union official determined to strike for wages growers can't afford and Dad—

I'm ashamed of myself. Dad raised Carrie and me alone when Mom left and I've never heard him complain once. Officer Haynes is wrong.

I get out my homework. The coffee table in front of me is cluttered with old photographs. Carrie's first grade class picture. Dad holding me as an infant. That picture is interesting because half of Mom's face is in it. People say I look like Mom, that I have her blond hair and dark eyelashes.

When I was little, Mom talked to everyone from Dad to my pediatrician about me. How Salem threw her brown rice on the floor. How Salem wrote on the walls. The conversations always ended with her asking how she was going to get to the important causes in life when I resisted her every step of the way.

Mom left when I was nine because she was unhappy. She left because one day she couldn't find the ground flaxseed and so she dumped a bucket of oats on the kitchen tile, shouting that flaxseed had healthy oil and that listening to kids whine while she made granola wasn't what she'd asked for in life. She was gone by nightfall.

I cried myself to sleep at night, thinking Mom wouldn't come home because of me. Eventually Carrie caught on to my guilt. Mom was an authority figure, she said. She had let us down. Carrie told me to stop thinking of Mom, and that's what I did.

I turn on my laptop. I hit up a website about John F. Kennedy and ditch it for an image-search of the phrase "upside down *V* tattoo." I find hundreds. In the 1950s, Hispanics created groups to support and protect victims of racism. Some of those groups still use the *V* symbol. Some are still peaceful. Some transformed into violent gangs. It's strange to think about—violence sprouting from the idea of trying to protect victims. Carrie would never have supported violence.

Finding nothing that ties the *V* to Carrie, I start an essay on potential JFK conspiracies. Homework is like running—a way to keep my thoughts at bay. It's dark when I finish, shower, and crawl into bed without saying goodnight to Dad.

Hours later, I'm awoken by the sound of my bedroom door opening.

Confused, I raise my head from the pillow. "Dad?"

"If I'm arrested, I doubt I'll have the money to post bail." Dad is lit from below by a nightlight he set up for me last week to stop my bad dreams.

"What?" I sit up, pushing aside a quilt made by my grandmother. I'm half-asleep and sore from my race against Slate.

Dad's hair is mussed like he's been trying unsuccessfully to sleep. "I went to talk to Officer Haynes again. I got back an hour ago. If I'm arrested, you'll move in with your aunt."

"What do the police have on you?"

"That . . . is the question."

Terror hits me. For the first time, I believe it. They might arrest him.

He walks to my bed and sits down. He taps his fingers on his lap. "I spoke with Officer Haynes about hiring a forensic expert so you can get past this idea that was Carrie murdered. I'm one hundred percent sure she wasn't."

His certainty confuses me, almost like him insisting it was an accident makes me suspect that it was *his* accident— that something he did caused Carrie to die. That something he did caused the police to think he killed Juan. And that something he did really *did* kill Juan.

I rub my forehead. It's stupid, but I'm angry at Dad. Furious. Like it's his fault he's made me think such awful, crazy things.

Dad takes a breath. "There's something I should have told you after Carrie died. Carrie used her college fund to hire a gang member. It was a joint account. She must have forged my signature. From what the police have gathered, she wanted him to protect workers from any agitators hired by the growers."

"Gangs." I whisper.

My chest constricts. She *was* involved with gangs. She was hurt. She was killed. I shake my head. I shake it faster and faster. How could she have hired gang members? She couldn't have done that—even to protect someone. Hiring violent people is what the growers were doing. It's what she hated about the growers. How could she have *done* that?

I'm so upset I punch my lap.

Dad sighs. "I don't know what she was *thinking*, trying to—"

I punch my lap again for Dad saying what I felt, because I feel the opposite too. Carrie could do anything she wanted—she was Carrie.

Dad tries again. "Officer Haynes found out about the plot last week. Twelve hundred in her bank account is gone. I guess I thought you'd be happier not knowing."

I try to talk. "The gang member—" I catch my breath, hugging my knees. I will not cry. "Did . . . did he hurt anyone?" Everyone knows gang members. She wanted them to protect people, but they're not going to stop at just shoving.

"Apparently there was a bonus involved—some condition that there never be any violence. That's Carrie. Trusting a gang member to play by her rules just because she wants him to. But it appears her plan worked."

"Who was it?" I ask.

"The guy she hired? Even if I knew I wouldn't tell you."

"Dad—"

"Salem, I don't know who it was."

"Well . . . if Carrie hired a gang member to protect workers, who's to say another gang member wasn't hired to kill her? Apparently gangs can be hired for anything."

"Maybe. But to me, it seems like Carrie died accidentally."

I explode in rage. "After what you just told me?" Rage feels wonderful. It feels directed and controlled.

"We'll know more if Haynes calls in a forensic expert."

"*If?*"

"Officer Haynes was willing to consider the idea, but not willing to give me a certain *yes*. There's something else."

Dad takes a breath. I find I'm bracing myself.

"When Carrie originally called 911, it was right after she dropped you off at cross-country. She told the police that someone was trying to kill her and then hung up."

I stare at the gray hair at his temples. I bury my face into my knees.

Dad rubs my back while I sob. The last thing Carrie did before someone came after her was drive me to a meet—always taking care of me.

"Just listen," Dad says quietly. "She changed her story when the police arrived. She said no one had tried to kill her, but instead, that her car had been vandalized. Haynes told me at the time that he knew she was lying about something. Maybe she was trying to manipulate the gang with made-up stories against them. I hope that's what happened. For me . . . for me, I hope she died in an accidental gas explosion. Until there's more evidence, I want you to remember it's possible the explosion was an accident."

The entire conversation has exhausted me.

He pats my back. "Get some sleep. We'll talk in the morning."

He leaves, shutting the door behind him and calling, "I love you," from the hallway.

"Love you too," I whisper voicelessly. I don't know who started our estrangement, me or Dad.

I lie down. I'm numb. Dad might be a suspect in a murder. A forensic expert could come, but isn't. I know part of Carrie's secret. She hired gang members. But what other secrets was she hiding?

My thoughts swirl in dizzy, looping patterns. Maybe Carrie was murdered. Maybe she wasn't. Maybe I'll never know. How can I live like that? My thought pattern loops tighter and tighter. I can't live like that. She was my sister. I can't wait forever, hoping the police or Dad will do something.

I have to investigate.

I have to find out for myself if Carrie's death was more than just an accident.

CHAPTER SIX

W hen the going gets tough, will you give *up*?" Mr. White's voice whines the next day.

Humidity rises from thirty bodies in the room, the way it does when sweat hits air conditioning. I finger the graffiti etched on my desk. In the front of the room, Kimi and Envy pass notes to each other. Cordero is seated behind me, breathing slow and even. I wish I knew where his gaze was focused. I wish I knew every shred of data about Carrie stored in his brain. I'm going to learn it all, whatever it is. Whatever it takes.

"Confidence," Mr. White declares. "You'll never win without confidence."

Doubt erupts at the teacher's mention of confidence. I'm unable to picture actually cornering Cordero.

"First you need to know how a mock trial works," Mr. White continues. "Let me introduce you to our class TA. He's a veteran of last year, Qorkhmaz Panakhov, a fantastic Azerbaijani name. Don't worry. His nickname is Slate."

Slate comes to the front of the classroom from within Mr. White's office. Carrie should have been with him. I drop my gaze to my desk. I swallow. I think of confidence and force myself to look up.

"This year, things are a little different," Slate announces to the class. "We aren't going to put a murderer on trial. History accepts that a young man named Lee Oswald shot President Kennedy. But did he act alone? That's where the mock trial comes in. The trial is made of two teams. Each team will have help from a community leader who has volunteered their time to help with the mock trial. The prosecution's job is to attack the idea that Oswald was part of a larger plan to—"

"Conspiracy! A larger con-*spir*-acy!" Mr. White shouts from behind his desk. He's grading yesterday's homework essay.

Slate grins at the class. "Mr. White really likes conspiracies."

The class laughs and Mr. White goes back to grading.

Slate continues. "I want to make sure all of you know the basics of the JFK case."

He sets up a projector that displays best to the left side of the room, motioning for those of us on the right to stand and watch. I rise from my chair, staying far away from Cordero. He catches my eye and I feel myself go red with uncertainty.

"Come closer," Slate instructs.

I obey. Cordero doesn't, staying at the back of the room. Slate gestures at him to come and then frowns, as if recognizing him. He turns back to the projector without saying more. I glance between the two, wondering how they know each other.

On the projector screen, President John F. Kennedy's avatar is next to his wife in a convertible driving in slow motion. The governor of Texas and his wife are in the front seat.

"Notice the top right window of the building," a man's voice narrates from the computer.

A man holding a rifle appears in the window of a brick building behind the president. At the sound of a digital blast, a bullet leaves the rifle in slow motion and lands in the street—a poor shot. A second bullet hits the president in the back of the neck and continues on, hitting the governor as well.

"Oh, no, no, no. My God. They're going to kill us all!" the governor's avatar yells.

A third bullet smashes into the President's head. The scene ends.

"That's terrible." AddyDay's fingers are over her mouth. "So . . . that proves the president was killed by one guy, right? One gun?"

"Well, watch this," Slate says, starting the next clip.

The same avatars appear inside the same convertible. The same man with a rifle is in the same window.

"Notice the second man," the male voice narrates.

In this version, a second man emerges from above a waist-high wall across the street, also carrying a rifle.

Both men aim their weapons and fire.

"Which sequence of events is correct?" the narrator asks. "The lone shooter or the tandem pair? The debate may well rage forever."

The scene freezes on a close up of Mrs. Kennedy. I can't stop staring at her. All that film footage and she still had to wonder who killed her husband, who else might have been responsible. Who else might have held the answers.

I turn. My eyes meet Cordero's and I realize he's already watching me. He lifts his chin in a cautious greeting. I get a vision of reacting to him the way I would if I didn't suspect him. I would smile at him. Or blush and look away, more likely. I hurry back to my desk. He's right behind me, taking a seat.

I lean forward, consumed by hatred for him. Maybe I'm wrong about him and he didn't harm Carrie. But maybe I'm right and he did.

What will I say to him to make him tell me what he knows?

"Okay," Slate continues once the class is settled. "Let's talk about the trial itself. The teams will assign students to be witnesses, say a scientific expert. Like Jeremy here." He gestures at the front row.

"Oops." Jeremy Novo takes headphones out of his ears, accidentally ripping the wire free from his phone.

A woman's electronic voice fills the classroom. ". . . in store for the peach strike . . ."

Jeremy cusses and fiddles with his phone.

"You listen to news clips?" Mr. White asks.

". . . with growers and migrant laborers rocked by murder," the voice continues. "The victim is Juan Herrera.

Despite evidence of gang involvement, police are not ruling out suspects who may have targeted Juan for his union affiliation. He was apparently beaten to death during a fist fight—"

Jeremy's phone goes silent.

Murder by fist—a crime of passion. And somehow Officer Haynes suspects Dad, the least passionate person alive. Granted, the suspect I'm fixated on hasn't shown much emotion either. Slate was the one frowning at Cordero, not the other way around.

At least Dad's name stayed out of the newspapers, except as the owner of the orchard. I was relieved. I'd seen him surfing news sites this morning, so I know he was worried too.

The bell rings to leave. I whirl to follow Cordero, but his tall frame—no hat today—is already halfway to the door.

Upset, I hurry out the door. Cordero is nowhere to be seen.

So much for courage.

At lunch, I buy a Coke and savor its coolness. In the center of the outdoor quad, Verona High's flag languishes on a pole, the only vertical relief to flat landscape that extends for hundreds of miles. I'm smack in the middle of the fertile Central Valley, the seedbed of one-third of the nation's fruits and vegetables.

Old-time Verona lives, eats, and breathes orchards. If peach growers succumb to wage-hike demands, the growers of plums, oranges, and cherries will be next.

Under the eaves of the administration building, two Hispanic guys wearing blue slowly scan their surroundings.

Do any of them know about the symbol on Carrie's car? None of them sport the upside-down *V* as body art. Still, they might know something.

I gather my courage, repeating Mr. White's words about not giving up. I walk to the guys. The soda can in my hand shakes. The guys lift their chins. I stop in front of the younger one, a guy in a white t-shirt and jeans so big they need five layers of boxers to hold them up.

"Do you know—" I realize my mistake and lose all my confidence. "I mean, *did* you know Carrie Jefferson?"

My interrogation skills are awful. I sound like a pushy gossip columnist. I haven't introduced the reason for my questions or given anyone a reason to want to answer.

My face flushes at their silence and lazy scrutiny.

"Carrie," I say louder.

The pair keeps their emotionless stares trained on me. Like territorial bulls, all the more menacing in their patience. They'll never tell me about Carrie. Because I'm not like Carrie, and I won't ever be able to be like Carrie. I don't have the confidence to fight the people who harm others. How could I have thought I could be like Carrie?

I hurry away in the wake of their low insults, said to my back in their native Spanish.

The heat of shame radiates from my skin into the swelter of the day.

CHAPTER SEVEN

The first time I saw violence, I was in fifth grade.

"Ew!" I was gripping the side of a dumpster, giggling. I had a brown paper sack in my other hand.

"Is that mine?" Carrie's worried twelve-year-old voice sounded like an audio recording found under the definition of "precocious." She was the one who convinced me to go dumpster diving.

Shuffling, she tried to get better footing on the pile of garbage. "Dad's going to kill me if I don't find my retainer."

"Must'a been a parent who packed this lunch. It's full of wadishes!" My *r* wasn't low enough in my throat to sound right. "Radishes," I whispered to myself. I didn't like anyone to hear me practicing, not even Carrie.

58

"There are so many aluminum *cans* in here," Carrie said, offended. She collected them into a corner. "Why doesn't our school recycle?"

The dumpster rocked as something hit it from outside, sending the stacked cans crashing. A stream of Spanish was followed by moans of unmistakable pain.

I froze, afraid and uncertain.

"Stop! Hey, you out there! Stop!" Carrie gripped the dumpster wall, moving toward the voices. She was going to face the trouble and stop it, not hide from it.

Seeing her, I knew what to do. I copied her actions.

Only I was a lot faster.

Using a metal hook as a foothold, I slung myself up and over the side of the dumpster. The lunch bag I'd had in my hand tumbled down to the pavement. I landed and looked up.

They were big. Big as adults. Junior high students with facial hair. They breathed heavy, kicking and punching. The chubby victim pitched this way and that on the ground, an over-sized, dark teddy bear.

One of the attackers heard me land, a tall guy with a split lip and a thin, brown face. He rushed at me, yelling words I couldn't understand. Teddy-bear boy was crying out in pain from his fetal position. Carrie screamed above us.

I stooped to grab the lunch bag I'd dropped and threw it into the fray.

"Run!" I shouted to Teddy-bear boy. I forgot to enunciate. "*Whun!*" My call sounded pathetic and immature.

"Careful!" Carrie screamed, watching from above.

I scurried backward, trapped between the dumpster and the chain link fence. Instead of coming after me, the tall guy yelled a sharp, foreign command. The aggressors retreated from their victim. Teddy-bear boy uncurled, his eyes jumpy. He flashed a grand frown, like an unhappy clown—a desperate joke.

The attackers laughed. They offered to help him up. Mouth open, I watched Teddy-bear boy sprint with them toward the junior high down the street. I climbed back up to Carrie and calmed her as she cried. Eventually, she told me what a gang initiation was, and then I understood.

Teddy-bear boy. Wide cheeks, eyes without pride. He'd been in on the whole thing. He hadn't just known the attack would happen. He'd requested it.

PRESENT DAY

"Gang initiations often involve brutal beatings," reads a link on the side of the Verona Bulletin's website. The main section of the website remains empty as my phone slowly downloads an article called *Murder on the Peach-Strike Express.*

Classes just ended, bringing the second day of school to a close. I'm sweating with a group of students next to the administration building, waiting for Mr. White to announce the mock trial teams.

As I wait, a chill rolls over the sweat on my skin. I want to know what happened to Carrie. How far would I go to know? Would I endure a brutal beating?

Mr. White arrives with quick strides. "I've assigned the teams. Leaders will be in charge of the video camera I will give each side, along with recordings from previous mock trials—analyze those videos carefully!"

The article I requested downloads. I hold my hand over the screen, blocking the glare.

Murder on the Peach-Strike Express

Elena Thornton
Verona, CA

Yesterday afternoon farm workers found the body of missing union official Juan Herrera, buried in a peach orchard two miles outside Verona's city limits.

While I read, Mr. White continues his announcements. "The partnership who scored second best in the homework assignment will lead the defense team. And it's . . ." He pauses dramatically. ". . . Envy Chiquoi and Kimi Tam!"

A few students clap while Mr. White reads off the names assigned to their team. He has to hurry so people can get to their sports practices and buses.

I block out the noise and keep reading.

"A labor strike is going to bring tension and crime," says union official Rick Thornton.

Thornton points to a fifteen percent rise in theft since the strike began. Coincidentally, the official's own house has suffered three attempted burglaries in the same time period.

I reread Rick Thornton's name. Carrie knew and liked Rick. I wonder if the house break-in means he's a victim of the same strike-violence that Carrie may have been a victim of.

"Everyone else, you're on the prosecution team," Mr. White says. "With leaders Salem Jefferson and Cordero Vasquez!"

I hear my name but it means nothing until AddyDay crashes into me, arms wide. "Oh, I'm *so* glad I'm on your team!"

A team leader—me? Carrie was the leader, not me.

Across the outdoor quad, I notice movement from the two guys I spoke to at lunch, who dress like gang members. Their faces are down, their arrogance gone. My gaze doesn't follow theirs but seeks whatever they fear. Something behind me. A person exiting the administration building in a waft of cool, stale air. A tall presence.

I turn and stare at an upside-down *V* tattoo shimmering in the sunlight, black and fierce. Like fuel waiting for ignition.

"Salem," Cordero says. His expression is calm and almost inviting. He seems confident and controlled, like someone I might trust despite his gang attire. The way he knows how to play his cards gives me more reason to suspect him of being involved with Carrie. Carrie would've hired someone smart.

"Gosh, um, Cordero!" AddyDay says, letting go of my arm. She smiles at him, hoping to get noticed.

Instead, Cordero holds my gaze, like something about me has caught his interest—in a good way or a bad way, I don't know. His facial hair is crisp and thin along the line of his jaw. Another trail of black outlines his dark mouth. I feel my face get hot, burning to verify he's connected somehow to Carrie.

"Did you know my sister?" I ask.

Cordero's smile disappears. His eyes flash with emotion. I get hot all over. He *did* know her. He knew her and I don't know what to do now. I have no practice in pressing someone for information.

He regains his cool. "Who didn't know Carrie?"

Slate calls to me from behind. He must have just arrived. "Salem, sorry I'm late. Great paper on Oswald's USSR ties. Mr. White let me read it."

Turning from Cordero to Slate is like falling from fire into ice.

Meanwhile, Mr. White hurries toward Cordero and me with wide strides, waving a manila envelope. "Salem. Cordero. Here are your team's phone numbers and addresses."

As the teacher arrives, Slate notices I'm not alone. His eyes lock on Cordero and his good mood vanishes.

Cordero greets Slate with a twitch of a smile. "Did you also like the paper *I* wrote?"

I throw strategy to the wind and step into Cordero's personal space. "You're in the gang that tagged Carrie's car, aren't you?"

Not one muscle of his face moves and yet it darkens under the harsh shadow of his cap, like the sunlight is frightened of him. I'm out of breath under his gaze.

No one makes a move until Cordero pulls the envelope out of Mr. White's hands, still facing me with an intense expression. "*I'll* make the trial assignments. *You* learn how to question someone." He strides toward the parking lot.

Slate turns to me with cold blue eyes. "Are you friends with him?"

"I don't even know him," I answer. "What's your problem with him? Does it have anything to do with Carrie?"

With a reddened face, Slate presses his hand to my back so that my shirt clings to my skin and glances at Mr. White. "Give us a minute?"

Other students whisper while Slate walks me to a bench several yards away.

I don't sit. "I know Carrie told you stuff about what she was up to. Did she tell you she hired a gang member?"

He's caught off guard. "You knew she hired Cordero?"

I lean forward. "She hired *Cordero*?"

It *was* Cordero who Carrie hired. That's why he reacted to her name. That's why he knows who I am and why he's arguing with Slate. I flush with success, finally learning something.

Then I think about what I've learned. I've learned Carrie really did hire a gang member—no question.

But how could she have done that? *How*? Carrie *knew* involving gangs would lead to violence.

Five and a Half Years Prior

After the gang guys finished beating up Teddy-bear boy, I went back to the dumpster and found Carrie's retainer. She thanked me three times.

"No pwoblem," I answered, still standing on garbage.

"I've seen that guy before, the one they were hitting. I think he's a year older than me." Carrie was still wiping away tears and calming down. "Salem, I'm proud of you. You stood up to those guys down there! Someday you're going to figure out who you are." Her words didn't sound ridiculous, even coming from a twelve-year-old. Carrie had been born confident.

She smiled at me. "I know you think you do everything wrong. But you're strong. You're going to help me like I help you sometimes. You . . . you just have this power."

"Well, I'm fastah than you." I was blushing. I had no idea what she meant.

"See? You don't even know." She turned and tried to find a foothold on the dumpster. "I wish I could be like you."

Present Day

"Look, are you okay?" Slate says gently, reminding me that I'm at school.

I keep picturing Carrie crying at the violence of the gang initiation. How could she hire a gang member? And why did she ever think she wanted to be like *me*?

"Salem?" Slate feels sorry for me.

Concerned, he nudges my elbow, and I sit. Heat from the plastic bench radiates through my cut-offs.

"What's wrong?" he asks, taking a spot next to me.

I fist my hands. "I think someone hurt Carrie. I think that's how she died." I tell him about the symbol on Carrie's car showing up on Juan Herrera's shoe and how the police might call in a forensic expert to reexamine the house explosion.

Slate shakes his head, rejecting my words as strongly as Dad had. "Carrie died because a pipe was leaking."

"But what if she was targeted by the gang she hired? What if she couldn't pay them, or knew too much about them?"

"Salem—"

"You should have told someone what she was doing, hiring Cordero," I say over the sound of my mental scream. *I* should have told someone how frightened she was.

I expect Slate to be furious that I've blamed him. Instead, I look up to cool eyes haunted by grief and isolation, looking like my own image in a mirror—my own grief and isolation, just the same. He understands what it's like living without her—the guilt, the pain, all of it.

Slate looks away from me.

"I did tell the police," he says in a thick voice. "But not until after she died."

"How could she?" I whisper.

"Don't hate her, Salem. She wanted so badly for that strike to go through, but she was very conflicted. She didn't tell you because she wanted to be a good example for you."

I press my lips together.

Slate takes a ragged breath. "I found out when we went out for dinner a few days after her birthday to celebrate. Remember that? We went to a restaurant at Mission Plaza and . . . well, Carrie talked to two guys—Cordero and someone named Tito . . ." Slate hesitates, as if the memory is troubling. "Tito's crazy . . . rough . . . not a good guy. He . . . hit me. We fought. Anyway, I avoid him now."

Mission Plaza is a strip mall a mile from Verona High. Lots of graffiti gets painted over down there. It's a hangout spot for local teens and gang members too.

I frown. "Do you think Cordero could have turned against Carrie for some reason? Carrie said there were gang members working for growers. Maybe it was Cordero—or another Primero. He could have . . . I don't know . . . betrayed her to the growers if they had more money than she did or something. That could have led to her being murdered."

"I don't think a gang blew up your house. I know Carrie made some mistakes, but there's no way she was murdered."

"Maybe the growers wanted it to look like an accident. You know how much they don't like her for making the strike popular."

Slate frowns. "It's true she was worried about the strike. She cared so much . . . she was going to fix the whole world. Someone just *couldn't* have wanted to . . ."

He looks away. "I loved her. I can't talk about this anymore."

He's gone before I realize he's suffering over the loss of Carrie and I accused and interrogated him anyway. Shame rolls over me.

I head to my locker. I pass Mr. White who gives me a manila envelope identical to the one he gave Cordero. Apparently he has one for each team leader. Didn't he say the addresses of all the team members were listed inside?

When I get a few yards away from my teacher, I tear into the envelope, my fingers shaking as I scan the top page.

"147 Benjamin Road," I say when I get to Cordero's name. I could go to his house, question him there.

I stand and gaze at the athletic field in the distance. I should be at the track already. Slate's headed there. I could make it to Cordero's house around the same time as him if he's walking.

I type 147 Benjamin Road into my cell. *Left on Main Street, 1.8 miles*, it says. I stash my backpack into my locker and settle into my distance pace.

I get to Main and run until the sidewalk ends in a crumble of concrete. My phone says to keep going north, but Main Street is one leg of my standard training route. Noticing a small gap of patchy asphalt next to a store made of pink stucco, I continue forward, my breath coming in long draws.

I reach the gap and look left. A street appears from nowhere.

Dilapidated homes are strewn in no order. Spanish-tiled houses smack in the middle of downtown—a world inside a world. Rap and mariachi music compete from open windows.

I turn onto the road, passing a tricked-out Cadillac and a chicken coop. The exotic surroundings play on my fears. Even the chatter of children is foreign. Their rapid Spanish dialogue is nothing like the plodding, stiff lines my class-mates and I repeat.

I reach the porch of a crumbling two-storied manor.

147 Benjamin Road.

I knock, and the door swings slowly open of its own accord, bringing a waft of stale smoke. I blink at the dozen teen boys inside. Shirtless ones, lounging in filth. Old mattresses spill their stuffing onto concrete subflooring. Costco-sized boxes of cigarettes. A carton of milk in the corner oozing something gray. Cordero is nowhere in sight.

No one notices me, too busy laughing while one of the tattooed men tells a story. His mouth is pulled into an exaggerated frown for his audience—the face of a clown.

I recognize his defeated eyes and chubby frame. I remember the first time I saw that face. The most recent time too. I was terrified in both instances.

The man notices me, locking his gaze on mine. I freeze.

CHAPTER EIGHT

I was sitting with Dad in a neighbor's kitchen the day after Carrie died. Officer Haynes was there with a grainy picture.

Dozens of shirtless males posed for the camera, making gang symbols with their fingers. I scanned the photo, recognizing a man frowning like a clown.

"This one." My voice sounded strange. I hadn't used it since seeing the charred house with Carrie's body still inside. All that crying.

"You recognize him?" Officer Haynes asked.

"From school a long time ago. Is he the one who tagged her car?"

Officer Haynes shook his head. "That's Oscar Garcia-Joya. He's been in prison for a few years, scheduled to get

70

out next week, actually. One of the bosses. He goes by El Payaso."

I translated the word automatically.

"The clown."

PRESENT DAY

Standing on the porch outside the house on 147 Benjamin Road, I stare in terror at El Payaso inside. He's still chubby, but more hardened than before. I doubt he recognizes me from school all those years ago.

In a burst of foreign yelling, El Payaso drops his comical expression and rushes toward me, gesturing for me to leave.

Carrie said I was the strong one.

El Payaso grabs the front door to shut it, but I dart into the house first, feeling a rush of air as the door bangs shut beside me.

"I'm looking for Cordero," I announce to the gang members' menacing faces. My voice reverberates through the sagging stairwell.

One of the shirtless boys stands. I step back, colliding with the doorjamb behind me, but he's not coming at me. No one is. One by one the figures head to the back of the house. It's like a man with a megaphone yelled "Cut!" but more organized because there's no man and no megaphone. Just teens who know exactly what to do in case of interruption. Teens who don't overplay the seriousness of the interruption.

El Payaso glares at them. Then he rolls his eyes. "We was done anyway," he says, rubbing his shoulder. He's not wearing a shirt.

I can barely breathe. "Does anyone know Cordero?" My voice is small.

I'm nothing to these people. My self-doubt begins to set in. I wanted answers from Cordero but expected to find him in a small trailer or a one-roomed home. Now I'm inside a massive house filled with possible gang members. This was not a good idea.

Half a dozen brown-haired children spill into the front room, like they were waiting to re-occupy the space. El Payaso sits on an overturned bucket near the front door, head in his hands.

"El Payaso," I say, desperate.

The man looks up. He's got thick, wavy black hair.

"Wait, you don't got the wrong house? Serious?" Confused, he looks behind him. "Yeah, like there's some other El Payaso, huh?" His laugh is big and contagious. He's in no hurry to make me leave. I wonder if he lives here too, like Cordero. Maybe they all live here, even kids too.

"I'm trying to be clean, you know?" He looks at me and spits on the wooden floor. "You don't know. Forget it."

His accent is Cordero's soft consonants tainted with backstreet, crass English. I assume he's talking about being clean from drugs, but he's nothing like the addicts I've seen on TV. He looks healthy and pudgy, like a big, brown baby.

"I'm looking for Cordero," I repeat.

El Payaso stands. "Who are you?"

"Salem Jefferson."

Grunting, he stretches, giving nothing away. A preteen girl with a toddler on her back races with other children around a couch situated smack in the middle of the room, like the walls didn't want it. Officer Haynes said El Payaso was in prison when Carrie died, but he might have heard something about her anyway. Does he understand my connection to her by my last name?

"I think Cordero knew my sister," I say.

El Payaso tilts his head like he's accessing an old memory. "Jefferson. Carrie Jefferson?"

I gasp. "You know her?"

The front door opens, hitting me in the shoulder. Cordero Vasquez walks inside, sucking the air I'd been breathing right out of my lungs. He fills the room with his unusual height and his demand for deference.

He lets his gaze linger a moment on my face, his only hint of surprise. The children laugh as they run. From outside, a car engine's faint rumble plays under their song.

El Payaso collapses onto the couch. "Man, why you always be comin' late?"

A thud sounds against a back wall that partially separates the once grand room from the kitchen. A small, compact noise. Hard. The whole house heaves, stilling in an instant.

A breeze that hadn't existed before comes into the room from an open window.

"Oh, no, no, no!" El Payaso tosses screaming kids behind the couch, rushing at them with his monster-clown face. He waves his arm at me. "Down flat!"

Cordero flat-out sprints away from us down the hall, no explanation.

Two more thuds. Thud. Thud. A window behind me breaks.

Screaming, I drop my nose to the wooden floor. Bullets fly around us. A girl begins shrieking. She's next to the couch, barely old enough for kindergarten. The front of her lavender shirt disappears into a slick, liquid stain that spills through her fingers in heavy drops.

Thud, ping, thud.

The girl's anguished cries make thinking impossible. Footsteps drum toward us from the hallway. Cordero rounds the corner and throws open the door, bringing a handgun to shoulder height. He squeezes off rounds, disappearing out the door.

"Help!" El Payaso yells before lapsing into a string of Spanish.

I get my cell from my pocket and crawl toward the children. Car tires squeal, fading into nothingness. The thudding stops. But the yelling continues.

". . . said get *down*!"

At El Payaso's command, I drop and army-crawl on my elbows. When I'm within reach, he drags me behind the couch by my upper arms, snatching the phone. El Payaso speaks to the 911 dispatcher. He peels children off him and scoops the injured girl into his lap, wrapping thick arms over her like he'll be able to force all the blood back inside. I'm on the floor shaking.

This can't be real. I can't be listening to her die. Not like I listened to Carrie die.

A Hispanic woman with a tight ponytail runs into the front room and tries to wrench the bleeding girl away from El Payaso. They argue. Another adult, a Caucasian man, staggers in on jean-clad legs so thin only a drug-addict could maintain them.

"This ain't right," the man says, dazed.

The Hispanic woman gets the upper hand on El Payaso and drags the girl from him in a trail of blood. Tears splash down her face.

"*Mi niña!*" she screams. The front door opens and slams shut. Cordero rushes around the couch to the shrieking girl.

"Your sister," El Payaso shouts.

The woman stands and shoves the girl at Cordero, screaming at him. Sweat glistens on his *V* tattoo. The gun hangs at his side. Expressionless, he refuses to look at the woman with her straight frame, so like his. I see the resemblance. The woman is Cordero's mother. The girl is his bleeding sister. 147 Benjamin Road, his address.

Cordero's mom screams at him. She holds the girl with one arm so she can slap him with the other. I cringe. Each movement is punctuated with awful, urgent cries from her dying daughter. They're intolerable. Around us, everyone is yelling. I pick up meaning from the Spanish in snatches.

"*. . . because of you they did this!*"

"*Mommy!*"

"*. . . hear? She needs pressure . . . come, come!*" El Payaso grabs a towel from the pile of laundry, shoving it against the dying girl. He tosses my phone back to me, and the girl's body convulses.

Silence.

The woman howls and collapses to the floor, taking the girl with her. Sirens clamor in the distance. My upper arm is caught by an iron grip. I look up.

Cordero has me.

He drags me across the wooden floor, into the kitchen. He waves the gun, backing me into a wall next to a window missing its glass.

I suck in my gut. I can't breathe.

The gun.

I dart sideways, muscles like springs. I'm fast. I don't know how Cordero catches me by the waist. For once he's not calm. He gets in my face.

"Get out! Get out of here!" He pushes me out the back door.

I land hard on my butt in a patch of weeds behind the house. I get my feet under me. I run.

Past a rundown, Spanish-tiled pool.

Over a livestock fence. Across a short stretch of horse-manure-laden pasture.

In my terror, noises play on repeat in my head—foreign sounds, screaming. *Carrie.* El Payaso knew her name.

Beyond the pasture, I hit the sidewalk on Main Street, my feet flying.

Cars zoom down the five-lane road. A guy in a chicken suit advertises a fast food restaurant at the corner. Men in khaki shorts, families unloading babies from car seats, the mortuary we coordinated with when Carrie died.

We had a funeral. We buried all the bits of her they'd found. But most of Carrie wasn't Carrie anymore. She was tiny floating particles of smoke. Pure carbon imprinted on house rubble. A collection of images and audio recordings indented on my brain.

Knees driving high, I change my course and head toward the police department. The sirens of cop cars and ambulances fade long before I arrive and go inside. My eyes adjust slowly. There's a bench and a counter with a glass panel crisscrossed by metal for security. The secretaries behind it don't look up. I lean heavily on the lip of the counter, my pulse pounding in my ears.

"I'm . . . I need . . . to talk to . . . Officer Haynes," I say through a hole in the glass.

A black woman nods for me to sit. "Gonna be a minute, hon. There was some drive-by shooting just now. Media's already there."

I might throw up. I run to a drinking fountain, water spilling over my chin. I gulp and gulp. I'll never be filled.

"Your lucky day," the secretary calls.

Drenched down the front, I straighten to look at her.

She hits a button on the wall to her left and a green light starts flashing over the door leading into the station's interior. "He says your dad's already here."

Dad?

I race to a large room full of busy policemen. Stacks of paper are piled over desks, file cabinets, and printers. Officer Haynes has a straight-backed chair waiting for me next to the one Dad's in.

I run to it, but don't sit. "Dad—there was this Primero—"

Dad stands. "Salem?"

"Are you okay?" Officer Haynes sets a coffee cup on the desk he's seated on.

I stop in my tracks. "You—" I look from the office to Dad and back. "You didn't arrest Dad, did you?"

"No one's been arrested," he says.

I start breathing again.

Dad puts a hand on my shoulder. "They've ordered a forensic expert. He's coming in two weeks."

"What? Why not now?"

"Scheduling."

I can't organize my thoughts. We'll know if Carrie was killed. We'll know. I turn to Dad. "Dad—he knew her name—Carrie's name. This gang banger guy. I couldn't ask how he knew her because the little girl—"

"Salem, calm down," Dad says.

"—was shot but I said 'my sister' and he said, 'Carrie'—I *am* calm!"

"Sit down," the officer says.

"But—"

"Sit *down*." He steps between Dad and me to push me into an office chair. "You were at the drive-by on Benjamin Street?"

I nod. Dad's face goes slack.

"Do you need an ambulance? Are you hurt?" The officer's questions keep coming. Did I see shooters? The car? Do I know what shock is? Dad somehow has my hand in his.

"So you left via the back door?" the officer verifies. He's writing everything on a yellow pad.

"Yes." I think of Cordero yelling at me to get out. Threatening me, holding a gun.

"What were you *doing* there?" Dad asks.

"What were you doing there?" the officer repeats calmly.

"No one will tell me what's going on. So I . . . I got Cordero's address and . . ." I realize too late I should have lied. I should have made up a reason.

Dad leans to catch my eye. "Oh, Salem. Did you call the police when you heard shots?"

"Yeah. El Payaso talked to them. He's the one who knows Carrie. He used my phone."

"El Payaso?" The officer puts a finger up and grabs a radio from his belt. "Dispatch, report of a 1340," he says into it. "Suspect Oscar Garcia-Joya, wanted for parole violation. A witness puts him at 147 Benjamin Street."

Static cracks and he turns off the radio.

"But El Payaso helped the bleeding girl," I say, troubled. Police shouldn't be after El Payaso. He was in prison when Juan died and when Carrie's car was tagged.

The officer waits for me to look at him. "Salem, El Payaso is dangerous. If you see him again, call. We'll send every vehicle in town to you."

I nod. Every vehicle in town.

"And don't go anywhere *near* that house again," Dad lectures, crouched on the floor next to my chair.

"Fine, but I want to hear everything about Carrie's case," I say, nodding at the officer.

Haynes sits on his desk. "We sent officers for a preliminary investigation. They took a look at her vandalized Volkswagen. It was burnt out from the fire, but they came across a can of black spray paint found almost undamaged near the collapsed wall of the garage. Carrie's fingerprints were on it, which means we now have proof she vandalized her own car. She told dispatch about a death threat, but changed her story. Whether anyone actually threatened her or not—killed her or not—I don't know."

"But . . . what if the vandal was wearing gloves?" I run my hand over the sweat-damp hair at my temples. My ponytail loosens, already a mess.

"Either way, an expert is coming."

"If Carrie painted her own car, she put that symbol there as a message," I insist.

Haynes takes another sip of coffee. "Well, we'll find out in a couple weeks."

CHAPTER NINE

The next day, our team—the prosecution—is supposed to meet in the gym during political science. I'm not sure Cordero will come to school after what happened yesterday. I want him to show up and I don't want him to. He knows more about Carrie than I do, but I'm terrified of him. I'm terrified of his gun and him yelling at me and gang members in general.

I searched news sites this morning and learned his sister was expected to live. The article said that the day before some websites had mentioned the Primero symbols found on Juan Herrera's body. Police think their enemies, the Últimos, figured the victim was one of their own and went on the warpath in retaliation, shooting up the house and hitting Cordero's sister.

I was blissful at the news. Jealous. Carrie didn't live. The little girl did live—a drop of innocence in gang-infested waters.

I'm almost to the entry of the gym when a guy in a black backpack cuts in front of me, blocking my path. It's Cordero.

"Salem, I want to talk with you," he says, his vowels open, his smile less so.

Flinching, I back away from him. "Go away."

I don't meet his gaze, but I notice everything—a scar twisting through the dark of his forearm and the ribbing of a white undershirt stretched over his chest. There's stale cigarette smoke and something sweet coming from his skin.

His fingers twitch at his side, gesturing at the parking lot and the next set of students arriving from campus. "I'm not going to hurt you. I only want to set up a mock trial practice. We must meet as a team outside of the school. My home and your home will not be good for this."

Offended by his casual attitude, I look up at brown eyes framed by dark lashes. "Oh, I thought you wanted to talk about how someone left a Primero gang symbol on Carrie's car right before my house burned down around her. Because that's all I want to talk about."

His eyes harden. Stepping back, he masters his emotion. "Also, I wanted to make sure you were okay after yesterday." His words become formal, exiting his mouth with the caution of one who wonders if they're correct, who wants them to be correct. "I guess you are. Do not come to that house again."

He walks to the gym doors and goes inside.

I don't follow him. My body is trembling in fear. The muscles wrapping my ribs are sore. What was that? Some kind of bad-cop, good-cop routine? I'm ashamed of myself for freaking out. Cornering me on campus wasn't a murder plan. I should have been kind and pretended to be his friend, so he'd want to talk to me. But even if I'd thought of that, I couldn't have done it. I'm barely holding myself together enough to attend school, let alone pretend to care about someone who may have hurt Carrie. I have to wait. Make it through today and talk to him when I'm calm. Stop giving him reasons to dislike me.

Squaring my shoulders, I enter the gym.

The air smells of perspiration, but it's somewhat cool at least. Cordero is at the top of the bleachers, left side. His focus is straight ahead, but I swear he knows I just arrived. He's pointedly refusing to look at me.

"Fear!" Mr. White announces as he strides toward the bleachers. At their base, I notice a video camera labeled with the words, "Prosecution Team Leader." That's me. I tuck the camera into my backpack.

"What triggers the idea of conspiracy?" Mr. White asks.

"Horror!" McCoy Case shouts, fisting both hands in front of his own face. The freckle-faced student is Jeremy's partner. "White-knuckled dread!"

A few students laugh.

I climb to the top benches nearest the double doors, as far from Cordero as possible while still keeping him under surveillance. I came to class terrified of him. Now I'm embarrassed of that fear even though I still have it.

On the gym floor, Slate jogs up to Mr. White with some urgency. "The community leaders can't meet with the defense team today after all."

"One second," Mr. White says to the class, bending over a clipboard Slate holds.

Out of nowhere, one of my classmates, AddyDay, comes to the bleachers in front of me.

"Hey, Salem. How's . . . how's everything?" Her pink fingernails rest on her side. A bandage extends from her left ear to her jugular.

I should answer, but I just stare at her, wondering what happened to her neck. As I search for the right words to say, a pair of seniors comes across the gym toward us.

"Hey, Marissa. Katelyn," AddyDay says.

Marissa is a pimpled, Hispanic Olive Oyl. She grabs AddyDay by the elbow. "What *happened*?"

"What *happened*?" Katelyn echoes. She's a short blonde with ribbons in her hair.

AddyDay tries to laugh, like her injury is a joke.

The girls take a seat, still talking about AddyDay's neck. The attention of the entire class shifts to her. Classmates with brains say nothing. Jeremy asks if Jack the Ripper posts his hits on YouTube these days. AddyDay ignores him and sits next to me.

Why don't her friends stick up for her? I wish I were brave enough to.

"Jeremy's awful," I say.

Confused, she frowns. "He's just kidding, Salem."

I shift on the bench, not liking her answer.

Jeremy leaves us to join McCoy on the far side of the bleachers. They walk along a bench, stopping at Cordero. I watch in my periphery.

"Well, howdy, pardner," McCoy says.

Cordero doesn't acknowledge him.

"I said howdy!" McCoy's voice hits the corners of the gym.

Shifting, I glance at Mr. White. He doesn't look up, shaking his head at Slate and pointing at the clipboard.

"Oh, you knew we were going to recognize you," McCoy tells Cordero. "A bright-eyed little homeboy like you? You and your friend made trouble last time I saw you. Mission Plaza? Last May?"

My ears perk up. According to Slate, Mission Plaza is where Carrie met with those Primeros. May is when Juan was killed.

Ever the prankster, McCoy circles his fists in mockery. He jabs at Cordero. Cordero stands and shoves McCoy with both hands, sending the redhead into the bleachers on his butt. AddyDay yelps. McCoy scrambles up from the bench, ready to lunge but Jeremy holds him back, looking at Mr. White. Unbelievably, the teacher is still talking to Slate. Everyone else is watching the fight.

McCoy breaks from Jeremy and pulls up three inches from Cordero.

"All right, pardner." McCoy breathes heavy into Cordero's face. He's trying to conceal his delight. "This'll be real, real fun."

Cordero stares McCoy down, smart enough to stand one step above the taller redhead.

With a final nod at Slate, Mr. White hugs the clipboard to his middle and addresses the class. "Welcome to your lair, prosecution team."

Cordero sits without a glance at McCoy. He and Jeremy sulk and move across the aisle, taking their seats.

I want to shake all of them. Shake answers from them like coins from a piggy bank. How do Jeremy and McCoy know Cordero? What happened at Mission Plaza?

"For the next two weeks, you will have total secrecy here in the gym while the defense meets in my classroom," Mr. White continues. "Was President Kennedy's killer acting alone? Prove it! There's been a change on the schedule, so I'm going to go orient the defense team and Slate here will take you through witness questions."

Introduction complete, Mr. White strides toward the exit.

"Well, we'll start with good news," Slate announces. "Because of the peach strike, US Senator Debbie Lethco has decided to speak next Saturday during Verona's Festival Hispánico. You are required to attend."

The class groans.

"Sorry." He smiles. "Now, for today, we're going to jump right in and put Oswald on the stand. Salem, let's have you man the camera."

I come down the bleachers. AddyDay and Jeremy volunteer to star in the video we'll be filming. There's some confusion as AddyDay tells Slate that she didn't know she should have written the answers to the witness questions she prepared the night before.

"Let's practice anyway," Slate tells her.

I'm supposed to be acting as a team leader, but it's Slate who has the pair sit on the gym floor, facing the bleachers. Jeremy scoots close to AddyDay, who shifts away.

"Tell us your name and about your childhood, Oswald," AddyDay says.

Rolling the camera, I pan out from her face. She's sitting cross-legged, clutching a sheaf of binder paper.

"I'm Lee Oswald, born in 1939." Jeremy leans into the screen, wafting the smell of whatever he last ate into AddyDay's face. I center the picture to include him. "And I was a butthead."

"Where did you go to school?" she asks.

"You were too stupid to write the answers to the questions you wrote, so I don't know where I went to school."

"Tell us about your personality."

"Is this a trial or a dating service?"

"But that's . . . you're not answering based on any of the facts." AddyDay's face flushes, and she looks up from her paper. "There was other stuff. Like the kinds of books you read."

"Romance novels." Jeremy pounces on the question. "The kissing kind."

"You said you were trying to find—what was it?" AddyDay abandons her paper and speaks from memory. "A key to your environment. 'I dug for books in the back of library shelves,' you wrote in your journal. 'I became a communist by the time I was fifteen.' Admit it, Lee Oswald."

Jeremy's eyebrows soar as students stop laughing and focus. She just cornered a hostile witness with real-time questions.

"Actually, if you'd read beyond Wikipedia, you'd know that my best friend, Edward Something-that-starts-with-a-*v*, claims that your little factoid is a lie," Jeremy answers, proving AddyDay wasn't the only one digging into research.

I shouldn't be surprised, but I *am* impressed. Jeremy and AddyDay are apparently in an AP class for good reasons.

Jeremy continues. "I was a lying, stupid butthead. I didn't graduate from high school. I was *so* stupid, I went to Russia even though the Soviets didn't want me. I convinced this total hottie to marry me, but had to work in a factory. Lame."

Jeremy rolls his eyes, his frustration becoming Oswald's aggravation. How the self-important extremist must have longed for a plot that would put him on the map of the powerful.

A plot like murder.

Slate has Jeremy and AddyDay switch roles. They debate, and before I know it, the bell rings. Cordero must have been watching the clock. He has moved to position himself in front of the closest exit, blocking the path out. His emotionless eyes survey the students now hesitating to approach him. He lifts his chin.

"In whose house will we meet as a team?" he asks, examining our classmates one by one. None hold his gaze except Jeremy and McCoy.

"How about mine?" Jeremy says. It's a challenge.

"At seven tomorrow." Cordero turns to exit, becoming a silhouette as sunlight streams around him.

I'm the only person he didn't look at.

Maybe he's sending a message. Leave him alone and he'll leave me alone. It's not a fair trade if he killed Juan or Carrie. He gets away with murder and I get to escape without harm? Besides, he's not the only person who might know what the union, growers, and gangs were up to. Jeremy and McCoy might know something. Granted, they might not be any easier to pry information from than Cordero is. Other kids hung out with Carrie, though.

I'm willing to question every person on campus, but I need to be smart about it. No more dropping by gang member's houses. Start with those I trust most and move out from there.

And stay away from Cordero.

CHAPTER TEN

I decide on Envy and Kimi as my best potential sources of information. The perfect time to question them is at a Students for Strike club meeting the next day. It's the first meeting since Carrie died, and I'm nervous and emotional.

Students hang out inside the classroom where the meeting is held, making chaos. Envy, now copresident with Kimi, sticks a laminated picture of Carrie on the chalkboard. It has text on the bottom that reads, "Always." She rifles through a folder, pausing now and again to think.

At the teacher's desk Kimi notices me and waves tentatively. Envy looks over. Setting her folder down, she runs up to me. Her ponytail is like a dollop of black whipped cream on top of her head.

"Is it okay to hug you this time?" she asks.

Grateful, I nod.

Envy's skin is soft and brown. Kimi makes it a group hug.

The club's advisory teacher announces to everyone that a school counselor is scheduled to arrive soon for grief counseling. She chokes up as she speaks.

"The accident that killed Carrie shows us how fragile and precious life is."

Anxiety shoots through me.

"I can't do this," I whisper to Envy. If we talk about Carrie, I'll cry—in front of all these people. Why did I come here?

She must notice my unease. She leads me away from the crowd starting to surround us, taking Kimi too. We huddle near a supply closet in the corner. People glance at us in pity.

"You don't want to stay? You don't have to," Envy says in a low voice.

Kimi smacks Envy's arm. "Counselors are good for people."

"So?" Envy asks.

"I can't leave yet, I . . . I wanted to ask you two something," I whisper. "Did Carrie ever mention Juan Herrera, the guy killed in our orchard? I just . . . it seems so strange, you know, that he was found so . . . so close to where she died."

They huddle closer for privacy from the classroom, their eyes serious.

"I never heard her say anything about him," Envy says.

Kimi just shakes her head.

"What about that new kid, Cordero?" I whisper. "You guys said you didn't know him. Did Carrie?"

"Not that I know of," Kimi says. "Is that who vandalized her car?"

"I don't know. What about . . . did Carrie ever talk about plans or strategy—something straight from the union itself?"

Envy looks at Kimi. "We never talked to anyone from the farm union, only Carrie did."

"I talked to President Benicio de la Cruz once," Kimi brags in low voice.

Envy smiles her soft smile. "You just answered Carrie's phone when he called her."

"Yes, and I said, 'Hello, Mr. President. Here's Carrie Jefferson.' Carrie needed an introduction. It increased her aura."

"I remember that." A laugh escapes me, which is better than a sob. When Carrie's fundraiser earned all that money, we got a letter saying President Benicio wanted to thank us and would be calling us the following day. Carrie was so excited.

"Carrie said she was going to name one of her kids after President Benicio," Envy says.

I take a breath. "What about . . . did she talk about . . . *hiring* someone?"

Envy frowns. "We tried to get everything for the fundraisers by donation."

I need to clarify, but I weigh my words. "I mean for underground kind of stuff. Hiring a guy . . . or . . . I don't know, like, a gang member to beat up a grower or something."

Kimi raises her eyebrows. "Excuse me?"

Envy hits my arm. "If Carrie were here, girl, what would she say, listening to you talk like that? Anyway, you were at all the meetings. We talked about how to get more Facebook shares for the union. How to fundraise."

My shoulders drop. "You're right. Of course."

"The counselor's here," Kimi says with a glance over her shoulder. "Want to stay?"

"Girl, get out of here," Envy tells me with a pat on my back.

I go to leave and Envy stops me for one more hug. "You'll come next time."

They escort me to the door, telling everyone I have a cross-country practice I can't miss. Everyone knows they're lying. I rush to a bathroom, fixated by the idea that I could go back to the club meeting and give up this obsession with learning about how Carrie died. Learn to accept she's gone. Grieve. Is that what she would want me to do? I enter the first stall and sob, swearing I would do what she wanted. If only I knew it, I would do it. But that's the point. She's not here to tell me. She's not here and I think someone took her from me on purpose.

. . .

After cross-country practice the next day, I wolf down dinner, shower, and head to Jeremy Novo's house for the mock trial practice. Dad lets me use the car because he has a bunch of technical papers to edit at home.

There won't be any teachers there, possibly no parents either, and Cordero is the one who set up the meeting. I have a vision of cornering him where he's afraid and I'm not—the exact reverse of our encounter in his house.

"Wi-Fi password is *babesdigjeremy*, no caps, no spaces," Jeremy says when I arrive, walking me to an office nook. The dark walls are lit by sconce lighting. Heavy drapes obscure a wall of windows facing the backyard. AddyDay and her friends Marissa and Katelyn are already here. They wave to me as the doorbell of the house rings.

Jeremy rolls his eyes. "*You* get it." He points at me.

I go to answer, picturing flashing, dark eyes. Instead, I find Slate waiting on the porch.

His hair is so black and thick over his eyes that their color would fade to nothing if they weren't so piercingly blue. When he sees me, his full lips widen.

"Heard about a mock trial meeting," he says.

I smile. "Glad to get help from our class TA."

He can't know just how glad. Slate doesn't trust Cordero any more than I do. It's like having a person to help me.

"Slate!" Marissa says when we reach the front room.

"Slate!" Katelyn says louder, not to be outdone.

They descend on the class TA, inviting him to pick a seat, pointing out water bottles provided by Jeremy's mom, and alerting him to the fact that they would have worn more makeup if they'd known he was coming. McCoy shows up with other boys on our team, shouting about connecting his laptop to an outlet.

Slate claps his hands together. "Hey, guys. Maybe we should turn the time over to Salem and get started."

Fourteen pairs of eyes land on me, annoyed.

"Um, we . . . um, should split into teams to research different things," I tell the group. "Oswald probably planned the assassination with the mob, the USSR, or the anti-communist Cubans living in America. So . . . um . . ."

"I already have made assignments."

I turn.

Cordero is standing in the open entrance to the living room with a black backpack hanging from one shoulder, cap gone, his gold necklace mostly hidden under the neckline of his t-shirt. His expression is confident.

Smiling at Cordero, McCoy twists his fist into the flat of his opposite palm. "You showed up. Awesome."

Jeremy laughs.

Becoming more guarded, Cordero ignores both of them and asks Marissa if the seat next to her is taken.

She looks up, surprised. "Go ahead." She grins at her friend.

He sets down his backpack on the brown leather couch, and turns to scan the room. He lands on Slate as a potential source of trouble. The two exchange cool glances. Cordero keeps his body angled to see Slate, Jeremy, and McCoy as he addresses everyone.

"Jeremy and McCoy will research the mob. You . . ." He nods to the boys surrounding the computer. ". . . will research the USSR like Salem. All of the others, the Cubans. I will research the forensics. Report to the class Monday. We will win. There was no conspiracy."

The room explodes in comments.

"How do *you* know?" I'm furious, as if he's talking about Carrie, saying she wasn't murdered.

"Good thing he cleared *that* up," Jeremy says to McCoy. AddyDay wants to know the source he's citing.

"A mob does not hire killers, not from the outside," Cordero explains. He doesn't raise his voice. His facial tattoo, height, and calm stare silence the room. "They have their own killers. The mob kills with mob people. Same for the Cubans."

A student named Philip speaks up. "You're talking about power structure." Excited, he turns to his friends. "He's right. If you have your own power—your own assassins—why hire someone from the outside? We can use that in our closing statement. It makes the whole idea of a conspiracy look dumb."

Cordero nods. "Conspiracy requires more money. More time. The risk of getting caught is higher."

"But conspiracies *do* happen sometimes," I say. "Especially when the money involved was big time. Havana, Cuba was the resort capital of the world back then. The Cubans—the mob—they hated Kennedy for not taking down the communist leader who shut down their casinos."

It's the most coherent thing I've said to my teammates since school started. Many are nodding, maybe jazzed at signs of life from the prosecution team.

"Whose side are you on anyway?" Marissa asks me from the couch. "You're going to make the defense team win."

"We can't just assume there was no plot," I say. "Kennedy was one of the most popular presidents ever. Maybe all the regular mob assassins refused the assignment."

"Mob members don't say *no*," Slate says in quiet calm next to me. "It's the mob's teachings. You serve the family and what the family needs, not yourself."

"Well . . . maybe that works sometimes," I say.

Slate frowns. "No. All the time. You do whatever the family needs."

Cordero's hostility toward Slate cools enough for him to nod. "He's right."

"You do what the family needs even if it makes you a murderer?" I ask, ready to hate Cordero regardless of his answer. Instead of responding, he tightens his jaw in a sudden frown, looking away.

Slate takes the opening. "*Are* you a murderer if you know that it's for your family?"

"Slate!" I cry. He can't mean what he's saying. He means other people, bad people—that's who murders for their family.

AddyDay cuts in from a kneeling position next to the couch. "Soldiers kill for their families."

"Mobsters are hardly soldiers," I tell her.

"I don't know. Maybe they think of themselves that way," she answers.

With a wave of his hand, Cordero dismisses us all. "None of you understand the mob."

Cheeks flushed, Slate stands and steps toward Cordero. "I don't understand mobs, but I understand family. I understand loyalty. So did Carrie."

Cordero stands. "You understand nothing!"

I glance between them, fearful of more fighting, thoughts spinning. Cordero doesn't shrug off murder like it's no big deal, that's for sure. He's certainly more conflicted than Slate about the idea of the mob making an assignment that has to be fulfilled no matter what.

A loud female voice shouts into the room. "Snack time!"

"Mother," Jeremy complains.

Across the room, a brunette woman with a wide smile steps into the living room, carrying a tray of cheese slices and crackers.

"I thought you all might like some," she says.

The company of boys at the desk head for the tray. Cordero won't step away from Slate for anything but the TA retreats, obviously coaching himself on the foolishness of making trouble. As they separate, each turns toward me. They realize their common goal and frown at each other. Again, Slate moves aside. Cordero smirks and steps in front of me to talk to me, like it's his place to do so. He is my partner, after all.

In confusion, my gaze finds his. His expression is dark and tense and alert to my scrutiny.

Could it be possible? Could Cordero have a moral code that's as important to him as anything I follow myself?

He speaks calmly to me. "Write out your arguments about the JFK case. We'll find a way to counter them one by one."

I nod. "Okay, I . . . but I . . . actually I wanted to talk to you."

"I'm not staying." He turns and walks toward the front door.

CHAPTER ELEVEN

When the mock trial practice ends, Slate is in no hurry to go. We review notes for ten minutes. Jeremy and McCoy start up Xbox games. After AddyDay and her friends take off, Slate leads me into the warm evening. Streetlights are on, but they don't compete with the glimmer of a summer sunset.

Slate glances at me when we reach the sidewalk. "Cordero giving you any trouble as your partner?"

"Well . . . not really." I don't say how I feel tricked for even considering Cordero might have a moral code. He grabbed a handgun and shot at his enemies. *That's* probably his moral code.

After failing to talk to him, I didn't even attempt to ask Jeremy or McCoy about Carrie. I can't ruin my chances by demanding answers in a room full of people. Slate and I are alone, though. It's an opportunity I can't pass up.

I swallow and try to look casual. "Did you know Cordero hung out once with McCoy at Mission Plaza? Was that the night you fought him?"

Slate stops with me next to the driver's side of the car I drove, Dad's Prius. "You need to leave this alone, yeah?"

"Listen, I—"

"What's Cordero going to do if he finds out you're asking questions about him?"

"At least tell me—"

"Listen." He shakes his head. "McCoy wasn't there when I fought. Not that I know of. It was another night McCoy got into it with Cordero. I wasn't there. Carrie was. She called me for a ride home and I was already in the car with Anna, my sister—she . . ."

He stops talking right in the middle of his sentence. His expression turns off. It goes from anxious to emotionally dead.

I wonder if he's afraid of emotion. Well, that's one thing we'd have in common, besides Carrie.

I wait, not sure what to ask even if he would answer.

"Anyway," he continues with a careful voice. "The night McCoy was there, Carrie seemed . . . she might have been frightened. I don't know. Just tired maybe—she wasn't her usual self."

"Don't you think Cordero knows what might have happened to Carrie? She hired him after all. He obviously would never tell police, but what if—"

"I don't get involved with people like him. Not even to find out about Carrie."

"I would just talk to him."

"Being safe doesn't mean I didn't care about her."

"I . . ." His words about my sister slash deep. He thinks I'm accusing him of not caring about her. I feel terrible.

I slump forward. "Sometimes I wonder . . . if I could just find out what he knew . . ."

"You want to know what happened to her, yeah? I know. I understand. But she'd want you to be careful, yeah?"

I nod. He's right. Of course he's right.

His phone rings. The screen is angled so both of us are able to see the picture of his sister flashing on the screen. Anna's features are much darker than his. Her smile looks sad. Carrie talked about Anna sometimes, about how she was so shy and pretty, but troubled. Something about a guy.

Slate's expression stiffens.

"Hello?" he answers.

When his sister responds, his shoulders relax. "Okay, I'll be right there," he tells her, waving good-bye to me.

I drive home, taking country roads that are unlit this far from town. I think of Carrie, how crazy she was about Slate and his whole family. Slate's mom was polite, but reserved and very religious—she wears the Muslim shawl while she works as a maid. I think for some reason of Cordero's mom. She sobbed over her daughter's gunshot wound, but didn't help her really.

At the thought, my mental image slides dramatically away from Slate—who has told me all he probably knows— and swings to Cordero—who likely has more information about Carrie's union plans than anyone else. I'm running out of people to question. I have to be smart, take my time, and create a good opportunity.

I have to get Cordero to open up to me somehow.

. . .

On Monday, we start our reports on potential conspirators. McCoy and Jeremy show everyone up, coming to class with dark sunglasses, shooting the bleachers with double finger guns, and telling us, "It's the mob, people. That's who was gutsy enough to kill an American president." They deliver a thorough lecture on primary mobster figures of the 1960s.

"So if you want to learn about the mob, do as the mob does," McCoy says as they finish, tossing small plastic packages to the bleachers. One falls near my sandal, and I pick it up. There's something fuzzy and black inside.

"What is this?" AddyDay asks. She's sitting next to her friends. Her Band-Aids are gone, replaced by a thin line of scabbing under her neck, like a knife wound.

"Fake mustaches," McCoy answers in a cheerful voice. "Gold necklaces are also standard mob-wear."

While students laugh, Cordero nods in approval. He doesn't direct the groups often, but when he does, it's with a confident voice. I glance at him twice. He catches me both times. I want him to instigate a conversation, but don't dare communicate that.

When AddyDay and her friends are up, they try to wear their mustaches as they report on Cuban suspects, but lose them as soon as they start talking. I hate speaking in public, so I speed through my information about Kennedy's Russian enemies. Cordero presents after me. His information is dead on, detailing the likelihood of the bullet that killed Kennedy entering from his forehead or from the back of his skull. I wonder if he used the school's computer. I can't imagine anyone in the 147 Benjamin Road house owning one.

As he speaks, I check the time on my phone and move to the exit when one minute of class remains. As usual, he's the first to the door after the bell rings. I stand in front of it, the way he did.

"We should . . . meet," I tell him. I stay calm and direct, the manner he usually adopts. "Outside of school. To study."

He glances at the other students beginning to head toward us. "We already did. At the mock trial practice at Jeremy's."

"But . . . I didn't even talk to you."

He shrugs and leaves.

I'm mad at myself for not following him to demand answers but grateful at the same time. I can't mess this up. I need to give him a reason to want to talk to me.

After cross-country practice I'm supposed to meet Dad at Mountain Mike's Pizza, where he's having a meeting with the Peach Growers Association. I arrive on foot, fifteen minutes early. I drop my backpack on a strip of grass near the restaurant and sit. Devouring three protein bars, I take out the prosecution team's video camera to watch scenes from last year's mock trial.

The screen blinks, and the first image I see is Slate sneaking a private smile at someone offscreen.

"You ready?" he whispers from the television speakers.

A girl giggles in the background. Carrie. I'd know her laugh anywhere. Carrie, full and strong.

I max the volume.

"I swear to tell the truth, the whole truth, and nothing but the truth," she says.

The camera angle changes. Carrie is on screen, her brown hair falling in curls. She's got her right arm raised.

"So help me God," Slate prompts her from off screen.

Carrie shoots him a look. "Let us not trifle with things that are sacred."

He stifles his laughter poorly. "Please state your name for court records."

"I am August Spies, born in 1855," she answers. "A union activist accused of conspiracy in the bombing known as the Haymarket Affair. I am for the union! Workers of the world, unite!" Carrie stands so that her head is no longer on the screen. A fabric belt sways at her waist.

The scene ends in a blue screen that lists recording options by date. For a moment, I'm back in time, when unions, explosions, and murder raged. Strikes aren't supposed to be like that anymore. But they are. The corpse found in our peach orchard proves it.

The list of videos goes through early May until the final one, on May 22, which was when last year's mock trial was held. The schedule for the mock trial changes dramatically every year.

May 22 was two days before Juan was buried in our orchard.

I grab the remote and navigate down to that recording, labeled 1:07 p.m.

The scene shows last year's mock trial teammates seated inside Mr. White's classroom. Carrie bursts onto the screen without noticing the camera is recording. Slate meets her, reaching behind her neck to fasten a necklace studded with clear-jeweled droplets.

"Do you like it?" Carrie asks.

"No, I bought you something I didn't like," he teases.

The scene pitches as the camera operator squeals. "Slate got you a present?"

Carrie laughs. "I made him give it to me now. I don't want to wait until we go out tonight."

Slate smiles. "It's for her birthday."

The screen goes blue.

I remember that night. I was home alone flipping channels while Carrie and Slate went to dinner to celebrate, even though her actual birthday had been a few days before. It's the night Slate talked about, the one where he fought Tito. I didn't realize how close it was to Juan's death.

I turn the camera off and put it in my backpack.

All this time, I've been chasing after anyone who might have information about Carrie's death and I never thought to wonder what anyone was doing around the date of *Juan's* death—what *I* was doing, even. Like the very next night— the night after Slate and Carrie's birthday celebration, the night before Juan died. I remember every detail.

I play through what I did during those days of spring like I'm watching one of the recordings.

CHAPTER TWELVE

It was the day after Slate and Carrie's dinner date, so it must have been May 23. There was blood. I called Carrie five times and I couldn't move because of the blood and she still didn't answer.

I held the door of Verona High's equipment closet shut from the inside, wanting to die of embarrassment. Trying to locate Carrie, I called my family's home phone.

"Hello?"

"Dad?" I asked.

"What?"

"Where's Carrie? I need Carrie."

"What is it?"

"She's not out with Slate, is she? They just went out yesterday."

"Salem Jefferson."

"Dad, just make her pick up her phone. I have to talk to her," I whined.

"But you'll have to settle for me."

"Just . . . never mind."

I hung up. I listened for footsteps from outside. Nothing. I wondered if I could leave the closet and run for the bathrooms. One of my teammates might see me.

My cell rang.

"Carrie?" My voice was breathless.

"You skipped your hurdles meeting?" Dad answered.

"You called my coach?"

"He said people are looking for you—"

"Dad! Why did you call him?"

"—and the track practice is over—"

"I need Carrie!"

Dad always downplayed my anxiety. "—and no one knows where you are, including me, I might add, and I'm just curious enough to be mildly nervous. I think I've actually released adrenaline into my bloodstream."

"I can't believe you called someone."

"I can't believe I've released adrenaline into my bloodstream. I'm a better parent than I imagined. I'm about to leave so why don't you tell me where you are?"

"Wait, you're coming? Don't come."

"Thanks for your confidence."

"Dad, I need Carrie!" My voice choked up so I couldn't say more.

"Are you crying?"

I didn't answer. I was crying.

"Salem, has it ever occurred to you that Carrie won't be at your beck and call forever? She's going to move on. Celebrate wedding anniversaries and baby's birthdays—with Slate in all likelihood. She knows this. She's trying to prep you. Why can't you see it? Salem?"

My tears stop flowing. I didn't want Carrie to move on.

"Where are you? Are you hurt?" Dad's worry was as fierce as his frustration.

"I need . . . a tampon. Or a pad." I cringed, my voice muffled by the equipment in the track closet. I'd been inside it ever since I felt the blood running down my legs.

"What? That's great," Dad said.

"What?" I wanted to cry again.

"I was starting to get worried. I thought you were running too much. How old are you again? Fifteen and a half? That's on the edge of the normal range, right?"

I was so surprised I couldn't speak.

"You and your theatrics," he said.

Later, when I finished changing, I found him waiting for me outside the locker room with two ice cream cones he'd bought on his way to get me. I refused to be happy and instead demanded we go directly to the car.

"Please do not walk on the grass," I read from a sign as Dad cut across a patch of lawn.

"I'm in a hurry," Dad said, hurrying like he had an appointment.

The sprinklers came on. Dad tripped on his way to the sidewalk and smashed ice cream into his face.

Maybe Dad was trying to convince me to change my attitude. Maybe the weather was too good for frustration. He laughed. I started to relax.

"Guess that's what I get for walking on the grass." He wiped soft-serve from his mouth. "Ugh. It's like getting kissed by a snowman."

His phone rang. He wiped his hand on the outside of his pants and looked at the screen.

"It's Carrie," he said, putting the phone to his ear to say hello.

I found myself smiling, just a little. I got out my own phone.

"Carrie always says I should kiss someone," I said. "Maybe a snowman would do. Say cheese."

Dad turned to me, shaking his head. I'd already snapped the picture of the ice cream on his face.

Laughing, I texted it to Carrie as she spoke to Dad. Then I emailed it to her and sent it to her over Snapchat, just to mess with her. I couldn't focus on their conversation, preparing myself instead to reveal my news to her. Dad gave me the phone a moment later.

"I just got my period," I told her.

I could hear her breathing shallow and quick. She didn't answer. A vague anxiety settled on me.

"Carrie, I got my period."

"Oh."

"Carrie?"

"Oh, well, that's . . . that's really good." Her voice was finally starting to be animated.

"Well, everybody gets it."

Something distracted her. "Um, sorry, I've . . . the union . . . we're discussing some options. Rick Thornton is here. I have to go. Bye."

Once home, Dad found a website about puberty and then grilled steak because the article recommended iron-rich foods. I planned to stay awake that night and talk to Carrie once she was home. Instead, I drifted right to sleep.

Present Day

In the parking lot outside Dad's grower meeting, I hang on to the memory of Carrie. She fought to be my supportive big sister even when she could barely focus on talking to me, and all that happened just one day before the union official Juan disappeared. Was she frightened? Did she know Juan was going to die?

My thoughts keep coming. On May 22, Carrie celebrated her birthday with Slate. Slate said they ran into Cordero and a guy named Tito at Mission Plaza on the same night. On May 23, she spoke on the phone with me. But where was she on May 24 when Juan died? And when did Jeremy and McCoy see Cordero at Mission Plaza?

I have to figure out a way to get information from Jeremy and McCoy. And anyone else who might know what Carrie was up to those nights.

Come to think of it, Dad might remember something.

His meeting should be over soon. I gather my things and hurry to meet him inside the pizza shop.

CHAPTER THIRTEEN

My muscles are sore from practice as I open the door to the restaurant where the growers hold their meetings. I enter alongside a man I recognize—Rick Thornton. He works for the Farm Workers Union and agreed to be an advisor for the Students for Strike club. Carrie adored him. He's the union official she mentioned meeting with the night before Juan died.

He holds the door open for me, his blond hair wild from cowlicks.

"Thank you," I mumble as I pass. Once inside, the smell of raw onions makes my eyes moisten.

"No problem," he answers. I don't think he recognizes me. He's one of the mock trial's community leaders this year, but he hasn't met with our team yet.

I leave him and climb the stairs to the banquet hall.

Dad is inside the dim room with two other men, a bearded man and a small, excitable man who feathers his hair back while he talks nonstop—my teacher, Mr. White. Dad talked about Mr. White once. Something about real estate prices dropping and how he planted thousands of peach trees anyway. If it's true, he has debt payments on land he can't sell and debt payments on trees he can't harvest. The strike must be killing him.

". . . convinced the market just can't pay that amount," Mr. White is saying.

Dad glances up at me, looking serious. "Salem, give us a minute."

Frustrated, I go back to the reception area where Rick Thornton is. I catch his eye and don't know if I should say hello.

"Ten more minutes for my pizza," he says. His face is wide and dimpled. He's got a laptop case over one shoulder.

"I'm Carrie Jefferson's little sister," I answer.

His smile plummets. "Of course. I should have recognized you. You and Carrie were the heart and soul of the club. Call me Rick. You're what, sixteen now? Time flies."

I nod. Everyone knows he goes by Rick. He's on school grounds a lot because part of his union job is to reach out to troubled teens as part of a gang-prevention unit sponsored by the police.

Troubled teens . . .

I glance at Rick.

"Um, hey." I clear my throat. "You knew Carrie. Did you hear about her car? It was tagged by this gang, the Primeros. I thought maybe it was because of something with the union, maybe something you knew about. She died right after."

With a glance at me, Rick shifts his feet, taking in the importance of my statement. "Hmm, that's no good. You think she was hurt on purpose?"

Rick hasn't told me I'm crazy yet. It's the best reaction I've had so far.

I nod. "I don't know. I just . . . wonder." I'm not willing to go into details about how she hired gang members to work for her. Carrie respected Rick. I feel protective, like I can't ruin his memory of her.

"I just thought . . . you're a union guy and people from the union have been hurt before," I continue. "You met with her in May, the day before Juan died."

He frowns immediately, like he's trying to remember. "I . . . I did?"

"Yeah, she mentioned it while I was on the phone with her." I'm disappointed he doesn't remember. "Aren't you frightened? Has anyone threatened you?"

He takes a deep breath, half-laughing. "Well . . . yes, I've been threatened. Of course I've been threatened. Usually it's hot air. But I can't say Juan's death hasn't given me pause."

His face is sad, maybe even traumatized. He was probably friends with Juan, now that I think about it.

After a moment, I say, "Um, I know Carrie worked with you on union stuff. While you talked to her, did she ever say anything about gangs maybe? Or Cordero Vasquez?"

Rick's face breaks into a smile. "Cordero? Did she know him?"

"You know Cordero?"

"Hey, now. You don't have to make a face. I used to have him over to my house when he was fourteen, fifteen.

My house is open to any troubled youth. Always has been, always will be. That place his mom rents a room in is infested with bad influences. These guys don't want to be in gangs. Not really."

I'm knocked back a bit at the image of Cordero as a younger teen, seeking refuge. I thought Cordero liked hanging out with gang members just fine.

"It's hard for kids to resist gangs," Rick continues. "It's hard to accept that the things you were taught growing up, the people who taught you, were wrong."

Footsteps sound in the stairwell to our left.

The bearded man from Dad's meeting rounds the corner and appears in front of us. Other growers are behind him, their voices approaching rapidly.

". . . in our counterstrike to the union rally next Saturday," Mr. White is saying. "Same time, same place."

"I might go back to the counter and order another lemonade," the bearded man calls in answer.

"A lemonade with extra ice," Dad adds once in view.

When Mr. White sees us, he looks from Dad to the bearded man, like he's fidgeting. He laughs too loudly. "Ice. Yes, it's hot today."

Neither one answers. Almost like all three men are trying to ignore Mr. White's original comment. Trying to bury it so it won't be noticed. What was it? Something about a rally? A counterstrike.

"So this is where you hold your secret meetings?" Rick asks, approaching the men. "I wasn't even sure they were real."

I turn to look at him. Rick is a union guy. He's surrounded by a bunch of growers. His cheeks are red, like his blood is fifty degrees hotter than it was earlier.

"Salem?" Dad looks between Rick and me. "You've been talking to Rick?"

Rick answers before I can. "I'm not going to take it out on your daughter."

Dad steps like he's going to pass Rick, but Rick puffs his chest out so they collide.

"Hey!" Rick's hands are fisted, arms cocked. He's muscular and young.

Dad backs up, but I can tell he's furious.

"What the heck?" I ask. A bunch of men acting like schoolboys.

"Now, Rick," the bearded man says, putting a hand on Rick's elbow. The man is tall and has an aura of leadership about him. I've seen him before.

Dad takes my arm. "Let's go."

Rick shakes off the bearded man's hand. He could take a swing at him, but apparently his issue with Dad is personal. He glares at my father. "Say hi to Elena for me."

I search my brain for the name. It sounds familiar. "What's going on? Who's Elena?"

"My wife." Rick is quick with his words and their underlying implication.

"His ex-wife." Dad is utterly calm. Nothing ruffles him. "We're meeting—"

"Give me a break!" Rick interrupts.

"—to talk about the strike," Dad continues. I watch his reaction closely. Everything from his round glasses to the pencils in his shirt pockets is scholarly. I relax. Dad would never date a married woman.

"An interview she shouldn't even be having. This strike!" Rick says, not addressing Dad anymore but the bearded man. "These migrant kids have nowhere to go. Their parents work to death. No wonder the kids fall into gangs. We're not helping them, keeping wages so low. We were just talking about a perfect example of this!"

He gestures toward me and then stalks out the front door, still without his pizza. None of the men's conversation makes any sense. Mr. White and the bearded man aren't shocked on Dad's behalf. They're not acting like Rick is jealous and prone to overreacting.

As soon as Rick leaves, Mr. White laces his fingers and looks at me. "We haven't even told you the good news, Salem. We remembered your dad's alibi."

"Alibi?" I spin to face Dad. The police wanted his alibi? I guess I should have expected that, but it's still unsettling.

He nods. "The police want to know where I was on the night Juan Herrera died. There was a grower's meeting in the early evening, but we're not sure how long it went, and I need an alibi until eight."

"Oh." I had envisioned the murder happening late at night. "Juan was . . . was dead by eight, then."

Dad shrugs, not unkindly. "That's what Officer Haynes says. I figure they're basing the time of death on when they found Juan's car, which was soon after that. Fortunately, after the grower's meeting, we stayed for pizza until 9:30. Thank heaven."

"*Good* pizza, if I remember right," the bearded man puts in. He has a full head of hair, wrinkles around his eyes, and a tie. "I myself had four or five slices." He extends his palm to me. "Bill Knockwurst."

"The mayor," I say, shaking his hand. I knew I recognized him. Carrie got her picture taken with him once for the Verona Bulletin. "You're AddyDay's stepfather."

He beams. "That I am."

Mr. White laces his fingers. "Good thing we finally remembered what we did during that May meeting. The recording of it is lost."

Confused, I look to Dad.

"The union official was there that night," he explains. "He records our negotiations."

I frown. "But Rick is the local union official."

Dad nods.

"Wait, so *Rick* lost the recording?" I ask, pointing at the door. "Rick Thornton?"

As I say his name, my memory triggers.

Rick Thornton. His wife, Elena—Elena Thornton. She's the journalist who brushed her fingers against Dad's wrist when the corpse was found. The article I read of hers mentioned Rick specifically. His home has suffered three attempted burglaries recently. I'm surprised I didn't notice at the time that their last names were the same.

So Dad and Elena are having an affair. But wait, I thought I didn't believe he was having an affair. I don't believe it, right?

Dad starts toward the door.

I hurry after him. "And Rick Thornton—who thinks you're having an affair with his wife—just happens to lose the recording verifying your alibi during a murder?"

We go outside into scorching air, Mr. White and the mayor following. I squint against the sunlight and look for Rick. He's gone.

Dad shields his eyes. "Apparently. We're the Peach Growers Association, Salem. Not the Supreme Court."

"He hates you," I say, noticing Dad's lack of comment on Elena. "Is there any evidence the recording was deleted? SD cards show stuff like that."

Mr. White stays on the sidewalk of the strip mall next to us. "They use a tape recorder."

I pause. "It's not . . . digital? Those things still work?"

The mayor smiles at Dad. "They do such a good job of making us feel old, don't they?"

Dad takes a breath, soaking in the heat of late summer like he's spent days realizing what freedom really means. "Rick lost the tape. Or maybe he never recorded the meeting in the first place. It happens."

We say goodbye to Mr. White and the mayor. Once inside the car, Dad sits lost in thought, thumb tapping the steering wheel. There's something about him suggesting that for all his relief, he feels guilty.

My suspicions whirl.

"Are the Thorntons divorced or not?" I ask.

Dad drives. The gravel crunches under the tires. "Salem, I'm not dating Elena."

"Are they divorced?"

The turn signal clicks off. "Rick won't sign the papers."

"And you and her—"

"Are not dating."

"No, I meant—"

"Have never gone out, met for lunch, or exchanged birthday presents."

"I meant you and her are meeting to talk about the strike."

"We're having dinner, but don't think she won't grill me. She's a journalist for one. Two, she and Rick don't agree on much, but they both want the strike to work."

"Mmph," I say.

Rick works for the union, so of course he wants the strike to work. But he does more than work for the union. He volunteers time at Verona High and pays attention to troubled teens and opens his house to gang members who want to change. He's dedicated, the way Carrie was. He believes.

Dad takes a breath. "This wasn't the way I was going to tell you."

I glance at him. "So it *is* a date."

He drives past the last stoplight and into the orchard-lined section of country road.

"If you were going to tell me, then it's a date." I don't know how to react.

"Can you get your own dinner?" Dad asks, tapping the steering wheel again. "I'm meeting Elena at six."

"You're nervous to see her?" I'm incredulous.

"It's that bad?" He clears his throat, making his nerves show even more.

"Stop it."

"But the way you're coaching me is so helpful." He pats his hair in the back. "It's not sticking up, is it?"

I realize he's acting nervous to make fun of me.

"Dad," I complain.

"What?" He laughs at me.

"Well . . . Rick's a lot younger than you. You need to date somebody old—old enough for you."

"Elena's thirty. Is that old enough?"

I do some calculations in my head. "If she were twenty-nine, she'd split our ages exactly," I say, horrified.

"Good thing she's thirty."

"Dad! Anyway, there's something wrong with her if she left Rick." Why would anyone leave a person who's like Carrie? "Did you know she wrote in one of her articles that someone is always trying to break into Rick's house?"

"*Her* house now. The break-ins are because he used to leave it open to gang members, which was such a great idea," Dad says sarcastically. "He lives in town now that he and Elena have split, but the old house is near us, just east of the Knockwursts' property. Supposedly, Rick's trying to transfer the, uh, *safe house* to his new place, but some gang members haven't gotten the message. Elena has a security system now that she lives alone."

"Well, anyway, I'm glad you remembered your alibi," I say, circling back to why I wanted to talk to Dad in the first place. "Before I even talked to you, I was thinking we should go over what Carrie was doing around the time Juan died too. In case the police need it, like . . . in case it helps them decide if Carrie's death was an accident." I speak cautiously.

Dad's jaw tightens. "I guess it couldn't hurt." He doesn't appear to think it'll help, either.

"Well, Juan died on Friday, May 24. The Wednesday before that, she and Slate went to dinner, for a late celebration of her birthday. On Thursday, you picked me up at track practice because I . . . I got my period. When I talked to her Thursday night, she seemed really worried. Do you know why?"

Dad thinks. He shakes his head. "It was so long ago."

"Any idea what she was doing Friday while you were at the peach meeting?" I ask.

He blows air out of his mouth. "I don't remember." He looks at me. "*You* don't remember?"

I pause. I hadn't really thought through the night after I got my period. Me on a Friday night?

"I had weight lifting for track from 5:30 to 7:00. Then I went home, I guess . . . did homework—wait, there was one day . . . that's probably it. One time I watched *Casablanca* right after practice. I bet it was a Friday. I . . . actually, I watched it twice."

I would never fess up to something like that under normal circumstances. I was alone and feeling sorry for myself. Alone and blissfully ignorant that Juan Herrera was beaten to death in our orchard. If I had ever looked out our sliding glass door that night toward the orchard, would I have seen anyone—like a gang member or Carrie or a union official living his last day?

"You watched a movie twice through and Carrie and I didn't come home in all that time?" Dad asks.

I nod.

"I guess she didn't see a murder after all," Dad says.

"What are you talking about?"

"Police found Juan's car at eight thirty that night, remember? They think the murder was done by eight. If Carrie didn't get home until late, there was nothing to see."

"Oh." I hadn't thought of that. "Maybe . . ." I can't think of any maybes.

"Salem, just let the police handle it."

"Great idea. They'll arrest *you*. Seriously, who buries a body in their own orchard when they can walk a quarter mile in any direction and put it in someone else's? What do the police think they have on you?"

I mean the question to be rhetorical.

Dad won't meet my gaze. As I watch him drive, I realize that he knows exactly what information the police have. I get goose bumps.

"I talked to Juan," Dad says finally. "His cell number was listed on the union website."

"When?" I whisper.

"Six days before he died. We only spoke a few minutes. I told him I wanted to chat with him about the strike and he said he'd stop by the house sometime. I guess he made a note to himself to visit me. The police have known about it since May. But he never came."

Neither of us says anything. No wonder the police suspect Dad.

Dad's phone rings from inside his shirt pocket. He checks the display and looks at me. It's Elena calling him, I bet, and he's not smiling. We're two miles from home, where he could answer without having to talk to her in front of me.

"I knew you were nervous," I say.

"I'll text her back."

"No—Dad!" I motion for him to answer. Doesn't he know to at least take her calls? "I'll . . . plug my ears."

Elena's voice is so loud I can hear her despite my half-hearted attempt to block my hearing. I'm curious.

"You are so lucky you get to spend time with me tonight," she says, her voice displaying a touch of accent. She's Puerto Rican, if I remember right.

"You've mentioned that," Dad answers, holding the phone at an angle so her voice doesn't blow his eardrum.

Elena has a snappy way of talking—not angry, but fiery. She's got attitude and confidence. All of a sudden I'm worried. She's smart and pretty and twelve years younger than him—of course he should make sure his hair isn't sticking up in the back.

I check Dad's appearance as he listens. Fortunately his hair is not sticking up. We pull in the driveway.

Elena continues. "Did you tell Salem about how I can help with her mock trial research?"

"Not yet." Dad motions me to go to the house.

I climb out of the Prius. I remember something and reopen the car door.

"One second, Elena." Dad fists his phone, annoyed.

"The police aren't going to arrest you now," I say. "I—I'm glad, that's all."

He shakes his head and leans to hug me.

I inhale the familiar smell of pencil lead on him and let myself realize how frightened he was. How frightened I was. This morning he was facing murder charges, and today he's going on a date with Elena.

And me? I go inside the house, steam some vegetables and rice, and dig into my plan to attend the required Festival Hispánico this Saturday. Who knows if Cordero will be there, but Jeremy and McCoy come to everything, carrying with them all they know about Carrie. I haven't found a way to talk to them in private at school, but with any luck, soon I'll know as much as they do.

CHAPTER FOURTEEN

On Saturday morning I opt for a ponytail, light make-up, and white capris. Casual. Classic. The perfect outfit to be wearing when I meet Dad's non-girlfriend.

Their non-date went so well it's getting a repeat performance. Elena invited Dad to the Festival Hispánico and, since I needed a ride there anyway, we'll all be going together. Oh, and then we're having dinner to "get to know each other."

Elena is not shy. Last night she told me through Dad that my mock trial group could meet at her house and use her Wi-Fi to get UC Berkeley library access—every FBI file ever released. The idea was tempting enough that I floated it on Facebook, but the team decided to continue meeting at Jeremy's.

After breakfast, Dad and I go pick up Elena together.

"Hi, Salem." She gets in the car and talks the whole trip. She's sort of interesting, like when she tells us about an interview she did with a family who donated their dead daughter's organs as transplants.

"Oh, that was hard," she says. "I cried four times."

Dad glances at her.

"What? I'm Hispanic and female. I can cry four times whenever I want."

He laughs.

I ditch Dad and Elena the second we park because I don't know what to do around them.

Under bright sunlight, I walk past teens in team jerseys and middle-aged women carting signs that read, "Pro-strike is Pro-gressive"—people who have never seen Verona on a map, let alone in person. They're here to support the peach strike. The pavilion is packed. I find Envy and Kimi shouting, "*Viva la* strike!"

I stand with them. They hug me, loving that I'm hanging out with them instead of pushing them away.

"This peach strike is about fairness!" United States Senator Debbie Lethco yells from the podium at the start of her speech. Her highlighted curves of hair shake. "This strike is about middle class creation! Opportunity! The American dream!"

The crowd in the pavilion comes to its feet with a stadium-worthy roar.

For the next hour, the senator is an aerobics instructor, leading everyone up, down, up, down. The temperature is the only thing that rises without falling. I map my route to shade during her every word.

"The union and I are proud to end this speech by announcing there will be a farm worker's march! Next

Saturday, pickers will march through peach country and then bus sixty miles to the Laborer's Rally in Sacramento!" Senator Lethco shakes a fist above her head, yelling over the growing noise.

The senator's announcement reanimates my overheated brain. A union event planned for next Saturday. That's what Mr. White was talking about. And the growers' counter-strike to it.

"We will march," Senator Lethco shouts. "We will start at the edge of peach country and will march with you to Sacramento. We will march with you right now. March with us! March! Workers of the world, we *are* united!"

The clamor is deafening. Senator Lethco continues yelling, continues throwing her fist forward rhythmically as she leads the march, snaking south. Envy, Kimi, and other club members dance on their way to follow her.

"*Viva la* march!" they shout.

The tide surges, sweeping me with it into the carnival area. There's an emotion to it—a frenzy. Someone may have gotten caught up by this emotion, the way Carrie had been, even hiring a gang member. Was this the emotion that killed her?

"Come on, Addy. You know you like me," someone behind me says as we walk. I turn to see Jeremy Novo a few groups of people away, holding AddyDay's arm.

"It's AddyDay," she answers.

"Aw, come on, *Addy*."

Doesn't he ever take a snack break? Tormenting people can't be as easy as it looks.

"Marissa, Katelyn, wait," AddyDay calls. Her friends from the mock trial slip farther ahead, not appearing to hear.

"A trip down memory lane," Jeremy says. The crowd has shifted so that they're closer to me. Only a pair of old women separates us. "You were my first, you know."

"Let me go!" Panic threatens to overcome the hate in AddyDay's voice as she struggles. She sounds like Carrie did the morning she died.

Furious, I sling my backpack in front of Jeremy's feet. A dude full of piercings runs into him from behind, and he trips to his knees, freeing AddyDay. The crowd splits around us and continues flowing forward.

"Stop picking on her," I say.

Jeremy gets up, checking his ironed shorts for grass stains. Satisfied, he faces me. "Salem Jefferson? What are *you* doing? Going to accuse me of being a Primero?"

AddyDay glances at me and bites her lip in pity. "Everyone heard you ask Cordero if he was in the gang that tagged Carrie's car."

I flush.

Jeremy laughs. "Oh, I bet now you think *I* hurt Carrie."

I'm embarrassed he thinks I suspect everyone, but I pull myself together. I stop glaring and try to act conversational. He brought up the subject, after all. "So, what makes you think Carrie was hurt?"

He smirks. "Uh, because she died and now you're going around accusing people of going after her?"

"I thought . . . I thought it was strange that the union guy Juan Herrera had been buried so close to where she died. McCoy mentioned you and he ran into Cordero in May. That's around the time Juan died—did you know that?"

He gasps, mocking me. "Well, and here I was, wanting to tell you all about that night at Mission Plaza, but no. You're not nice. You tripped me."

"Jeremy, stop being mean," AddyDay says.

He rolls his eyes. "I'm not your friend, Salem. See ya later, *Addy*." He puckers his lips at her before disappearing into the stream of people.

I grab my backpack, and AddyDay and I make our way over to the ferris wheel. The fence around it makes a wide oval, lined with observers we can see on the other side. To our left, the thoroughfare is thinning. Senator Lethco's impromptu march is taking it to the streets, literally.

"He is the worst!" I lean against the chain link. "Why does he have it out for you?"

AddyDay leans next to me. "You don't know? Everyone knows. I lost my virginity to Jeremy in seventh grade. He promised he wouldn't tell anyone and when he did, they made fun of him for sleeping with garbage."

Horrified, I watch AddyDay finger her neck, now featuring a narrow white scar, blaming herself rather than the popular kids she wants so badly to please.

AddyDay misinterprets my look of disgust.

"I didn't have a lot of self-esteem back then," she says defensively. Her shoulders slump. "My only time. I've regretted it ever since."

"Just stand up to him, like you did at the mock trial practice," I say, wishing I were skilled enough to convey my sympathy correctly.

"I don't know. I just . . ." She shrugs. We stand in the hot sun for a minute, and she turns to me. "But what did you want to know about the night at Mission Plaza?"

I push off from the chain link. "Wait . . . you were there? You saw Cordero?"

"Mm-hmm."

I smile. "Well, forget Jeremy. Was Slate there? Carrie?"

She smiles. "Carrie. And Slate, but only for a minute because Carrie called him for a ride. Anna came with him—you know, his little sister? So what happened was, Carrie got there when we were having dessert and we—"

"Who's we?"

"My best friends, Marissa and Katelyn . . . some kids from the drama club . . . McCoy and Jeremy."

"You were hanging out with Jeremy on purpose?"

She shrugs, embarrassed. "Marissa and Katelyn really like him. He's not mean all the time. He's just mad now because he wanted to leave the festival early and no one else wanted to. He was fine at Mission Plaza, just ignoring me was all."

I frown at AddyDay's definition of *fine*.

"All of us had been at the restaurant for hours, just hanging out, you know?" she continues. "It was probably eleven by the time Carrie came. Right after that, out of nowhere these two guys showed up. I'm sure now Cordero was one of them. He kept shouting his name and pointing to himself. Weird, huh? He would go in English for a bit, then Spanish.

He introduced the other guy too. Tito. He and McCoy got into it, shoving and all. McCoy hates gang guys."

"Tito," I say, pouncing on the name. Slate mentioned Tito. That's who he duked it out with two days before Juan died at Mission Plaza. "Did Tito look like he'd been in a fight?"

"Oh, yeah. Swollen eye. Everything. He's got this gold tooth. He's freaky."

If he had a swollen eye, it's possible he'd already fought with Slate. "Did Cordero say what he and Tito wanted?"

"No, they barely stayed ten minutes before they left. Right after that, Carrie called Slate for a ride home."

My shoulders slump. I've learned nothing, and it sounds like Jeremy and McCoy won't have any more information than AddyDay. I picture Cordero and Tito, at Mission Plaza, fighting Slate one night and then returning another night. Why?

"We offered to take Carrie home ourselves, but she wouldn't come," AddyDay continues. "She was acting kind of funny. Sort of . . . spacey."

Spacey. "She wouldn't answer for several seconds and then she'd say something totally normal."

"Exactly! Yes!"

"Do you know the date? Because it may have been May 23. She was acting that way with me over the phone that day. I was at a track practice."

"Ooh, I'll look." She gets out her phone.

"You put it on Instagram or something?"

"And Snapchat." She scrolls down her screen. "Oh, look." She shows me a picture of puppy dogs with bow ties.

"I just love that one. Wait, here. It wasn't May 23. It was May 24."

I lean to see a selfie of AddyDay with a restaurant napkin tied around her forehead like a headband. Carrie's profile is in the dim background. The time-stamp is 11:38 p.m., May 24. "And you're sure you posted this the day you took it?"

She takes her phone back. "Posted it the minute I took it."

"May 24 is the night Juan Herrera went missing."

"Oh, wow." She's obviously heard of the man buried in my orchard.

I tap my lips. "11:38 is pretty late. Police say the murder happened around 8:00 p.m. Sounds like Cordero doesn't have an alibi that early."

AddyDay nods. Then she frowns. Her eyes are serious and disappointed. "Wait, you don't seriously suspect Cordero, do you? He saved us. All of us. At the gang house during the drive-by."

Gang house. 147 Benjamin Road.

A wave of fear hits me.

"How do you know about that?" I say in disbelief.

"I was there. I tried—well, I *did* try to tell you. That's why I went up to you the next day in class. To see if you were okay."

I notice the bandages on her neck and touch my own neck. "You were shot?"

Her fingers shake as she touches her own neck, tracing the injury. "No, I followed you in my car. I saw you running down Main Street, and I've been to Cordero's house before with my stepdad—you know, with outreach programs? I didn't want you to start the mock trial research without me. I parked in the driveway and got out. This low-rider pulled up and this guy started shooting. I stared right at him. He shot out my driver's side window. And right then Cordero came out of the house. He scared the guys. They drove away. I didn't even know the glass cut my neck until they were gone. Cordero ran back into the house."

"Did any of the people inside the house come out later?" I'm so shocked I can't stop my questions. "Did El Payaso come out? Did anyone mention Carrie's name? There was a girl who got shot, Jimena."

"Cordero's little sister, yes." AddyDay is eager to provide whatever information she can. "Cordero was with her and he was so calm. And there were all these people screaming and crying. Neighbors . . ."

Nothing makes any sense. How can AddyDay talk about Cordero like she's not afraid of him? How could *I* have considered not being afraid of him?

"Cordero is dangerous," I warn her, reconverted to the idea by my memories of the drive-by. "He had a gun. He shot at the enemy guys in the car."

"He saved my life." She lifts her chin, casting a shadow on the faint scab on her neck. She's become the AddyDay of the mock trial video, the AddyDay who will stand up for something. But I haven't told her what she needs to hear. She needs to dislike him and suspect him without proof, the way I do. Because I'm frightened of him. Because I need someone to blame for Carrie's death.

"Look, there she is," Elena Thornton's voice calls from several yards away.

I turn to see Dad and Elena walking toward me. Dad doesn't see me yet as he smiles down at Elena. His goofy, carefree expression clashes with his professor spectacles.

I wish I could talk to AddyDay longer—to convince her or be convinced by her, I guess. How can she trust Cordero?

"Hey, Salem," Dad says as he arrives.

"Hi, girl!" Elena says to me. She's happy. She's really happy. I want to feel relaxed around her, but I don't.

She turns to AddyDay. "I'm Elena."

"AddyDay," she answers. "I'm your neighbor actually."

Elena puts her hands on her hips. "Well, of course. You should come to my house for dinner with Salem. Unless she wants to ask Mr. Tall, Dark, and Handsome, maybe?"

"You've got an admirer," Dad explains in a quiet voice, nodding across the ferris wheel enclosure and looking for my reaction with interest.

What? I look across the chain link fence.

My heart stops.

There, his gaze dark and fixed not thirty feet across the enclosure from me, is Cordero.

CHAPTER FIFTEEN

Even from across the Ferris wheel enclosure, I can see Cordero's right shoulder is drooping. He's got a bandage covering where his upside down *V* tattoo is.

The instant my gaze reaches him, he pushes away from the fence and heads right toward me.

I stumble backward, even though this is the perfect place to question him. That's what I wanted, right? He must know something.

"Cordero's going to say *hi* to you?" AddyDay asks in awe. "He never chats with anyone."

"How cute! You're blushing." Elena says. "Just focus on something else. Then, right when he walks by, smile at him."

Sunlight glints off his gold necklace as he steps in front of me. He's got a cap on, black, facing forward. "Salem, do you have minute?"

Though his body language is as open and friendly as I've ever seen it—maybe more—I don't answer. I don't know which Cordero I'm dealing with—the AP student always one step ahead of the curve or the gang member who keeps a handgun and isn't afraid to use it.

"What's your name?" Dad asks Cordero.

I tense. Cordero turns to face Dad. Half my school wears more gang paraphernalia than Cordero is currently showing, all in the name of fashion. Dad doesn't seem to recognize him as anyone tied to Carrie. More than anything, Dad seems curious.

"My name is Cordero," he answers. "I'm Salem's partner at the school."

Dad smiles blandly. I find the tension in my neck dissipating. Dad doesn't recognize Cordero's name, even though I said it at the police station.

"Nice to meet you," Dad tells Cordero.

Elena takes Dad's arm. "If you'll excuse us, I have my eye on a cotton candy vendor."

Dad glances at me, letting me know he approves of Cordero, at least for now. They leave.

Cordero focuses on me, breathing in. His gaze is not casual. It's not menacing, but it's not casual.

AddyDay clears her throat. "Okay, well, I'm going to go . . . I'll—I'll call you, Salem."

He spares her a moment of attention. "Your neck is okay?"

"Um, yeah, it's getting better." She gives him a smile, which he returns, and for a crazy moment I'm stung with jealousy.

As soon as AddyDay leaves, Cordero drops his polite façade and steps close.

"I want to have the mock trial meeting at Elena's house—you understand?" His tone is so low and full of emotion I can hardly catch his words through his accent.

Confused, I step away, hitting chain link with my lower back.

He adjusts his hat, adopting a more controlled expression. "You said it yourself. Elena has access to better trial information. We should meet at her house." He nods toward the direction Dad and Elena took. They're nowhere to be seen.

Yes, Cordero must have checked the Facebook page. Yes, he knows meeting at Elena's house was a possibility. But he doesn't care about the mock trial practice.

"I know you hung out with Carrie," I say suddenly, the words taking all of my breath.

Cordero narrows his eyes. "Change the location of the practice."

Now that he's close, I notice the black tip of his *V* tattoo peeking out from under overlapping butterfly bandages. The bandage doesn't completely cover the cut that's under it—a deep cut as thin as a knife-blade. Like he guesses my thoughts, he touches the bandage and steps back from me. He glances almost by instinct at a group of guys a stone's throw away from us.

There are three of them. The two younger ones are the Primeros I spoke to at school. The third one is older. He has a broad neck and the wide-set eyes of a fetal alcohol baby all grown up.

The older guy notices Cordero and comes over to us, laughing cruelly. His gold tooth flashes in the sunlight, reminding me AddyDay's description of Tito. I think I'm looking at the banger who fought Slate and then two days later showed up at Mission Plaza on the night Juan died. The younger boys follow him.

Tito turns to me just as I realize I've let myself become surrounded by gang members.

"Lookee at *mamacita* here," he says to me, his smile a promise of violence. "Yeah, I know who you are. You're that girl. You think you can come into my house, huh? Just any time?"

I feel all three of Cordero's friends looking at me. All of them have heard me asking for Cordero, heard me making myself a target.

"I need to go." I push past Cordero to head toward the carnival crowd.

Tito lunges and catches me by the arm. Using both hands, he twists my wrist like he's wringing all the blood out of my skin. The pain is excruciating.

"Ow!" I stop struggling.

"Oh man, look it! She's so scared!" Tito laughs with excitement.

Cordero tries to get Tito to let me go, rattling off a string of Spanish. The younger guys glare at me, nervous because I'm here.

Tito gets into Cordero's face. "You think we gonna leave some girl alone 'cause o' you? *I'm* the leader, yeah?"

Cordero's jaw clenches, but he lowers his eyes, as if forcing himself to submit.

"Didn't I teach you your lesson this morning? Obey me, *ese*," Tito shouts, nodding at the bandages on Cordero's face. "You wanna go to school for nothing, that's your problem." He shakes my arm. "Bringing this girl in my business, that's mine."

Once he's composed, Cordero looks up directly at Tito. "Make me stop." His voice is low but distinct. He stands still, challenging Tito only with his eyes. The challenge is fierce, though. The younger boys spread out behind Tito, one to the left and one to the right. They fist their hands, looking more nervous than ever. I can't tell whose side they'll take.

"Oh, you wanna—" Tito relaxes his grip on my wrist.

Cordero grabs my opposite arm and yanks me behind him. He's so quick. Tito stumbles before losing hold of me completely. Using Tito's momentum, Cordero shoves him to the ground and spins to hold my elbow.

We run.

He propels me past ice cream cones fisted by girls in black braids. We don't stop until I see Dad and Elena in the distance with their back to me, facing the Octopus ride. Behind us, Tito stops near the bathrooms, eyeing a security officer strolling nearby. The older boy points at Cordero like Cordero's going to get it later and sulks off with both younger boys.

Cordero spins me to face him. "I'm going to Elena's house."

I can't think or breathe. His face is inches from mine, dark, intense, and shaking. Only it's me that's shaking, by his grip on my arm. I glance one more time to verify Tito isn't following us. Cordero might be hurt for helping me escape. My heart rate is maxed.

"Óyeme. Listen to me." Cordero's low, urgent words blow into my cheeks. "Tell everyone we're having the mock trial at Elena Thornton's house."

"Elena Thornton's house," I repeat. "You mean *Rick* Thornton's house—before they separated."

As soon as I say it, my thoughts become steady with the sense of it. Elena's soon-to-be ex-husband worked with troubled youth, giving them a refuge from gang members. It's not the class Cordero wants—it's the house. The house that someone tried to break into three times.

"There's nothing—" He stops. His calm denial comes a beat late. For once I'm sure my guess is right. "Why do you—"

I become furious—him helping me doesn't matter. Finding out what happened to Carrie matters. "So you're going to break into Rick's house? Why? Because someone like Tito told you to? Why won't you talk to me about Carrie?"

Cordero's eyes flash. "Tito is a bad leader—"

"Oh, you think?"

"In the gang, there are the leaders and there are the . . ." He's losing his cool, watching me lose mine. He'll explode if he can't find the word he wants fast enough. ". . . the followers."

"Who cares?"

"Me. I care. I . . ." He switches to Spanish. I only catch a few of his words. *Palo,* stick. *No son complicados*, they're not complicated. I can't translate fast enough.

"Was it a gang leader or a gang follower who killed Carrie?" I scream, losing all control.

"Quiet!" he says in a harsh voice.

Bystanders stare at us.

Composing himself, he backs away from me and gives the people around us a small smile.

I don't care about them. I step toward him, ready to shout again.

He shakes his head slowly, but his eyes remain as intense as before. "Calm down."

He waits, watching me shake and breathe heavily. He's right. I'm causing a scene. No one will talk to me, not even Jeremy, because I lose control. I swallow and rub the back of my neck. People watching us lose interest.

Cordero approaches me with a smile and friendly attitude. He even puts his arm around me, like we're an item.

He whispers in my ear with the same intensity in his eyes as before. "Let's walk."

I want to shrug his arm off my shoulders, but only because I want him to feel rejected. My body takes instantly to the warmth of his presence and the feel of his breath on my hair. Even the faint smell of cigarette smoke coming from his clothes makes me think about the house he lives in and the company he keeps, whether he wants that company or not. I think I respect him. I might even sympathize with him.

Still, he may be covering for someone who hurt Carrie. I keep my back stiff.

"Our guys don't cut gas lines." Baseball cap pulled low, he leans close to me and puts his finger to his temple. "They—boom." He pulls his finger-trigger.

I shake my head, refusing to listen. "I know someone killed her."

"Of course someone killed her."

"Someone who—" My gaze shoots to the line of his brows. "*What?*"

He nods, serious and motivated. He cares very much about this topic. "Of course someone killed her."

We meander through the carnival—his arm around me, my face turned to drink in his lowered gaze, like we're some loving couple. He knows she was killed. Finally, someone believes me and it's the wrong someone—it's not a cop who can investigate and punish, it's a gang member who's skilled at acting and owns a gun. But he believes me. He knows she was murdered.

"How do you know?" I whisper. "The police don't even know."

He matches my intensity. "How do *you* know?"

"Because . . ." I'm not sure if I should tell him about the markings on Carrie's car matching the marking on the victim's shoe. "Because Juan Herrera is from the union. Because Carrie hired you to protect the union."

Cordero's arm becomes lighter, almost leaving my shoulders. His anger is cold. "How did you know that?"

"Who tagged Carrie's car?"

"Who told you?" Cordero demands, pulling me closer. He even slips his hand around my waist. At his touch, my chest threatens to burst from the need for air—the good kind of need. I feel like it's wrong to react positively to him. Like maybe I'm betraying Carrie.

"I'm not . . . I won't answer you until you answer me. You never answer," I say, flustered.

Air escapes his nostrils, but he eases his grip on me by degrees, like he's unsure what to do with me. His black cap is low. He stops walking.

We stay like that, me in his arms, testing each other visually.

"I want inside Elena's house." His dark eyes prove it—telling me just how much he wants it.

"If you—if you show me what you're taking from the house, I'll get you inside." What am I doing?

With the darkening of an already dangerous expression, he backs away from me, folding his arms in refusal. My shoulders and waist feel cooler without him, but I'd move closer again if I could do it somehow without him noticing. I miss the closeness.

I swallow. "If you show me—"

"Today," he demands.

"Wait—go in Elena's house *today*?"

"You're friends, right? Take me to the house."

"I can't. We barely know each other," I say, even as I throw together a plan to do exactly what he requested. I'll be eating dinner at Elena's in just a few hours. I could get Cordero inside.

His eyes narrow.

"Um, Cordero? Salem?" a voice asks.

At the interruption, I step back from him. Only then does my world include the carnival. The crowds are sparse in the dead heat of late afternoon. AddyDay toys with the scab on her neck while Cordero dons his aloof expression.

"Um . . ." AddyDay continues. "Well, I saw your dad coming and thought I'd give you a heads up . . ."

I look. Fifty feet away, Dad and Elena stroll toward us, eating cotton candy.

"Today." Cordero tells me. He keeps his voice low in front of AddyDay, who hums softly—a little tune called "Minding Her Own Business."

I try to match the confidence in Cordero's gaze. "How will you even know when to come?"

"I'll know."

Cordero leaves, walking in Tito's direction, which happens to lead right past Dad and Elena. He falters on his first step, his right shoulder rolling forward. I'd forgotten about his injuries, and he's likely to get more after helping me. He straightens. Elena calls to him in Spanish, steering Dad toward him for a hello. I could die of embarrassment. Cordero actually stops to talk. How will he know when to come to Elena's, or how to get inside? My shoulders tense. Will he watch her house the whole time I'm there?

"Are you okay?" AddyDay asks me. "I said Cordero was, you know, not evil, but don't go dating him or something."

"Are you kidding?" I ask, wondering which part of, *I think Cordero might be a murderer* confused her in our earlier conversation. Still, I blush.

"Good—then you're not mad I interrupted? What were you talking about?"

I hesitate, not sure I want a sidekick. "Before Carrie died, she . . . hired Cordero to protect union members."

"Oh, that's so nice of her."

"No—what? It's not nice. It's kind of a big deal. Cordero's in a gang and he was supposed to intimidate anyone the growers hired to intimidate strikers. Do you understand? Carrie hired a gang member. The growers have millions of dollars on the line and Carrie hired a gang member to stop their plotting. I think that's why she died. I think one of them killed her."

"You . . . you think the fire at your house was on purpose?" Her eyes are huge.

"Cordero thinks so too. And now he wants to get inside Elena's house, but I don't know why. He was talking about Carrie too. Gang members used to hang out at Elena's a lot, back when she was married to Rick Thornton. You know Rick, right?"

She nods slowly, still overwhelmed. "Everyone knows Rick."

"Well, I told Cordero I'll help him get inside Elena's house if he tells me what he knows about Carrie."

"Okay. Okay, let me think. It's all so crazy." She taps her lips. "So you need access to Elena's place. That seems doable, really."

"I'm eating dinner there," I remind her. "I could crack a window before I leave."

AddyDay makes a face, not sure about the idea. I'm not either. If I let Cordero inside and he hurts Elena, that would be my fault. But Cordero's given zero indication that he wants to harm anyone while inside the house. He could harm Elena anywhere. There've been other break-ins, so it seems like he's trying to find something.

What is it, then? An old cell phone of some gang member, with the contact list still intact? Cash?

"Anyway, I can't let Cordero inside without me." I say. "He might not show me what he takes."

AddyDay tilts her head. "Of course, you *could* look for it yourself—whatever he's looking for."

"I don't know what it is. Anyway, how will I search the house without Elena and Dad noticing?"

I glance at Cordero as he nods goodbye to Elena and Dad and jogs stiffly away. What if I *could* find what he's looking for? No negotiation with him. And if I can't find anything, well then, partner with him.

Across the way, Dad raises his eyebrows, noticing how I'm watching Cordero's tall frame recede into carnival crowds. I look away, more embarrassed than ever.

"Distract them?" AddyDay says as Dad and Elena head toward us.

"What? Oh." I shake my head. "The three of us won't be at Elena's house that long. Right after dinner, she and Dad are going to a movie."

"A movie? Wait, that's perfect! I have a plan."

"Should I be worried?"

AddyDay gives me a knowing smile, like I was joking with her. I hadn't been.

Dad stuffs his wallet in his back pocket as he arrives with Elena. "You get your study schedule all aligned with *Cordero*?" he asks me.

"Of course." Elena sends a wicked look at Dad over her cotton candy. "Think how important good grades are."

Dad's suspicion of my interest in Cordero must be so amusing to her.

"It was nothing." I try not to look nervous talking about Cordero, which makes me more nervous.

I'll never get him inside Elena's house if Dad finds out he's a Primero. Dad is smart enough that he'd be suspicious of every move I made after that.

"Hey, remember how you asked me to dinner?" AddyDay asks Elena. "Well, I was thinking—maybe I could come still?"

"You want to?" Elena answers. "I have enough food to feed ten of Salem's friends."

"Oh, good," AddyDay says. "I'm just *so* excited about the UC Berkeley library access Salem told us you have. You and Salem's dad are going to a movie later, right? Can Salem and I stay and research on your computer while you're gone? Do you really get access to all the FBI files?" Her innocence is astonishing.

I hold my breath even though Elena's face is breaking into a wide grin.

"I'm not sure about that," Dad answers.

"I *do* get access to the FBI files—everything they've released. As a journalist, I find the subscription fee is worth every penny." Elena turns from AddyDay to Dad, like she's asking his permission too. "Oh, they'll be fine."

"Well?" I ask Dad.

"Well." Dad takes a breath. "All right."

Just like that, whatever is inside Elena's house—and all it might tell me about Carrie's death—is hours away from being discovered.

CHAPTER SIXTEEN

I sit next to AddyDay in the back seat on the way to Elena's house, scowling at all of Elena's questions and amused hints to Dad about my love life. AddyDay chats freely, but I have no attention for anything but Cordero.

He argued with me when I said Carrie was killed by a gang member—but he wasn't arguing that her death was accidental. He was saying the killer wasn't a gang member. Does that mean he knows who killed her? He spoke in Spanish for a while. Maybe he said something important, thinking I wouldn't understand.

I pull up the Internet on my phone and search for the phrases I remember him saying about gang members. *They'll hit you with a stick. They'll shoot you. They're not complicated.* There has to be something that I'm missing.

Cordero's words keep ringing through my head. The way he phrased it. He'd said, *they*. Not *we*.

The gang. Could he be planning to leave it?

"Are you?" AddyDay asks me.

I look up in confusion. The air smells nauseatingly sweet. In the open window behind AddyDay, row after row of peach trees rush by, heavy with overripe crop. Carrie would be so proud.

AddyDay is staring at me. "Salem?"

"Um, yeah, I am," I say, not sure what I've just agreed to.

"Me too. *So* excited." She talks to Elena in the front seat. "That much FBI information, and I think we'll be able to prove Oswald didn't have time to meet with conspirators before he killed President Kennedy."

Once I'm sure they're talking about the mock trial, I lean back, still picturing Cordero's dark gaze. Could he really want out of the gang? Three attempted robberies on the Thornton house and I'm secretly planning to welcome inside the Primero who is likely responsible. Granted, only if I don't find the item first.

When I think about it, I know that searching without him is doing to him exactly what I think he'll do to me—I'm making a deal to get what I want and planning to go back on my word if I can get away with it.

My phone vibrates.

> Slate: How was the festival? Envy and Kimi are here at my house with mock trial questions.

> Me: Good. Cordero was there. I think he wants to meet to work on the trial, like maybe at Elena Thornton's. Just the two of us.

> Slate: lol. I'm going to get you back for that.

Perfect. He thinks I'm joking. If something terrible happens at Elena's, though, he'll have a hint of what happened.

Cordero's words are still running in my head. *They'll hit you with a stick. They'll shoot you. They're not complicated.*

One of the gang members is complicated. Cordero is impossible to figure out. I can't let myself trust him. I wonder, though, if I'm kidding myself—if I already do trust him.

My phone screen shuts off automatically and I drop it to my lap.

The possibility frightens me.

. . .

After dinner, AddyDay and I see Dad and Elena off.

Elena's house is huge and falling-apart old. The ironic part is that it's smack in the middle of peach orchards. I'm told the property ends at the edge of their small lawn, but every harvest they get to see pickers laboring in the heat as Rick and the union fight for higher wages for them. Still, there's fresh paint on the walls and very little clutter. Some of the walls are adorned with decades-old cut-glass mirrors, truly stunning antiques. The only thing out of place is a stack of packing boxes with labels like "Rick—HS years" in the entryway. Looks like he's still in the process of moving things from Elena's house.

"Listen, you two, be on your best behavior," Dad tells AddyDay and me.

"We will," I answer.

Elena grabs a set of keys from a hook. "I won't set the alarm—it's pretty sensitive. Ready?"

Dad leads her out the door. It's still light outside. The movie will last two hours, but I might have even more time than that if they stop somewhere for dessert.

Once they're gone, my anxiety elevates a notch because I don't know when Cordero is coming. I want time to search for what he's looking for without him.

AddyDay claps her hands together. "Well?"

"First we're going to check the entrances. And the windows. I want to make sure everything is locked." I turn the old-fashioned deadbolt on the front door, and head for the back rooms.

She jogs to keep up with me. "Wow, does your dad do yoga? My stepdad isn't flexible enough to come through a window, even to spy on me."

"Not Dad, Cordero. He could break in, knowing the adults are gone. You heard Elena, the alarm isn't set."

"Well. You and I just disagree about Cordero, don't we?"

I pause before going inside the first room, a master bedroom decorated in cans of drywall plaster and paint. It feels intrusive, invading Elena's personal space. This is the place where Rick used to live. Does Dad want to occupy this room someday? Why can't I relax about him dating her?

AddyDay and I check every possible entry point one by one. The house seems secure.

Back in the main room, we pause.

Now what? Is he even coming? How long can I search on my own?

"Let's go upstairs," AddyDay says.

She climbs up the wide stairwell, which twists back on itself at a landing halfway up in order to meet a balcony hallway. Once upstairs, we can look over the railing on either side and see the main floor below us, the front room on one side and the entryway on the other. Natural sunlight fills all but the farthest reaches of the hallway, which extends in both directions. We try the left side.

"What do you think he'd be looking for?" AddyDay asks, opening the first door. It creaks, revealing a bathroom with a pink stand-alone sink and a hole where the toilet is supposed to be. "What if he's looking for a secret message? Like written in code?"

"I think that only happens in Nancy Drew books."

The second door is a mini-gym.

"Let's try the other side," I say, retracing my steps.

On the other side of the balcony hallway, we each take a door. I find a bedroom without furnishings. I run my hands along the empty shelves. Only minutes have passed, but still I want to race downstairs to check the entrances again. That would just waste time. What if Cordero is trying to get inside, though? Will he call me? My number is listed on the team info sheet. I check my phone, but there are no notifications.

AddyDay calls from the room she's in. "Wait, Salem, come here."

I race to her, entering a room with two dressers and a twin bed. AddyDay points at a poster that reads *Hip-Hop* in gangster-style print.

Heart pounding, I pull open the top drawer of the first dresser. Empty. I open the rest, making a racket. All empty.

"There's nothing in the other one, I already checked," AddyDay says.

"No, there has to be something here."

We check a dusty hamper, the desk and some shelving. I look inside the garbage can and move white curtains to see the warbled wood of the window ledge.

Kneeling on the hardwood floor, AddyDay looks under the bed. "If gang guys stayed at this house, they stayed here. But there's nothing in here."

I check all the drawers again. I don't know what I'm looking for. Anyway, Elena could have moved something.

Wait, what if she moved *a lot* of somethings? Like a bunch of belongings in four boxes stacked by the front door?

"I'm such an idiot," I say as AddyDay leans past me over the bed.

She reaches for a red LED light glowing from a switch on the headboard. It's labeled, *Panic.* "What's this?"

"Don't!"

She pulls her hand back just in time. "Whoa. Do you think the police would come if I hit that?"

"I guess," I answer. "If the alarm company can't get in touch with Elena. I bet there's one of those buttons in every room."

There have been three burglary attempts on the Thornton home recently. I don't know what Dad would do in the face of three burglary attempts, but I'm pretty sure panic buttons would be involved. I'm less sure what his reaction would be to AddyDay and me hitting one accidentally while at his new girlfriend's house.

"Come on," I say.

Once we're downstairs, I heft the first box off the top stack and set it on the floor. The one under it is labeled, *Rick: football.*

"Look," I say.

AddyDay's face lights with a smile. "Of course. If any gang members left something here, Elena would give it to Rick." She takes that box and sets it on the tile.

We line the items along the entryway so we'll be able to repack everything correctly. I empty out a late-model printer, a photo of Rick in a Verona High football uniform—he signed it *#5*—and a bunch of newsletters from the Peach Growers Association. I repack it.

"Would Cordero want Rick's old wallet?" She brings the wallet to her face, laughing. "Oh my gosh, is that a *perm*? He's sixteen in this driver's license picture!"

"There's got to be something in one of the others," I answer, switching my box for the next one.

I pull out a plaque I recognize. It reads, *Rick Thornton: World's Best Union Club Advisor* and is signed by Carrie, Envy, Kimi, and me. I didn't want to have any attention on me, so I didn't stand with the other girls last year when they presented it to him at a Students for Strike meeting. I feel a grin compete with a wave of sorrow. Carrie wanted this year's plaque to read *Rick Thornton: World's* Only *Union Club Advisor*, but she'll never order another plaque. I miss her. I'm not on the verge of sobbing, and that's a relief I wasn't expecting. But I miss her.

I continue emptying the box, which is full of union stuff, most of it from the Students for Strike club. I move a stack of Verona Bulletin newspapers, stopping when I notice the top one.

"Wait, that's Carrie," I say, staring at the picture on the front page.

Mayor Bill Knockwurst is smiling at the camera, shaking Carrie's hand. I remember the photo. Carrie looks terrible in it. She's not ready for the snap of the camera, looking off to the side with a flat, almost worried expression. She got on the front page alongside the mayor for winning a teen community service award. She joked that God had humbled her by allowing that picture to go to print.

AddyDay stops laughing and comes over to look. "Oh, I remember that. That's my stepdad."

"I didn't remember the article being so close to when she died," I say. The newspaper is dated May 22. "Why does Rick even have these newspapers?"

"Well, Elena *does* work for the Verona Bulletin."

I check to see if Elena wrote the article. She didn't. I take the first page of the newspaper, and tuck it into my back pocket.

"You're paranoid," AddyDay says.

"We need to hurry." I dig into the box again.

It's mostly cassette tapes. Pearl Jam, Nirvana—each with handwritten labels. An old-fashioned tape recorder sits under them. The tape inside has "PGA Mar/Apr" written in permanent marker on it.

PGA—the Peach Growers Association. The missing recording of the grower's meeting.

I stare at it, mouth open.

AddyDay laughs. "What is it this time?"

"Dad's alibi," I say.

"What? My stepdad is your dad's alibi—Bill. Bill and Mr. White."

"And this might be the recording that proves it." I push play. Amazingly, nothing seems to be broken. The batteries even work.

". . .the union is asking for increased wages," an authoritative voice says. "Or in ten days they'll vote to strike."

AddyDay tucks hair behind her ears. "That's Bill."

I nod, talking over the tape. "If the union is going to vote that soon, then this is the May grower's meeting. This is the night Juan died."

Her eyes widen.

"But we take all the *risk*!" a speaker on the tape interrupts the meeting's formality. A speaker with a high-pitched voice.

"Mr. White," we both say.

"We buy the land and the trees," Mr. White continues. "If the crop fails, we get *nothing*. Does the picker work and get nothing? Don't be absurd!"

"You don't live at the poverty level. Pickers do," Rick Thornton's voice answers, loud and quick. As the official union representative, I doubt it's wise for him to get that angry at a group of growers.

"Only because I work another job—one I'm allowed to make money at!" There's a thud as Mr. White slaps the table, one of the varnished ones they have at Mountain Mike's Pizza. How many times have I been in that room?

A familiar voice interrupts calmly. "Rick, you and the union want this discussion to be about the plight of the worker. So let's talk about these workers. How will they earn money when peaches are grown, canned, and shipped in from overseas?"

"That's my Dad," I whisper to AddyDay.

She nods, equally entranced.

"Let the illegals follow the crop to China. Solves two problems," someone answers rudely.

"It's people like you that make your whole organization rotten!" Rick Thornton shouts.

A flurry of angry voices creates a dull hum in the background. I picture the *XII* and upside down *V* carved into the bottom of Juan's shoe. I picture the men and the handful of women that I've seen at the banquet hall, the way they're usually bored and wishing the meeting were over. No one is bored now. They're angry and emotional. Enough to kill?

I speak over the voices on the tape. "Dad needs to listen to this."

Dad is going to freak when he finds out I've gone through Rick's things, but I don't care. The tape might identify someone with a serious grudge. It might even prove that Rick was hiding the recording on purpose, though I suspect it proves the opposite. If Rick wanted to frame Dad by getting rid of the cassette, he wouldn't leave it lying around in his soon-to-be-ex-wife's house, certainly not now that Dad is dating her.

"Wait, did you hear that?" AddyDay nudges me.

"What?"

She rewinds the recorder and hits play. Mr. White is speaking, his voice warbled as the tape restarts.

"Some party is scheduled tonight. Now we can't stay for dinner after the meeting."

AddyDay gives me a significant look. "He's announcing that they have to leave when the meeting's over."

"That can't be right," I say. "The growers stayed for dinner—that's Dad's alibi. Anyone who left before eight has no alibi for when Juan was killed."

"Do you think . . . I mean, could the growers have remembered wrong?"

Doubt lurks in the corners of my mind. A professor, a teacher, and a mayor—Dad and those growers didn't get together and guess whether or not they'd met in May. They understood the importance of an alibi. They either pinpointed something that made the date certain or—

Or they lied.

Before I can answer, my phone vibrates with a call from Dad. Also, a second person has just sent a text.

Unknown: You want to know about Carrie? Let me in the house.

Cordero is here.

CHAPTER SEVENTEEN

W hat's wrong? Is Cordero coming?" AddyDay asks, leaning to see my phone. She looks as spooked as me. Dad's call goes to voicemail while the two of us stare at Cordero's message.

"You have to go home," I tell her. Meeting with Cordero is one thing. Dragging AddyDay into it is another.

"So you can be totally freaked out and alone?" she asks. "In movies, that's a really bad plan."

I don't answer, tucking my phone away to dig through Rick's last box instead. Trophies, camping equipment. Nothing.

What does Cordero want? The cassette? Impossible. If Rick doesn't know where the tape is, the odds that Cordero somehow does are astronomical. I stop the tape recorder and shove it into AddyDay's hands.

"I—you need to keep this," I tell her.

"Salem," she warns. "You can't expect Cordero to open up to you when you're hiding—"

"Cordero probably doesn't even know about this tape and if he does—if he's coming here to destroy it—AddyDay, this could be the only evidence of who's missing at that meeting. Whoever killed Juan could get off if we let Cordero take this."

"Well . . ."

"Take it home. I'll stay here to see if he's looking for something else."

She nods. "All right. I'll record it on my computer."

"No way. You could mess up the tape before the police see it."

"But we'll never know what it says if we hand it straight over to the police."

I hesitate.

"Fine. Hide the recorder in your laptop bag," I say, shoving it into her hands. "Send me a text when you're home."

Cheeks flushed, AddyDay pats her zipped bag. "I'm ready."

I unlock the front door and follow her into warm twilight. Long, thin peach leaves droop in the orchard, more gray than green in this light. Cordero is out there, waiting to make a deal with me—a trade. Information in exchange for access to something unknown. I'm getting the better end of the bargain, I tell myself.

AddyDay dashes into the orchard. A minute later I get the text that she's home.

That's when I see him, stepping from the shadow of the third row of trees. Dark and tall.

I run inside and press my back against the closed door. I think of getting a weapon, a knife from the kitchen, but I can't use a knife on someone. He'll take it from me and become armed himself. If he's not already.

Thoughts like that are crazy—Cordero helped me get away from Tito today. I trust him. I do.

If only I were certain.

My phone rings. It's Dad.

I stare at the screen. I hit the ignore button and pull up the voicemail he just left.

"Salem Jefferson, stay away from Cordero," his message says. "We ran into Mr. White at the movie theater. Why didn't you tell me he's a Primero? Salem, stay away from him. *Stay away from Cordero.*"

Three knocks vibrate the door behind me. Cordero.

I nearly drop my phone.

This is my chance. My only opportunity to make a deal with him.

Steeling my emotions, I crack the door open with my foot wedged against the inside.

He stands on the porch, cap gone, tattoo still hidden under bandages. His backpack hangs from one shoulder. He should look like any other student, but he doesn't. His face is cautious and calculating. And confident. I'll never be able to mimic such a face.

"Before I let you in, why did Carrie hire you?" I say, bluffing confidence.

His gaze flits to the entryway behind me and then back, silent. I get nothing until he's inside.

I swallow. "I want to know why your friend Tito fought with Slate at Mission Plaza too. I—you won't get in otherwise."

He says something about Slate in rapid Spanish. While I try to translate in my head, he uses my distraction to shove the door open and slip inside.

I back away from him, a safe distance. I don't know the word he used in talking about Slate, *quita*. "You mean I should stop hanging out with Slate?" I ask. "You think he's dangerous?"

Cordero smirks. "I think he's a coward."

Twisting the deadbolt into place, Cordero sets a chain lock above it—a chain lock I didn't notice before. I could have kept him outside until he answered one of my questions. I curse myself.

As soon as he's inside, he heads for the stairs.

I follow, hot on his trail. I knew it. He's not going to tell me anything. He's not working with me—he's using me. I charge up the steps. What do I do now?

The house is darkening rapidly now that the sun has set. At the top of the stairs, a loud voice begins talking. "And you're back—"

I jump. Cordero spins around, muscles ready for a fight. The lights come on.

"—with Channel Five News," a female reporter-voice continues, permeating the house from a television in the living room under us. "Coming up: a live view of Senator Lethco touring Verona businesses that support the strike."

The television and the lights are on some kind of automatic timer. An anti-theft device supposed to make the house look inhabited.

The interruption has left me trembling. Cordero glances at me with a serious expression and heads down the hall. I follow him.

"You have to answer my questions," I say.

He keeps going, past the first door. There's only one left.

"You're not even listening." I pass him and position myself so that we're face to face in front of the final door. His gaze is steady and dark.

"Tell me how you know Carrie."

He pauses long enough to make me anxious. "I work in the fields sometimes. She came once with some union officials. She decided to hire me."

"You must have told El Payaso about her then. He knew her name."

He blinks in surprise. "Talking to El Payaso was not smart." He leans closer. "I've never talked to him, about anything. Because I *am* smart."

I roll my shoulders to try to release the tension in them. "He knows Carrie."

His dark gaze holds a warning, maybe even a sense of concern for my safety. "But he was not her friend. He's no one's friend."

"We . . . we saw El Payaso's gang initiation," I admit. "Carrie and I did. He's only a year older than her. Maybe he just knew her name from school."

He nods in approval, like I've just admitted I won't go cornering El Payaso. "Now I've answered your questions." He takes hold of the doorknob to the bedroom.

I move closer, which makes my arm brush the hand he holds the knob with. "You told me you were going to show me what you took too."

A dangerous glint gleams in his eyes. "I never said that. *I* am going in the room. *You* are not."

"There's nothing for you to take in there anyway. I already looked."

Cordero leans over me with dizzying speed, accent thicker because of his emotion. "I'm not taking anything."

"You're lying."

He drops his act, expression probing. "How involved do you want to be? There are things you can't unsee."

I'm not expecting this. So I'd be in danger, knowing what he knows?

"I have to know what happened to her," I say simply.

He hesitates, with almost compassion showing in the corners of his lips. Then his eyes harden. "Too bad. I don't trust you."

I reach for the door handle, but he's too fast. The door is open and he's inside the room slamming the door in my face before I can blink. The handle is smooth, with no lock mechanism.

I burst into the room to follow him. "*Me?* You don't trust *me?*"

He's across the room, on the other side of the bed. Stooping, he lifts the top mattress, sending the pillows rocking. His backpack hangs from the crook of his elbow, unzipped, waiting to house whatever he's looking for between the mattresses—the most classic hiding place ever.

"You have searched the room already." Hidden by his fist, Cordero's coveted item falls into his backpack with a jingle. He straightens with a smirk at me. "Are you trying to say you trust *me*?"

We square off with me solidly in front of his only exit from the room. The item jingled. Keys? A bracelet?

"It doesn't matter who I trust," I say, pressing the small of my back into both my hands clutching the door handle and stalling for time. "You have all the cards here. You have all the cards everywhere."

I hate myself, my fear, my stupidity for not looking under the mattress. I hate the power of Cordero's presence, a power I can never match.

I hold the door handle tighter and nod at his backpack. "You show me what's in there and you lose nothing. You know it."

His jaw twitches, perhaps in fear. "You have no idea."

I frown. "Yes. That's that point. I have no idea how my sister was murdered." Even as I speak, I process what he could have meant. He's afraid. Cordero doesn't have power everywhere, and I already know that. Tito beat him up. Who is Cordero afraid of now and why does the item he's taking matter?

He jukes left then right. I don't fall for it. I stay right in front of what he wants—escape.

"Move away from the door," he says.

"I know you won't hit me." I'm sort of bluffing.

He's furious. "Move."

Turns out I was right about him not hitting me. If I trust him, how can I get him to trust me?

"We can't stand here all night," I say. "Dad will come home. Find you. Find what's in your backpack. Probably call the police. Let me help you. I won't say a word to anyone."

With a glance over his shoulder at the bed and window above it, he backs away a step, the coveted backpack swinging on his arm. I realize he's thinking about escaping through the second-story window. He's definitely on edge.

"The police?" I ask. "That's what you're afraid of?"

His eyes blaze. "I didn't hurt Carrie."

"Then show me what you're taking."

"Don't you remember? You don't trust me. I don't trust you." Another glance at the window. The way it's situated above the bed gives him an advantage in getting there, but the stained wooden frame is heavy and looks swollen, partially obscured by limp white curtains. No way he can open the window and keep me away from the backpack—not without a serious fight. Anyway, I believe him. That he didn't hurt Carrie.

But he definitely is afraid of something. It's a two-story drop from the window, and I'm hardly a physical threat. I wrack my brain for an answer.

He opens his mouth to answer me, and then makes a break for the window. I'm a step late, thinking he'll double back to the door, but he kneels on the bed. He muscles up the windowpane eight inches, bringing the sweet smell of peaches. The backpack is cradled in front of him like a bundled infant. I follow him, my emotions snapping.

"I have every right to see what you're taking—more than you!" I yell, bouncing onto pillows next to him, reaching for the backpack. In my maneuvering, I nearly hit the blinking panic button on the headboard with my wrist. I gasp when I see it. If he gets out the window, he'll be gone from the house in two minutes.

How fast can an alarm company get the police here?

"Leave!" His biceps twitch with effort. The window gives once more, this time opening up two feet of clear space. There's not even a screen. Just a waiting bush far below in the dusk next to a concrete path leading to grass.

"You used me to get into the house. You think I won't use you?" I hold my hand over the panic button, still unsure.

He notices my focus.

With a sudden twist, he shoots a hand toward the headboard, no doubt to block me from the panic button. He must think it's an item that I could threaten him with.

"Wait," I cry.

Too late he realizes his mistake. His open palm slams into the button and an alarm blasts with debilitating volume.

His gaze meets mine, panicked.

"I wasn't going to hit it," I say. I wasn't, was I?

He winces in fury. At me? At himself?

I rip the button's cord from the wall. The alarm doesn't stop.

"Don't follow me!" he yells at me, uncertainty in his eyes. He scrambles off the bed. He runs to the now unblocked door.

I race after him.

"I'll distract anyone looking for you. We're on the same side!" I shout over the noise of the alarm, pulse racing. I have to get to that backpack.

He runs across the balcony, ready to hit the stairs with a fifteen-foot head start. Pausing at the top of the stairs, he points at me like I'm a misbehaving child and yells in Spanish.

I translate automatically. "Stay here for my own good? Are you kidding me? For *your* good, you mean." My phone vibrates in my pocket. It's probably Dad, this time calling because the alarm company has contacted Elena about the panic button being activated. "You think I'll never learn who killed her so I'll be *safe*?"

He turns from me to bound down the stairs, now only ten feet in front of me. I'm still on the balcony itself, not the stairs—not good enough, not fast enough. Still running, I glance over the balcony railing at the view of the first floor. If I were down there already, I could cut off Cordero's nearest escape. I could make him see reason.

I change my momentum.

I palm the balcony railing and vault. With the banister still at my fingertips, I know I've made a mistake. I'm about to overshoot the couch below me. Frantic, I clutch the railing, trying to reign in my momentum. I pull too hard. My lower half whips toward the wall. My legs crash into the cut glass mirror mounted below. Pain makes me lose my grip. I free fall. My body scrapes down the broken mirror, which makes a popping noise. It jolts, threatening to break free of the wall.

The couch resists my arrival with a will I hadn't expected.

I scream as I'm pitched face-first into cushions on the back of the couch. There's blood splattered from the back of my wrist up to my shoulder and a blaring voice to my left. I look. It's the news program on TV. The volume is deafening. It nearly drowns the sound of the alarm. No one would have the volume that high unless they truly feared intruders. Senator Debbie Lethco's features fill the flat screen, earrings swaying with each emphatic nod of her head. She's in a parking lot filled with crowds under temporary lights. I recognize the location. Mission Plaza, just a few miles from here.

Before I can move, I sense movement above me and look up. I've knocked loose the heavy mirror above me. It's precariously skewed, hanging by a foot of metal wire extending up from its lowered left side. Much of its glass is broken—shattered in places. Tiny shards fall onto the couch around me.

Cordero sprints down the last steps of the stairs with thundering strides. He turns his attention to me, stunned.

We're equally far from the front door.

I plant my hands on the top of the back of the couch, ready to spring.

In a sudden burst, the sound of an explosion fills my ears.

CHAPTER EIGHTEEN

Screams and the noises of detonation swallow the blare of Elena's house alarm.

Covering my head, I drop. I roll against couch cushions. I can't feel the heat. Did Carrie?

". . . a bomb has exploded at Mission Plaza—" a female reporter's voice says.

I slowly let go of my clutched knees. The noise of explosion disappears.

"—not one hundred feet from Senator Lethco. We're here live. Again, that's an explosion at Mission Plaza. We now have—yes, here's another look at the initial blast."

I uncover my head to stare at an undisturbed desk across the room from me. There's no damage, no fire. My adrenaline makes it impossible to believe—the explosion is miles from me, not in Elena's house at all but featured on the TV screen where Senator Lethco's face appears.

". . . in support of the Farm Workers Union." She's giving a speech at a podium in the middle of a parking lot. "We now—

With a gasp, Senator Lethco ducks. The camera swerves left and pans to the Taco Shack in the dark distance beyond.

Screams sound as a microphone closer to the scene is turned on. A fireball shoots from the shattered glass of the shack's windows. Figures block the screen as they flee. The noise of the blast ends as quickly as it came.

I'm not the only one mesmerized by the televised explosion.

Cordero is next to the couch, his sharp features illuminated by the TV's shifting light.

"—obvious questions," the reporter continues. "Could this be an effort to intimidate peach strikers? Or is this another tragedy in the battle for control of drug trafficking in Verona, where Mission Plaza stands as a gateway for Primero and Último gangs?"

Loud, popping sounds twang above me. Cordero stays focused on the screen, but I look up. The ten-foot long damaged mirror has broken free. It's falling like a pointed dagger from the balcony, directly at Cordero standing next to the couch. It's big. The right edge of it could hit the cushions I'm still on.

"Corde—!" I scream before I can think, diving off the couch.

My shoulder slams into the coffee table. The mirror crashes into the back of the couch with the crack of a thousand fissures. Shards rain like sand in a desert storm.

Shrieking, I scramble over the varnished wood, covering my head with my arms.

The frame of the mirror teeters against the couch. One side slides to the floor while the other rises from the cushioned armrest, like it's reenacting the final scene of the sinking Titanic.

Finally, glass stops breaking, leaving only the house alarm and the reporter's voice.

I drop my arms from my face and see Cordero's dark form on the worn wooden floor.

He's sprawled on his back with his forehead touching the base of a wooden hutch. He's covered in glass and not moving. There's an angry bump above his left temple— from the hutch. He must have collided with it when he jumped back to avoid the glass.

His hand twitches against the backpack half concealed under his hips—the backpack with the evidence he took.

I stand. Debris rains from me. He could be hurt. He could need medical attention. Ten seconds with that backpack and I'll call every ambulance in the county for him.

I take a step, and he rolls to his side in a crunch of glass. He spits on the floor, rising onto his knees. I dart forward and jerk the backpack from under him. The newspaper article in my back pocket comes free and falls to the wooden floor. Carrie's fearful face stares up at us. He turns to look at me with eyes that are coherent, determined. The backpack strap jerks me back, burning my palm. Cordero leaps to his feet. He's got the backpack.

I give up. I'll never get the backpack by force.

"Tell me," I plead, still clutching a strap. I point with my free hand to the newspaper on the floor. "She was everything to me."

"That's Carrie?" He glances at the photo. The police are on their way, presumably. He doesn't have much time.

I can't look at him anymore. "Just tell me why someone would kill her." I hate the desperation in my voice and the tremble of coming sobs.

"That is the man who threatened her," he says slowly, nodding at the mayor shaking Carrie's hand.

My gaze flies from the newspaper to the firm line of his lips. "Did he kill her?"

"I don't know who killed her." Cordero's eyes have no hint of aggression in them, just dark solemnity. He's telling me something real.

There's a jingle from outside the front entrance. The door springs forward, stopped by the chain lock Cordero set. The rounded blades of a pair of wire cutters twist through the door's small opening.

"Drop your weapons or I'll shoot to kill!" the former owner of the house, Rick Thornton, yells. He must have gotten a call from the alarm company along with Elena when I pulled the panic button.

Fear laces every curve of Cordero's features. He runs for the back hall.

"Why'd he threaten Carrie? When?" I grab the newspaper and scramble after him.

The wire cutters click against the chain lock.

"You have to go to the police," I shout.

"And if the police work for the mayor?" Cordero yells back.

He veers right, going toward a bathroom with a window too small for anyone to fit through. I noticed when I searched the house earlier. The hallway is black, like the whole world is going dark at the mention of dirty cops.

I hesitate. If Cordero's arrested, could he actually be in danger from dishonest cops? And even if Verona officers are all moral superstars, would he go to the grave before he'd tell them anything about Carrie?

I sprint the opposite direction down the hall. "This way."

There's no time to see if Cordero is listening. I run into Elena's room just as I hear the front door burst open. Rick yells incoherently as he enters. It sounds like he's going upstairs. I bounce onto the bed and open the window. Cordero's shoulder brushes mine.

I look at him. "You trusted me."

He answers my gaze as we kneel next to each other on the bed. The pause lasts forever. He seems troubled or guilty or some other emotion I don't recognize—a feeling he both likes and doesn't like. Something he hasn't given himself permission to feel.

Breaking our eye contact, he opens his backpack and produces three keys on a ring. The top of one is rusted and dark. I realize I'm looking at blood. I realize he's showing me the evidence he took and I'm looking at blood.

"Juan's keys," Cordero says, tapping one of them. "It's to a Honda. It's not a smart key. So, old. The media says Juan owned a 1996 Honda Accord.

"And that's Juan's blood?" I ask.

"And me and Carrie's fingerprints."

"No," I breathe.

His brown eyes are intense as he leans into me, making sure I'm coherent. "I trust you. Do you understand? You trust me. Be careful around your father."

With that, he grabs the top of the windowsill and swings his feet so they burst through the screen. Landing, he runs into the orchard, taking the keys and all that he knows with him.

I slump on the bed, my whole body shaking. There's a cluster of my own hair tangled between the fingers of my left hand. What do the keys mean—dotted with blood and fingerprints? How did Cordero get them? No wonder he had to trust me before he'd show me anything—the evidence incriminates him.

The house alarm stops. I can't hear Rick Thornton's voice anymore, just the announcers on the television.

Be careful around your father.

". . . just received news that police have found a hand-written note one block from the blast," a male newscaster is saying. "It reads, *Stop persecution or suffer an explosion in Sacramento Saturday.*"

A second announcer's voice answers. "Do police think the person is threatening the Laborer's Rally?"

Did Dad kill Juan? Is he capable of that? I picture him angry. I picture him beating Juan to death and burying him in our orchard. Impossible. Even if Dad were involved, someone else must have delivered the blows. And then there's Carrie and Cordero. Somehow their fingerprints got on

Juan's car keys. But Dad couldn't have killed Carrie. That's even more impossible than him killing Juan. Although, he *is* wracked with guilt that he caused her death. What if his mistake in getting her involved got her killed? Is that why he feels such guilt?

No, I refuse to believe my father is involved.

Footsteps pound against the tile in the entryway. "Salem? Salem?" Dad's frantic voice calls.

I scramble off the bed, tucking the newspaper into my pocket. "I'm here! Dad!"

Rick's shouts echoes from the front of the house. "Stop!"

"Dad?" I run into the entryway across glass fragments that crack underfoot.

Dad is in the doorway, his hands up. Rick is on the landing of the stairs with his gun aimed at my father. When Rick hears me, he swings the gun from Dad to me, his eyes red with fury.

I skid to a halt, screaming, staring up into the barrel of a handgun.

Dad's yelling, "That's my daughter! That's my daughter!"

Rick sees me and jerks the gun up. "I'm not shooting. I'm not!"

Our breaths are audible. The announcers on the television are loud.

"Organizers of the Laborer's March say they plan to gather for a rally at five o'clock on the steps of Sacramento's capitol building, threat or not," one of them says.

I lower my arms. Saturday at five o'clock. That's right around the time the mock trial will end. Our class will exit the courthouse just a few blocks from where the bomb will be.

"Put that gun away," Dad commands Rick as he runs to me.

Rick leans forward to set the safety on his gun. "Easy for you to say. You and the mayor are staging these break-ins."

I throw my arms around Dad, feeling his fear. Dad could never be involved in break-ins or murders.

He pulls back slightly. "Salem, are you bleeding?"

"Just a little."

"What else am I supposed to think you're doing?" Rick's voice trembles with anger. "Having secret meetings. Planning a counterstrike. *Same time. Same place.*" He mocks the words Mr. White used while talking in private to Dad and Bill.

His phrasing triggers my memory. I stay in Dad's embrace, fighting mental images. Rick, at the pizza restaurant, outnumbered by Mayor Knockwurst, Mr. White, and Dad, who were planning secret meetings to beat the strike. Growers with secret meetings apparently fabricated Dad's alibi. Who's to say growers with secret meetings couldn't plot a murder? Mr. White words were *same time, same place.* The grower's counterstrike could be at the same time and place as the Laborer's Rally next Saturday, in downtown Sacramento. That's exactly where the next explosion has been threatened.

What if the counterstrike Dad and his friends planned *is* the threatened explosion?

Terrified, I retreat from Dad, glass snapping against the entryway tile under my shoes.

"What happened? Salem?" Dad reaches for me. On the stairs, Rick secures his gun behind his back.

I sprint to the bathroom and lock it.

I don't know what to do. I hug myself. I'm getting blood on my shirt. Blood. Is any of it Cordero's? I don't remember him bleeding. If he was, he may have gotten some on me. I need to get rid of it before police test it. I can't let anyone know Cordero is digging into the secrets of the growers and their hush-hush meetings.

Tossing my phone onto the sink's counter, I turn on the shower and step fully clothed into the water. My white capris are dingy and dotted with blood smears. Shallow cuts from the mirror burn my face and arms as the water runs pink down the drain. I'm shaking. Cordero thinks Dad is dangerous.

Dad calls from outside the door. "Salem, it's okay. Open up."

"Faking an alibi doesn't make him a murderer," I say with chattering teeth into the warming shower stream. Anyone facing a murder charge would try to get away from police suspicion. Of course he coaxed his grower friends into remembering he was with them.

The water is hot now. I turn it off. The front side of me is soaked. I pat my back pocket and retrieve the damp newspaper picture of Carrie accepting her award from the mayor.

Mayor Knockwurst didn't need Dad in order to kill someone.

"Salem," Dad calls outside the bathroom door.

But if I'm wrong and Dad is involved? What then?

"Salem?" The door handle jiggles.

If I'm going to keep Dad from suspecting I know more than I'm telling, I'll have to be rational, calm.

I rip the newspaper into small pieces and run water over them in the sink.

"I'm all wet." Shoving the destroyed newspaper into my back pocket, I unlock the door and dodge having to face him by kneeling to search for a towel under the sink. "I was washing off the blood. It was such a dumb idea."

"Salem?" Dad kneels down behind me and puts his hand on my shoulder. "Everything's okay. Stop."

Somehow I do it. I give him a hug and tell him that I'm not very hurt, that I'm not very frightened. Paramedics invade the house in a haze of iodine wipes. Elena arrives. She'd been outside, checking for a defect in the alarm and then detained by the police who entered before her. She gets me a change of dry clothes while Rick corners Officer Haynes.

"How could you take so long to get here?" Rick demands. "Elena could have been hurt."

"Your security system has had several false alarms, Rick," Officer Haynes responds.

"The young lady here—she *was* hurt."

"And you must have heard about the explosion at Mission Plaza downtown," Haynes continues calmly.

I stare at the officer as a paramedic wallpapers me with tiny Band-Aids. Officer Haynes could be the one Cordero thinks is bad. Does it really take two weeks for a forensic expert to arrive or is he trying to delay so the details of her death don't come to light? I'm so drained. I can't tell what I think.

All patched up, I find myself sitting at the kitchen table giving a play-by-play of events that seem surreally possible. I was studying alone in the main room after AddyDay left. I heard something upstairs and ran to the bedrooms on the second floor to check. I heard a guy yelling.

"I—I was scared," I say. Officer Haynes is taking notes next to me. Dad is seated on my other side, with Elena and Rick looking uncomfortable next to each other across the table. "I pushed a panic button in the bedroom. I was trying to go downstairs, but a guy was on the balcony, blocking the path to the stairwell. So I . . . I hopped the balcony railing. I knocked the mirror down and it—it got glass everywhere. I don't know where the guy went. Then Rick got here."

I describe the perpetrator with ease. He was medium height with medium-colored hair. He had a mask on.

Dad turns to me, serious and worried. "Was it that guy you were talking to at the festival? Mr. White says he's a gang member. Cordero Vasquez."

My pulse kicks into high gear. "No."

Rick looks upset as he glances from Dad to me.

Dad shakes his head, but doesn't press the issue. Why doesn't he make me tell him the truth? I've always been an open book. Does he not want to know if I'm consorting with gang members? The real question is why doesn't Dad want me around Cordero? Because he's a bad influence or because of what he knows about Carrie's murder?

The answer could well be recorded on the audiotape of the grower's meeting. A recording now at AddyDay's house—the house of the mayor, the house of the man who threatened Carrie.

CHAPTER NINETEEN

I wake up Sunday thinking how Cordero suspects Dad. He has to be wrong. Mayor Knockwurst is the one who threatened Carrie. He should be hauled to the police station this second—and arrested this second and sentenced to jail for life this second and maybe executed tomorrow. I'm not even sure of my views on the death penalty, but I figure one day is plenty of time to decide.

I stew on questions. If the mayor is the killer, I can trust Dad, right? What about the police?

I get through breakfast fueled by physical pain. My cheekbone only hurts when I put pressure on it, but my hip and shoulder throb no matter what. Bits of antibiotic goo from my shallow cuts get stuck in my hair, so I shower twice. The lady who treated me kept saying I might have been exposed to the blood of the perpetrator, who surely has all sorts of diseases. I prefer to think this is inaccurate, but don't protest when Dad takes me to the hospital for a battery of blood work.

We get home to a message from Officer Haynes that police have lifted perfect fingerprints from Elena's house, but don't have the match in their system. I'm relieved. Seeing Cordero is as important as getting my hands on that grower's tape. We're a team now. AddyDay is on my side too. Ordered to rest for the day, I'm unable to go to her house. I leave a voicemail for her explaining the official version of the house break-in in case her mayor stepdad intercepts it. She doesn't respond, which worries me.

Monday morning finally comes. I tell Dad I want to go to school.

"You sure?" he asks, nodding at my face.

"The cuts have sealed. I think makeup will mostly cover them."

"Well, okay." He's been cautious around me since the break-in. Willing to give me anything I want, even space and silence.

I put on twice my usual amount of foundation, a pair of quick-dry running pants, and a long-sleeved cotton tee. I stare at my reflection. I look puffy and red, but more boy-troubled than assaulted.

At school, I find out both community leaders are at the gym to meet with the prosecution team—Rick Thornton and Officer Haynes. Both the men who were with me Saturday night.

Mr. White calls to me the moment I step into the gym. "Salem, get ready to record a round of witness questions."

Nodding, I sit next to AddyDay on the bleachers. We glance at each other significantly, but we have no privacy for chatting.

Cordero doesn't arrive by the time the bell rings. Mr. White begins class.

"Team, your community leaders are here to help you hone your courtroom skills," he announces. "In this scene, Officer Haynes will be a prosecution lawyer and Rick will be Lee Oswald, the suspect accused of killing JFK. Officer Haynes will deviate from the script written by your team and ask his own questions. Take notes on what kind of information he digs for. Uncover strategies you haven't thought of. I'll play the role of the judge. The mock trial is Saturday. That's in only six days, people."

The Laborer's Rally in Sacramento is in only six days, also. Plus, by then it will have been two weeks since Officer Haynes requested a forensic expert to come. By Saturday, I could know with certainty if Carrie was even murdered at all.

"Men, start the court scene." Mr. White gestures to me. "Salem, record."

I start filming. Officer Haynes appears on screen, seated in uniform on a folding chair next to Rick Thornton.

"Did you beat your wife, Lee Oswald?" Officer Haynes asks Rick.

Rick squirms. Officer Haynes remains steely-eyed. Behind me, the students on the bleachers go quiet at the incendiary start to the witness questions. AddyDay takes notes.

I have to tell her about her stepdad.

I don't want to tell her about her stepdad.

"Did I beat my wife?" Rick looks up from the script in his lap. "The answer to Officer Haynes's question isn't here." He's right. I know because I wrote the script. "What do I say if I don't know the answer?"

AddyDay answers without looking up, writing with furious speed. "During the trial, say so—that you don't know. For now, say yes."

"Yes, I hit Marina." Rick straightens against his folding chair, perhaps uncomfortable with his role as an abusive husband.

"Interesting that she didn't leave you and end the marriage," Officer Haynes replies.

I glance over my shoulder at the double doors. When is Cordero going to *get* here? I can trust him, but I can't feel relaxed around him, not even at the thought of him. What kind of expressions will he wear now that we trust each other? I keep trying to picture treating him like any other friend and failing.

The officer continues. "So, Oswald. You married Marina in Russia and she stuck with you even in the States. Why? Did she value your fight for communism?"

"Objection," Mr. White calls from his observation point under the basketball hoop. "Speculation. The witness doesn't know what was going on inside Marina's head."

I watch Mr. White lace his hands behind his back. If Dad doesn't have an alibi during Juan's murder, neither does he. If he was involved, he's a more skilled actor than I imagined.

"Salem," AddyDay whispers.

I glance at her. She's holding out her phone so I can see an unsent text message to me from her.

Come 2 my house today after cross country practice, it says.

I shake my head. I'm not going any place where her stepdad could find us.

I type her a text I don't send, simply showing it to her. *Meet in orchard behind your house. I'll call.*

She frowns, but nods.

"How can you object to that question?" Officer Haynes asks Mr. White. "Oswald was married to Marina. Wouldn't he know her views on politics?"

"Like a husband cares what his hot wife's thinking," Jeremy calls out from the bleachers behind me.

"You'll keep that opinion to yourself, Jeremy," Officer Haynes fires back with a policeman stare down.

A few students snort. I'd love to watch Jeremy squirm, but lean into AddyDay instead. "Have you listened to the tape, yet?"

"I couldn't." She's not really paying attention. She's looking between Jeremy and the officer with her lip in her teeth.

"Officer Haynes, just ask Oswald his opinion," AddyDay says. "Did you *think* Marina believed in communism? That sort of thing."

The officer mutters that he's glad he's usually on the other side of courtroom questions, and then turns to Rick. "Oswald, did you *think* Marina believed in communism?"

"Objection," Mr. White calls again. "Relevance."

Officer Haynes blows air out of his mouth.

"All right," Mr. White says, coming to center court. "I'll stop picking on you. Students, don't forget. The real mock trial is in front of a real judge. I'm giving you a hint of the standards Judge Steele will have."

"Steele?" Jeremy asks with sudden interest. "The judge who's going to rule on the peach strike?"

I look up from the video display. Just this morning, I read some of the reports on Judge Steele myself. The peach strike is headed for the courts, and he's the assigned judge. The growers are all up in arms. They want their case to land before someone else's bench because of a lenient ruling the judge made on immigration last year. Growers like Mayor Knockwurst specifically. His name is on the lawsuit.

"That's the judge," Mr. White confirms. "Now, Salem. You've got your teams ready to split into two?"

"Um." I turn off the video camera and lower it. "Well, we're doing three groups today, not two. I thought Slate would be here to lead a team. And . . . well . . . Cordero too."

Mr. White checks his watch. "Follow your plan. Slate will be here. And the third group can move ahead without Cordero."

"Okay." I stand and face the bleachers, hating every minute of the class's attention. "You guys know which witnesses you're in charge of. So . . . finalize the order of the questions we'll be asking and make sure the phrasing is admissible in court." I turn back to the community leaders. "Um, Rick, why don't you go with Marissa's group? Officer Haynes, you'll be with Jeremy for the Oswald questioning. AddyDay and I will go with Slate."

The students separate by group. AddyDay and I head for the far end of the bleachers.

"You didn't have to put Jeremy with the mean officer," she pouts as soon as we're away from the others.

"I don't understand why you think Jeremy's your friend." I set my backpack down and take a seat. "So, what happened yesterday? The recording's safe?"

Sitting, she sends an elaborate look around the gym to make sure no one's watching. She starts whispering, her eyebrows going up and down.

"I can't hear you," I say.

". . . so, *so* sorry," she says upping her volume. "I mean, everything's fine, but we're Mormon. Sundays are like . . . church, hymns, no computers—and *no* phones. Not in my family anyway. Mom's very proud of that rule. I couldn't even explain why I couldn't talk to you. Are you ready to kill me? What happened? Your cheeks are kind of puffy."

I tell her that Cordero took something from the bedroom and wouldn't show it to me. "I tried to follow him to see what he'd taken. A mirror sort of fell on us."

"Ouch."

I get my laptop out so it looks like we're working. I explain what happened, hesitating when I get to the part about Cordero retrieving the keys. I decide I can fully trust her, filling her in completely.

"I have to know why Cordero has the victim's keys and why his and Carrie's fingerprints are on them." I say when I finish. "And the tape recording—I need to listen to it."

"Their fingerprints are on those keys, and so is blood. That's so creepy." After a sufficient amount of time shaking her head, she digs through her bag, bringing out a notepad and a pencil. Its eraser is badly chewed. "Listen, the second I'm home, I'll record the tape. Then we can hand the original over to the police and figure out—"

The metal bleachers thunder with the steps of someone running up them.

I lean into AddyDay. "Sh!"

AddyDay rattles on. ". . . which growers don't have alibis—"

I raise my hand to cover her mouth, stopping her mid-sentence.

Slate sits in front of us. "You were in a house burglary?" he asks me.

"I'm—I'm fine." I can't think what to do in the face of his worry.

"What happened?" He looks from me to AddyDay. Her huge eyes don't keep secrets well. Frowning, he looks back at me. "What's going on? Alibis? Weren't you talking about the mock trial?"

In a hundredth of a second, I take stock of what I want. I want Slate to approve of me, like his approval means Carrie would have approved of me. But more than that I want to be understood by him.

I glance at Officer Haynes and Rick, the two men who were with me Saturday night at the break-in, each surrounded by a group of students.

"Before the break-in, I found a tape of the peach grower's meeting," I say quietly. "It's from the night Juan Herrera died."

Slate looks from me to AddyDay in utter shock.

"We both found it," AddyDay adds, taking some blame. "By accident. And then . . ."

He shakes his head. "You took something that could be evidence? Promise you'll stop. Getting involved in this— that's what's making you a target. Stop."

"I . . ." Why can't I feel satisfied by whatever the police say about Carrie—like he is? Like all of Carrie's friends and Dad? Almost no one around me but Cordero is on a personal mission to figure anything out. Of course Carrie was murdered, Cordero told me that day at the festival. *Of course* she was murdered.

AddyDay twists her fingers in her lap. "You're right, of course. I just . . . I really, really want to listen to what those growers said. I never thought about it before . . . but Carrie dying . . . finding out how it happened—it's research. I'm good at research."

"The recording is important for my Dad's alibi," I say. "Police think he killed Juan."

He runs a hand through his hair. "Then turn it in to the police. What if you've made it inadmissible in court? How could you have even touched it?"

"Mr. White," AddyDay snaps to us in warning, leaning to write in her notebook.

Slate glances at the teacher making his way to us. "Scoot over."

I make room for him, hitting the touchpad on my laptop to wake it from hibernation.

"So, what research are we delving into?" Mr. White asks as he approaches.

Slate peeks at the open document of witness questions on my laptop. "Uh, Silvia Odia, one of Oswald's potential co-conspirators."

I attempt to focus on anything other than the grower's tape, which I can't imagine handing over without analyzing no matter what Slate says. He leans to scroll to the top of my notes of Silvia Odio, a witness in the JFK case.

"What's the weakest part of Ms. Odio's testimony?" Slate asks me. Mr. White watches.

"Her timing," I answer. I believed her story myself until I read about the mistake she made. "She said Oswald came to her house in late September but there are pictures of him in Mexico City at that time."

Slate points at my laptop screen. "Perfect. But you ask about the timing here, and you should ask about it last. It should be your main point."

"So what questions *should* we start with?" AddyDay asks, scribbling notes. "We need to get every idea we can, and there are only ten minutes of class left."

"Ten minutes?" I lose my smile, glancing at the double doors again. Twin rectangles of sunlight pour in from the double doors' windows. Doubt fades to certainty.

Cordero isn't coming.

"Salem?" Mr. White asks.

"What?" I say, bringing my attention back to our group.

Slate's focus is just leaving the doors as well. He clenches his jaw and refuses to look at me. He must realize I've been waiting for my partner all this time.

"Salem, I want you to run your witness affidavits to the defense team before class ends," Mr. White says. "You'd better leave now."

Slate leans into me right in front of Mr. White. "Are you working with Cordero off campus?"

"Of course not," I say, blushing.

"No matter how careful you are around him, be more careful. And Salem, just . . . think about trying to be safe about the *other* thing too." He gives me a significant look, obviously referring to the recording AddyDay and I have.

Face hot, I nod at Slate and grab my things. He didn't make me commit to anything specific. AddyDay shoots me the call-me-later sign as I head for the exit.

I wade through oppressive sunlight. Campus is deserted.

The heat makes my cheeks burn more fiercely. Why didn't Cordero come to class? He does trust me, right?

Frowning, I knock on the door to Mr. White's classroom. It's a mock trial rule.

Envy pokes her head out of the room, black braids jangling with beads. "Yo."

"Affidavits," I say, holding out a manila envelope.

"Girl, check you out." She opens the door all the way. "Come on in."

"I'm supposed to be your enemy."

"Well, time to get our consorting on." She comes outside, letting the door fall shut. Her soft brown eyes become suspicious. "Mmph." She looks at me for a long moment, arms folded. "I was gonna talk to you anyway. You still a member of the Students for Strike club?"

"I paid my dues."

"But are you trustworthy? Kimi is starting to not be okay with sharing our plans with just anyone and you didn't come to our last meeting. But I'm going to tell you something. If you want to be in, you're going to come Saturday morning to the Laborer's March. It'll still be in Verona, you know. The marchers are going to camp here."

"I know." The organizers picked a state park smack in the middle of peach orchards.

"Now there's going to be something special there," Envy says. "It's a secret. So that's why you're gonna come see for yourself."

"Does it have to do with Carrie?" I ask, one hundred times more focused now that she's mentioned the word secret.

She shakes her head. "How come you want to know so much about what happened to Carrie, but you don't want to support the cause she loved?"

The question hits me hard.

The bell rings and students pour out of the classroom next door, probably hoping to get a head start on lunch.

"See you Saturday." Envy disappears inside the classroom.

Wandering away, I get out my phone and cover it to see the screen against the brightness. I don't go to the club meetings because I can't face them. I can't hear Kimi poking fun at Envy for some lapse in judgment and not ache that

Carrie's voice isn't right on its heels, sassing Kimi for being bossy.

I want to know what happened to Carrie. I have to know. I could pour myself into supporting the union if I could just know.

Sunlight pounds my hanging head. As I slowly walk, I'm overtaken by two mock trial students, Marissa and a guy named Philip. They're in the middle of a heated exchange.

"The growers planted Saturday's bomb," Marissa says.

"Nope. Gangs did," Philip answers. "I work there. We've never had any problems with anyone but gangs."

I perk up somewhat, speeding my pace to keep Marissa and Philip within hearing range. Philip works at the Taco Shop? Does he know the two workers who were injured by what the bomb police are now calling an amateur IED? Improvised explosive devices aren't used by street gangs, certainly not in small-town Verona, California. News crews are flocking to cover the unusual crime. I want to shake them. What about Carrie, blown to bits?

I can't wait around and do nothing. I can't. If Cordero won't come to me, I'll go to him.

I snatch my phone from my backpack and type.

> Me: Meet me in the orchard behind AddyDay's house at 5.

No answer. What if he's hurt?
What if he's dead?

I trip as I put my phone away. That's . . . impossible. Of course he's not dead.

After classes end, I speed to cross-country practice to get there early. Coach Johnny is setting up cones for relays on the grass field.

"Can I do today's run on my own?" I ask him.

He looks up and frowns when he sees me. Apparently my stress shows on my features. He nods kindly. "Get in five miles."

I duck my head in gratitude and text Dad a lie—that I'll be at a mock trial practice until after dinner. Tucking my phone into a zipped pocket of my running shorts, I run. I cut through orchards, going slow since the trees have created a minefield this year. Massive pits hidden inside rotting peaches—an ankle injury waiting to happen.

Eventually I hit the section of the orchard Dad cleared last fall. There are no peaches littering the clumpy dirt dotted with holes, which will be filled with saplings in a few months. The dirt itself is left in the sun for a whole season, to kill off mold. Juan Herrera must have been so easy to bury. Just hollow out a pre-made ten-gallon hole, dump in the body, and scoot loose dirt on top.

I reach the end of Dad's property, cut through a dozen more rows, and enter the mayor's orchard. His mature trees form a three-dimensional canopy of green above me. AddyDay's house appears from behind the trees just as I hear a branch snap behind me.

I whirl.

My invitation worked.

Cordero is twenty feet away, stepping free from foliage so I can see him.

CHAPTER TWENTY

Cordero's appearance is so altered it's shocking. His black cap is gone. Filtered sunlight falls on two days' worth of stubble and eyes dark from the lack of sleep. His expression is hesitant, almost vulnerable as he stands a quarter mile from the spot where Juan Herrera was buried.

I'm so relieved to see him I hurry to meet him. Breathing deep from running to catch me, he approaches as well, until dust floating on rays of sunlight are the only things separating us. His temple is still bruised from where he collided with the hutch.

"You didn't answer me," I accuse.

"I couldn't." He reaches for the back pocket of jeans hanging well below the line of his hips and produces a phone. The screen stays blank when he hits the on button, proving it's out of battery. "It died when I got your message."

I breathe in relief. "I thought something happened to you."

"You were worried?"

"Come on," I say softly.

He pauses with his phone half-tucked in his back pocket, and we share a look. I don't know what it means, but it feels significant and makes me breathe faster.

"Salem, is that you?" AddyDay's voice calls through the orchard from the direction of her house.

Cordero steps back from me as AddyDay ducks between trees to get into our row. "Holy—holy Cordero. Wow," she says, pausing with her hand on a branch.

I wonder how AddyDay will feel about my plan to bring Cordero into our sleuthing party. Granted, she trusts everyone.

AddyDay lifts a laptop bag off her shoulder. She's also wearing a purple backpack. The tape recorder with audio of the grower's meeting is partially visible in the outside pocket.

Cordero glances at me.

"I already told her everything," I say.

He nods and then steps toward her, demanding. "Who did you tell that I was searching for Carrie's killer?"

"What?" AddyDay asks with a step back.

"Cordero," I say, trying to get him to look at me. What is he doing?

He's watching her like he's hungry. AddyDay's eyes will probably start watering soon, staying so wide for so long. Cordero finally switches his focus to me.

"When I went to my home Saturday night, El Payaso and Tito were waiting with knives to attack me," he explains. "Carrie was right. Someone is hiring gang members. The man who killed her, I guess. Tito was stupid, so I heard them talking. He said they were hired to make me stop talking to anyone connected to Carrie. They don't seem to know who killed her, but whoever is hiring them is protecting her killer. I couldn't stay to hear more. They started coming down the hall. I took off through a window."

My mouth goes dry. "How would they have stopped you from getting involved?"

Cordero won't look at me. "Make me want to see things their way. I'm one of them. They won't kill me."

I eye the thin cut going through the *V* tattoo on his cheek. "But those knives weren't just a threat."

"You don't understand us," he tells me flatly. He turns to AddyDay. "Sorry to accuse you."

I grab AddyDay's arm, picturing Cordero in a face-off after dark with El Payaso and Tito in that banger house full of switchblades and guns. "You're *sure* you didn't say anything about Cordero being at Elena's?"

"No—I swear," AddyDay says.

I turn back to Cordero. "I know *I* didn't. I told police . . ." What did I tell them? "I told them it was a masked guy inside Elena's. Dad asked about you, though, because I'd seen you at the festival. I told him it wasn't you."

He shakes his head. "Someone knows I want to learn about Carrie."

My skin is clammy. "I'm the one going around making it obvious I'm investigating, not you. But maybe someone knows Carrie hired you."

Cordero ponders that idea. "Maybe. I don't think Tito ever knew Carrie hired me. Not at the time. Definitely El

Payaso did not know. He was still in prison. It started in May, a few weeks before she died. She gave me two hundred to go to Kelly Farm. To figure out who was intimidating the union workers. Names. Who hired them. But no one would talk."

"Kelly Farm is a corporate farm—lettuce, tomato," I explain in a hollow voice to AddyDay, remembering how Carrie talked about it. "Someone attacked three union pickers for wanting to go on strike."

Cordero nods. "Carrie wanted me to try again and I made her a deal. For one thousand, I would talk to workers at ten farms. If I discovered who was hiring the gang members, I got another thousand. But I only got the first."

I nod. That fits exactly with what I already know. There were twelve hundred dollars missing from her account.

"Slate made her cut off the deal," Cordero continues. "Not because of Juan. Juan died afterward." Cordero's face hardens as he speaks about Slate. "Slate talks about protecting family, but he protects no one."

AddyDay protests before I'm able to. "He was trying to protect Carrie."

Contempt flashes in his features, but he says no more about Slate. "The biggest thing Carrie wanted was for no violence to happen." He continues, saying something in Spanish.

"Violence is for the unimaginative," I translate.

That's exactly the kind of thing Carrie would say. She paid attention to things like that because she *was* imaginative. She had dreams. Dreams she can't pursue anymore because one of the unimaginative, violent people she worked so hard to outsmart killed her.

"Then what happened?" I ask.

Cordero pauses. "One night . . . Carrie called me, very upset. It was May 24. She said the strike was in trouble. She asked me to come to the orchard behind her house. She said she might need an alibi."

Cordero clenches and unclenches his jaw. His breathing seems more rapid. My own breathing keeps pace with his. He's talking about the night Juan died.

AddyDay nods. "That's why you were yelling your name at the restaurant that night."

He doesn't continue. The sunlight and the sticky sweet air press into us despite the shade of orchard trees.

"An alibi?" I echo gently to prod him. "What does that mean? You got there at 10:30. Juan was murdered between 6:30 and 8:00. Besides, Carrie wouldn't need an alibi."

"I didn't ask why Carrie wanted an alibi," Cordero says flatly. He pulls the keys out of his front pocket. "That's when I got these."

AddyDay leans in to see better. "Juan's car keys."

I look too. The keys are inside a clear plastic bag. They appear shinier than before, like they're no longer stained by blood. I suppose he and Carrie's fingerprints are gone now too. Which is probably why he cleaned them—to erase evidence that might implicate him.

"But what . . . what *happened*?" I ask.

Cordero won't look at me. The stubble on his face should darken it, but he looks pale. A sheen of sweat makes his *V* tattoo shiny. "By the time I got there, all Carrie would say was, 'He said he'd kill me if I don't get rid of it.' I didn't know what she meant. Then I saw the flies . . . the body."

I step toward him. "The body—*Juan*? Carrie saw *Juan*?"

He looks at me. "Carrie and I buried Juan."

AddyDay cries out. I hold my stomach and lean over, unable to make a sound. Carrie buried Juan? She was with his body? Was she in on his murder? No, then she wouldn't have had to die herself. I force myself to stand straight. I feel dizzy. My skin is hot all over.

How could she have seen Juan's body and not told me? How?

Cordero looks to see if I can handle more. "She wouldn't tell me who the killer was. It wasn't until later I knew why the killer left—it was to move Juan's car from your house. The killer must have moved it hoping that no one would know for a while that Juan was dead. But instead, someone found the car right away. That's how the police knew the time of death."

"Carrie buried a body," I say, forcing myself to accept the idea. Fear washes over me. "What did the killer do to her to convince her to bury a body?"

"I don't know, but he was already planning to blame the gang. I saw the symbol on Juan's shoe. He put *XII* for Primero and a *V*, probably because it's a traditional union symbol. He wanted to intimidate anyone planning to go against the union. He probably didn't know I'd just gotten a *V* tattoo myself."

He taps his cheekbone. His face is haunted by the dark of a May night when he sweated in a plowed field and dug a shallow grave alongside my sister.

Cordero continues. "I found the set of keys in Juan's pocket and kept them. He must have had two sets because the killer used a different set to drive his car. The keys were the only thing he had on him except clothes and shoes. After we finished, we needed to clean ourselves, but Carrie was afraid to go home. She didn't want to be seen by anyone. I remembered Rick Thornton lived close and kept his doors open."

Of course. Rick Thornton and his safe house for gangs.

Cordero rubs his forehead. "His house wasn't open the way it used to be. I used a window to get inside. Carrie needed a new shirt. I got her one of Elena's."

"But a body . . . she . . . well, she must have called the police," I say.

He holds my gaze. "She didn't." He sniffs and continues. "We cleaned up, but we thought we heard someone. I hid the keys under the mattress so I wouldn't be found with them. We left through a window. We went to Mission Plaza, but I needed those keys back. Our fingerprints were on them. I went to get them and the house was locked. I tried again. Elena set up an alarm system. I tried a third time and was almost caught."

Three burglary attempts. Everything makes sense. Everything except why Carrie witnessed a murder. Why did she witness a murder?

AddyDay nods. "I guess asking politely to go inside *would* be sort of suspicious."

"When Carrie saw her friends inside Mission Plaza, she . . . woke up," Cordero continues. "She went straight to them. I didn't want to look like we were together—that we had come together—so I got Tito to meet us there. We made it look like we were messing with some guys Carrie joined with—McCoy and Jeremy. Carrie stayed there and I left."

"Carrie left too," AddyDay adds. "Almost right after you."

Cordero nods. "A few days later I heard about Juan's disappearance on the news . . . I knew that that's who we buried. I called Carrie. She wasn't in shock anymore, but she was very afraid—afraid to talk to me . . . afraid to go to the police. She wanted Juan's family to know he was dead. There was a lot of guilt in her. She knew who the killer was but she wouldn't tell me. She planned to turn him in. She talked about justice and about being smart . . . about telling the police what happened. She wanted no trouble to come to her family or the union."

His words shake me into a response.

"Wait . . . *that's* what she was doing—talking to someone about the crime," I cry, remembering her words with me on the phone. "The day she died. She was so worried. She said . . . she said she was going to talk to someone about righting a terrible wrong. She must have been talking about Juan's murder. She'd been different and anxious all summer—ever since he died— and then she decided to talk to . . . well, she said it was someone important. I can't believe this . . . the very day she was going to talk to someone, she died? The killer must have found out she was going to tell on him—he probably raced to our house to stop her. She called the police, but before they got there, the killer arrived . . . he forced her to tag her own car and change her story with the officers."

"*Carrie's* the one who spray painted her car?" AddyDay asks. "With the same symbols left on Juan's shoe?"

I nod. "Her leaving that symbol was a message. Her last. Because the killer broke the gas line . . . and the house . . ."

Gone is all my numbness. I shake with emotion, remembering the horror of the day, the smell of the smoke, the realization Carrie really wasn't ever coming out of the blackened house.

"I'm so sorry," AddyDay whispers, putting a hand on my arm. I can't look at her.

Cordero remains silent, giving me a moment.

Waves of sorrow and relief hit me as I process so many details. Throughout Cordero's story, Carrie was still Carrie—that means the most to me. She was my same sister who had unimaginably terrible experiences. I wish I could comfort her. Bear her fear with her. At least she had Cordero for part of the time. None of that was easy on him either.

It's such a relief not suspecting him, now that I owe him so much. Not just for telling me about Carrie, but for saying nothing about the fact that I accused him unfairly. During the first week of school, I insinuated to the whole mock trial class that he vandalized Carrie's car, and I didn't bother to apologize once I knew Carrie may have spray painted her own car.

I breathe deeply, becoming aware of the flies and the heat. Finally, I look at Cordero.

"I suspected you at first," I confess to him as if he didn't know. "Because of your tattoo."

He traces the black *V* on his skin with his index finger.

AddyDay looks at him. "Oh, you're for the union too?"

"I am not against the union. But it was not for the union that I got myself this tattoo. Before Carrie hired me, already I was thinking of getting the *V* symbol. It is a symbol of power. It's very old. It says, 'I am for the old rules, the old power.' It stands as a warning to leaders who become corrupt." He looks at me. "Tito is a leader who needs to be warned."

I nod slowly.

Cordero's entire persona seems to transform as he talks. The light in his eyes isn't defiance, it's passion.

"The *V* says, 'Alone, I am weak, but if you treat me wrong, I will bond with others against you and be strong.' The union has a similar message, but Carrie is the one who used it the right way. It was brave to write that symbol on her car. She was strong."

Just like Carrie's trust in the union, Cordero's conviction for these old rules he talks about is almost faith. And apparently, I'm a believer. I'm filled with pride in how right Cordero's message feels. Carrie was brave and strong. It's crazy she could talk to me on the phone with a murderer after her. Sure, sometimes her true emotion showed, but then she teased me about kissing a guy. She was pretending to be fine, the whole time keeping me from coming to the house so I wouldn't be hurt, talking about being brave enough to go the police all by herself.

Maybe she was grabbing her keys, checking out the curtains because the killer was watching. Or maybe he was in the house with her, breaking the pipes, escaping just in time, all to stop Carrie from talking to her trusted person . . .

"But, wait," I say. "The killer—how did he know she was going to reveal his crime *that day*? After all that time— practically the whole summer."

Cordero nods. "She must have told someone. She trusted someone she shouldn't have."

AddyDay grimaces at the idea of someone betraying Carrie. "*Or* the person she trusted was betrayed as well."

"*Somebody's* bad," I say. "*Somebody's* betraying people."

Cordero nods, eyes flashing. "I have to find the killer now. No one hires Primeros to fight against each other."

I fold my arms, not at all comfortable with what he's saying. "But you're not . . . I mean, I thought you didn't want to be one of them anymore."

"What are you talking about?" he asks. "I'll always be a Primero."

"But . . ." I stare at him. "Well, you should get out. They're willing to hurt you. One of them could have killed Carrie."

Cordero shakes his head. "The morning she died, every-one in the gang was at a meeting."

"A meeting? For, like, gang business?" I ask, genuinely curious. How can I convince him he doesn't need his gang anymore?

His face is unresponsive. Yes. The meeting was for, like, gang business, which is none of *my* business, apparently.

"When Juan died, Tito was at a party," he says. "He broke up with another girlfriend. All of the top guys have alibis. El Payaso was in jail."

"*And . . .*" AddyDay pats her laptop bag. ". . . I've got the grower's meeting right here. I guess . . . I mean, we're going to do this, right? You want to hear what the growers were doing on the night of the murder."

Cordero and I look at each other. He told me what he knew. Terrible as it was, I know more about Carrie than ever. I'd smile or say thank you if the mood allowed it. Instead, we're both determined, somber, and sweating profusely in sunlight filtered by branches weighed down with half-rotten peaches.

He motions for AddyDay to play her copy of the recording.

I steel myself for whatever the recording is going to say about my dad, the mayor, and their alibis for murder.

CHAPTER TWENTY-ONE

The sun hangs suspended far above the horizon, out past the orchard. We nudge peaches aside with our feet, clearing a spot of shade for us to sit in.

"I don't see why we can't go into my house," AddyDay says, opening her laptop on her crossed legs.

I kneel beside her. "You said your stepdad is home."

"Ugh, but it's so hot out here."

It's killer hot, but we can't be in AddyDay's house if her stepdad is a murderer. I can't tell her that because I want to listen to the tape before I make any accusations. I still don't know when or why AddyDay's stepdad was threatening Carrie.

Cordero sits next to me. His white t-shirt brushes the sleeve of my running outfit. We're partners now, no going back. I'm determined to be on my best, most trusting behavior.

Cordero shakes a fly off his foot and his folded leg fidgets. It fidgets again.

I've never seen him fidget before.

"Do you want . . . I don't know, a protein bar?" I wonder where he's getting his food from.

His gaze finds mine. He's embarrassed, but not enough to protest. He nods, his shoulders expanding in the kind of deep breath that comes from relief. The sun is spoiling the peaches as we sit here. They smell syrupy and rotten.

"Oh! I've got sodas. What kind do you want?" AddyDay shuts her laptop and brings cans out of her backpack.

Cordero drinks half of his in one long swig. Heat like this kills people sometimes.

The protein bar I offered is in the zippered pocket of my shorts, opposite my phone. I always carry one on me. Cordero opens it with the usual bumping of elbows that comes from being in close quarters. He looks down at me twice, probably because I look up at him. I'm not in the habit of eating snacks with boys, gang members or otherwise. He seems as aware of me as I am of him.

AddyDay hands Cordero the last two sodas and sets up her laptop on her empty backpack.

"I listened to the recording right after school." AddyDay moves her cursor over the beginning of a line depicting the recording. A bubble of text tells her she's at minute four. "The digital copy is way easier to navigate than the tape. I'm going to skip to the important parts. Now, the growers didn't stay after for dinner, but I found out the meeting went late—until just about eight, so everyone who stayed until the end has an alibi."

She hits play.

". . . twenty-one of us here today, May 24," Mayor Knockwurst's voice says. "Oops, twenty if you don't include Rick Thornton here. Welcome, Rick. Unfortunately, he brings news from the union that they'll strike if we can't agree on laborer wages . . ."

"It *is* the May meeting, the night Juan was killed," I say, disbelieving. The mayor's voice continues, confident and affable, so much so that a chill runs up my spine.

"I knew you'd want to hear that part." AddyDay stops the recording and heads to minute one hundred and fifteen, the very end. She leans past me to face Cordero. "So, my stepdad and Mr. White told the police Salem's dad was at the growers' meeting while Juan was being killed, but they were wrong and this clip proves it. But that doesn't make him a murderer. Here's the clip."

Cordero brings his gaze to mine, grape soda paused near his lips. I search his features for any clue of his thoughts. Does *he* think Dad is a murderer?

Mr. White's voice fills the room, getting louder and louder. He must be walking toward the recording device. ". . . for the wages—oh, I think that tape player's still recording. Right there . . . yeah, that'll eat up the battery."

There's a muffled response.

"Great, I'll let you get it," Mr. White answers. "Brian never came back, did he?"

"Brian's my dad," I whisper. Cordero nods, listening intently.

"No, he left an hour ago to forge his own negotiation," a female speaker says. I don't recognize her gravelly voice. "He's meeting at his house with a union official—"

The recording ends.

"Wait, like, that very night?" I cry. "Dad had already left to meet a union official at his house that very night?"

"The official is Juan Herrera, isn't it?" AddyDay asks, biting her lip.

I knock over my empty soda can onto the dirt as I stand. Dad didn't have an appointment with Juan the night I got my period during the track meet, the night before the murder, like he told me. Dad had an appointment with Juan the night the man died. At the place he was buried.

"That's . . . impossible." I pace, unseeing. Carrie buried a body. Dad met with the victim at the time of death.

Cordero stands as well. He's dark and somber and unshaven because he's been on the run from dangerous people—maybe Dad.

"Your dad would not kill Carrie." Cordero is asking me, or telling me. I don't know which.

"But would he cover for a friend who did?" I put my arms over my head. Dad lied to me. I'm sickened by the image of Juan Herrera at the door of my old house, waiting to meet Dad fifty feet from the orchard where his body would be buried.

"You two haven't heard everything. Listen." AddyDay motions for us to sit back down. "You heard the roll call, right?"

I take my arms off my head. I wring my hands, one of which collides with a fly. It buzzes away.

"Salem?" she asks.

"Yes, I heard the roll call," I say.

"There were twenty-one people at the meeting," Cordero's dark gaze gauges my emotional state. He warned me about Dad, but that doesn't mean he's happy about the news.

"Twenty-one. Exactly." AddyDay mouses to minute thirty-seven. Cordero and I remain standing. "That's how many people were there at the beginning of the meeting. This next part is halfway through. We heard some of it back at Elena's house," she tells Cordero as she starts the recording.

"It's people like you that make your whole organization rotten!" Rick Thornton shouts, starting a flood of angry voices.

"Let's take a break," the gravelly-voiced female suggests.

"Don't bother," Rick answers.

"Very unfortunate," she says. "How about an informal poll to calm us down? We'll go . . . balding versus a full head of hair. I'm the latter."

A few people chuckle.

"Looks like it's, let's see . . . nine . . ." a man says. "Nine to ten."

AddyDay points to the monitor still on her lap and looks up at us, excited. "Did you hear it?"

"Nineteen," I say, meeting her gaze and then Cordero's.

"Twenty-one originally," Cordero agrees. "Two people left early."

"Exactly," she answers. "Two people left with plenty of time to make an eight o'clock murder. Lots of people who

214

were arguing never speak again, like Salem's dad, Rick, Bill, the guy who said illegals should move to China."

"Not Mr. White, though," I say. "He spoke at the very end."

Cordero frowns. "That was Mr. White?"

"He's a grower," AddyDay says. "You didn't know that?"

I look at Cordero. "Do you suspect him?"

"Not if he has an alibi."

"Mr. White? Seriously?" AddyDay asks. "Anyway, the person who left the meeting could have been someone who never spoke at all. I bet your Dad forgot he left early."

"Or he and the mayor left and killed someone," I say.

"Okay, that's it," AddyDay dropping her hands beside her lap, disturbing two flies. "Just because someone's a grower doesn't mean they're a killer."

"Growers have motive, AddyDay, they do. And opportunity. And . . . and your stepdad threatened Carrie."

"What are you talking about?"

Cordero nudges me with a frown. "Her stepfather?"

"He's one of the growers who could have left early," I explain. "The mayor—Bill. Tell her what he did to Carrie." Tell *me* what he did.

Cordero grabs my upper arm, incredulous. "Her stepdad is the mayor? Does he know we're out here?"

I look at AddyDay's house in the distance. "I . . . well, that's why I didn't want to go inside."

Cordero drops my arm and kneels in front of AddyDay, gesturing at her laptop. "Erase this."

I know the implications and dangers of having a copy of this tape as well as Cordero. I should never have let her make a copy. I should have known it'd be too dangerous.

I kneel next to him. "AddyDay, erase the recording."

"It's my only copy," she says.

"*Ya!*" Cordero demands, leaning to flick the base of the laptop so that it rocks, a warning of what can happen if he doesn't get his way.

AddyDay looks from Cordero to me, fear settling on her features.

In a few clicks, she makes the recording disappear.

CHAPTER TWENTY-TWO

What were you thinking?" Cordero asks me. The three of us are once again standing because the peach guts don't make a great carpet. We form a circle of tension. AddyDay's laptop is still set up on top of her backpack on the spongy dirt, covered in flies.

"I didn't know about Bill when I gave her the recording," I say, defensive.

"Didn't know what about Bill?" AddyDay asks.

I look to Cordero.

"I was supposed to meet Carrie a week before she died," he explains. "I waited for her at Mission Plaza. She arrived in the backseat of a blue sedan. I hung back. But I heard what the driver said as she got out. He said . . . what was it? 'If you don't back off, young lady, I will make you stop.'" Cordero nods at AddyDay. "Your stepfather was the driver."

AddyDay's face goes red. "Okay. Okay, I knew Bill didn't want Carrie leading the pickers to a strike, but that doesn't mean he like, physically harmed her."

I turn to her. "Wait, you knew he threatened Carrie?"

"Salem. He *talked* to Carrie. *Everyone* was talking to her. She controlled the Students for Strike Club Twitter and Facebook accounts—the ones that were giving the union so much attention. Bill said she was better at media control than the union president himself. She was becoming a leader in a strike that might . . . you know, kill a whole industry or whatever. He wanted to give her a better way to lead. He invited Carrie to be his teen representative, but she had said no. That's probably what he was talking to her about right then."

I fold my arms. "First he asked her to join his side and when she didn't, he threatened her, and then someone killed her." I turn to Cordero. "Tell her how suspicious that looks."

Cordero looks at the orchard with a long, ponderous stare—lips pressed together, the setting sun behind him.

He shakes his head at me. "We need more evidence."

My shoulders slump. He's right. I've got to stop condemning everyone on zero hard evidence. But Bill *was* having secret meetings. I snap my fingers in realization. AddyDay and Cordero don't know that yet.

"Listen, I overheard Bill, my dad, and Mr. White talking when they didn't realize I could hear. They have secret meetings together. They said they're planning a counterattack against the union next Saturday. Maybe we can catch them in the act. I don't know what they're up to or how far they're willing to go to stop these strikes."

The question of how far the growers would take their counterattack Saturday hasn't left my mind since I heard about the bomb threatened against the Laborer's Rally, also planned for Saturday. At the time, it seemed so clear that the growers were the ones planting the bomb, but now I hesitate to suggest something that vilifies them so much. Not after I accused AddyDay's stepdad. But I still want Cordero's thought on the subject. I speak cautiously.

"Also . . . you know, another thing we could look into is the taco shop bomb at Mission Plaza," I say. "Whoever set it up is targeting the union and . . . well, that could be the same people who murdered Juan in the first place."

Cordero hesitates and then nods. "Tito and El Payaso were missing the night of the bomb until midnight."

My voice is heavy. "And then they came after you, possibly on orders from Juan and Carrie's killer." The potential connection is too tight. I can't keep my suspicions quiet any longer. "That counterstrike the growers were talking about is on the same exact day as the bomb threatened against the Laborer's Rally."

AddyDay stares at Cordero and then me. Her jaw drops. "You think growers are planting *bombs*?"

"I don't know," I say. "I don't want to think it—my dad's one of them. But someone killed Juan and probably Carrie. And someone's planting bombs."

AddyDay puts a hand on her hip. "Okay, if these growers are all crazy murderers like you say, why would they warn the union about the bomb?"

"The peach strike," Cordero and I say together.

"If the union gets scared enough, they'll fold," I continue. AddyDay makes a face because she knows it's true. "For all we know, the killer wants to hurt as few people as possible. Also, maybe not *all* of the growers who are helping really know how violent things are getting. I'm not saying Bill personally is the killer." Although, if I'm honest, I suspect Bill the most. It keeps Dad from being my primary suspect.

"Salem, Bill would *never* kill someone." AddyDay points at the recorder still in my hands, brown hair falling from behind her ears. "I understand you don't know Bill, but I think you even suspected Jeremy a while back. And you *do* know Jeremy. He'd never hurt anyone."

"*Jeremy?*" I ask. "This is why people like him pick on you. Because you tell yourself people are good even when you've seen them do things that are bad."

She frowns, stubborn. "That doesn't make them murderers. You didn't have any evidence against him besides coincidences, and you don't have anything but that against Bill. Look."

She gets out her phone and thumbs over it furiously.

Cordero sends me a wild glance.

I make her turn to me. "Are you calling your dad?" I cry out.

"Bill Knockwurst, Brian Jefferson," she says, sounding out the names as she types them.

Cordero breathes in relief. "A list of suspects."

"Oh," I say.

Cordero leans over my shoulder to look at the list. His chin stubble brushes my hair. "Add Slate."

"What?" I look up at Cordero to find him close, already watching me, like he was expecting my bias.

"Um, let's keep the list manageable." AddyDay says, voice cheery.

"Slate was . . . at track when Juan died," I say in my calmest manner. "We had double practice for weight lifting that whole week."

"He never missed any?" Cordero asks. With a flicker of his lashes, his gaze sweeps the length of me, coming back to meet my eyes with more emotion than I expect. Cordero seems to think I know why he's upset.

I step back. Confusion and pleasure make my thoughts cloudy. "Why are you even asking about Slate?"

I think back to what Slate said of his whereabouts. Slate wasn't at every practice last spring. He missed at least one to celebrate a birthday with Carrie. Cordero must notice a change in my expression.

"He *did* miss a practice," Cordero says in triumph.

"I'm not putting him down on the suspect list," AddyDay says.

"Don't put him down," I agree.

Cordero looks at AddyDay. "You weren't there the night he fought Tito. I broke up their fight. Slate was . . . not angry . . ."

"Furious?" AddyDay suggest. "Fuming—totally out of control?"

Cordero shakes his head. "Afraid."

My thoughts jump to the fear Slate showed when he got that call from his sister Anna after the mock trial meeting. What exactly is he so afraid of?

"No matter what," I say, "Slate has an alibi for Carrie's murder. I was with him at the cross-country summer-conditioning. *That* I'm certain of."

So there, I tell Cordero with a look. He refuses to meet my eye and waves away a fly. It's almost like he has an emotional reason for being at odds with Slate—a reason he now wants to hide from me.

"Any other suspects?" AddyDay asks.

I hesitate. "There are lots of other growers."

Cordero refocuses on the case. "We don't have to worry about all of them. The suspects are the people Carrie feared. The ones who have no alibi. The ones who know we are investigating, and told Tito or El Payaso."

"Okay, right." With a direction to go, my brain sifts through data. "I think we have to suspect Carrie might have feared the mayor, if she thought he was threatening her that day at Mission Plaza. And . . . well, and Dad. On the night of the murder, she was with you, Cordero, and you say she refused to go home. Granted, after she left you, she did eventually show up back home—with Slate. So maybe she wasn't afraid of Dad," I add quickly.

"We'll take your dad off," AddyDay says.

"Keep her father on," Cordero insists.

She frowns, biting her lip. I don't protest. I'm upset, though.

"Your father knew we were investigating," Cordero points out.

"So did Officer Haynes," I counter.

"Officer Haynes is a cop," AddyDay says, confused.

"Exactly," I say. "He could be a bad cop."

AddyDay actually gets angry. "You have gone insane."

Cordero explains. "Haynes came to the house when Carrie called the police the morning she died, the very day she was trying to tell someone what happened to Juan. Maybe Haynes didn't like her story. Maybe he was already paid off by the killer. Maybe he even killed Carrie himself."

AddyDay bites her lip. "I don't like that idea."

Frowning, I wave away a fly. "You know, I never thought about that. That Officer Haynes was at the scene of the crime."

"Well . . ." AddyDay says. "I still can't imagine an officer being bad, but that *is* another thing the killer had to have. Access to Carrie's house. You said the firemen who investigated the explosion at your house didn't find anything to suggest it had been broken into."

My shoulders slump. "My dad had access to our house." Supposedly he was driving to Reno for a business trip. What if he never left Verona?

"Well, *and* the officer, if Carrie let him in," AddyDay says, trying to reassure me, but keeping her frown. Neither of us likes the idea of a cop murdering Carrie.

"Well, other people *can* go to a house, right?" I say. "Push the door open if Carrie didn't lock it or something. Rick and Elena live super close to us. We're looking for someone who figured out last Saturday that Cordero was involved. Well, both of them heard Dad accuse me of working with Cordero."

AddyDay lights up her phone, and then pauses. "Add Rick and Elena as suspects? Really? Rick works for the union. Elena supports the strike all the way. They're no enemy to Carrie."

I shake my head, disappointed. "Don't add them."

"No one else knew I was at Elena's house with you?" Cordero verifies.

"Well . . ." I think of the text I sent Slate. "I guess . . . I guess Slate could have suspected something."

Cordero's glare is a gunshot straight at me.

"He thought I was joking," I say.

AddyDay pauses with her thumbs suspended above her phone "Oh, Salem. We *can't* write down his name. You were *with* him when Carrie died."

"Keep his name off." I sigh. "So that's it then. Your stepfather, my father, or a policeman. Great choice. Or a pair of them—or all of them. And that's not to mention the person Carrie wanted to talk to the day she died. That's not someone she feared, it's someone she trusted. That could be anyone—an officer, a teacher, some city official besides the mayor threatening her. Is there anything else we haven't covered?"

Each of us ponders as flies swarm around our ankles. All I can think about is how Carrie would have trusted Slate and Dad.

"Oh my gosh, *fine*," AddyDay says. "Bill's having meetings, but they're not secret. They're just . . . private. I don't know what they're about. Anyway, he's not having any more until this really big one in Sacramento, right after the mock trial. A whole bunch of growers are coming to the trial too. Some of them have children in our class, and the rest of them want to check out the judge they'll be facing—Judge

Steele . . . but, anyway on TV, investigators concentrate on the victim too, and try to learn why a victim was killed . . . I mean, there are dozens of union officials . . . do either of you know why Juan Herrera was even the one targeted?"

I look at Cordero.

The surprise in his eyes shifts quickly to calculation. "I have friends. Laborers. I'll talk to them."

AddyDay nudges my arm. "You and I can go to the Laborer's March when it gets to Verona this Saturday. We could ask club members about Juan there. Or even officials from the union—like super subtle, though. Just kind of bring up how sad it is that he died."

"Good idea," I say. "I'm going to make a timeline. Everyone around Carrie or Juan, every place they were the week he died and the day she did."

She nods at the recorder next to her laptop. "What about the growers' tape?"

"Slate?" Cordero demands of me. "He knows about the tape too, doesn't he?"

"But he—" I lower my eyes and think of what AddyDay and I told Slate during class. I nod.

Cordero shakes his head.

Slate didn't want me to listen to the tape because he was worried about my safety. The way Dad is nervous about me spending time with Cordero. All that safety, all for me. Right? Or is one of them just covering his own tracks?

AddyDay picks up the tape recorder and hugs it to herself. "We had planned to give the recording to the police, but we can't now. It kills your dad's alibi." She won't look at me. "Plus, it either makes our dads liars or it makes them very forgetful."

"You could test the police, yes?" Cordero asks. "See if they use the tape or not."

"I want to keep it. For now." I glance at Cordero like he's going to protest, but he doesn't. I get to make the decision. I feel another notch of gratitude for him. "The most important thing is following the growers to that meeting Saturday after the mock trial. It should end around five, right when the Laborer's Rally starts."

Cordero nods. "I'll be there."

"And me." AddyDay shrugs. "What? I'm going to prove Bill isn't doing anything wrong."

"Will you be in class tomorrow?" I ask Cordero, hoping to coordinate with him then.

"Too dangerous." He turns like he's about to leave. "I will find you if I need to talk."

"No way. Where and when are we meeting? And give me your phone." I open my palm.

He glares at me.

I drop my hand, amazed I could forget how intimidating he can be. "So I can charge it for you? Someone's got to have a cord that matches yours."

With a cautious expression, he reaches around and hitches his shirt up over his back pocket. He meets my gaze.

I look away, flustered that he's caught me looking at him again. It seems like that happens so often. "Then you can text me, and I won't worry that you're dead."

I can feel his focus. He's not angry anymore, but his eyes are intense with something else. He brings his phone in front of him so I have to step toward him to reach it. His fingernails are creased with dirt. I take it quickly.

"How will I get it back to you?" I tuck it into my left pocket without looking at him.

"Moffatt Bridge," he says, naming a freeway overpass.

"After school tomorrow? Six o'clock?" I ask.

Cordero steps closer to me, the black of his upside-down *V* tattoo inches from my face. "If the killer is sending El Payaso and Tito to find *me* . . ." he says quietly.

"Then he might be on to me too," I say, emotions shifting. The thought has been close to surfacing for a while.

AddyDay puts a hand to her chest. "Oh, Salem."

"I'll stop talking about Carrie every second," I say.

"Be careful," he warns over his shoulder. With a final glance at me, he leaves, heading south.

"Oh my gosh, wait," AddyDay calls after him. "I forgot. You have to be in time-period clothes to get into the mock trial Saturday."

Cordero turns back to us. He has a particular glare on hand for just this moment, one that says, *go ahead and try to make me wear dress-up clothes from the 1960s.*

"No, Mr. White can't have an excuse to kick you out," AddyDay insists.

He rolls his eyes and leaves without responding.

AddyDay and I watch Cordero's tall figure weave between the rows of trees. He's capable in so many ways, but he's surrounded by people like Tito and El Payaso. Maybe that's why he's conflicted. One minute he hates the idea of violence, the next minute, he's a bullet already shot,

hot from ignition and ready to act. What kind of person will he become?

No one can stay undecided forever. In or out. With his gang or against it—for real, forever. What kind of choice would that be?

AddyDay turns to me. "I have to get home or my parents will worry."

"So will my dad," I say.

We look at each other. Our whole conversation has centered on how her stepdad or my dad might be a murderer. We don't have to say it. We're in this together now.

AddyDay rubs her hands together. "What do you think? Should we go like *West Side Story* with Cordero's mock trial outfit? It's like the *High School Musical* of the 1960s. Turned up collars . . . gold chains . . . sideburns?"

"I think *he* will choose who he's going to be," I say.

When Cordero least expects it, the knife blade he's balancing on will tip, sending him to one side or the other.

. . .

After saying goodbye to AddyDay, I jog into the orchard in the opposite direction Cordero took.

Surrounded by the heavy smell of peaches, I think of what Rick Thornton said about gang members. He said they had to learn to accept that the things they were taught growing up—and the people who taught them—were wrong. Cordero sure seems affected by some gang mentality that's wrong. Like the idea that he has no choice about being a gang member even when he's running for his life from them.

I think of me running for my life from someone I trust. Would I figure out I was in danger soon enough, or would it be over before I took the first step?

I stop in the orchard and search Officer Haynes's address on my phone. The destination is only a mile away, and the day's heat is finally wearing down. I know I should turn in the tape.

Still undecided, though, I walk in the direction of his house while I play the entire grower's tape. It gets dark as I spend nearly two hours pacing through the trees, listening. AddyDay already played everything significant. Halfway through the recording, my phone vibrates. Dad is calling me. I text that I'm at a mock trial practice. He texts me to come home. He calls again. I don't answer. I can't imagine talking to him. He'd know right away something was up. What if he's refusing to see the dark side of people he's helping?

I can barely see my hand in front of my face when the tape finally ends. Using my flashlight app, I head for a road with streetlights.

I step out of the trees.

Despite the streetlights, I'm freaked out by the darkness and the solitude of the neighborhood.

Maybe AddyDay is right. Maybe a series of coincidences tying you to a crime doesn't make you a murderer. Maybe there's a reason Dad met with the victim at the scene.

But maybe AddyDay is wrong.

My teeth chatter from nerves as I navigate to Officer Haynes's blue split-level in the middle of suburbia. Cordero suspects the police, but I just can't seem to match his suspicion. I can't. I'll test them the way Cordero suggested, but I can't believe Officer Haynes is murdering or covering for murders—not because I know the officer well, but because when I see a crisp police uniform, I trust it. I've been trained that way since birth. Like how Cordero trusts gangs. Because you trust what you know.

Feeling sick, I stick to shadows. I wipe the tape recorder and cassette clear of fingerprints with the corner of my shirt. The mailbox in front of Officer Haynes's house creaks when I shove the proof of Dad's broken alibi inside.

I sneak away, wondering how the gang members change, the way Rick said they do. How do they act once they suspect that the things they were taught and the people who taught them could be wrong? Even evil? Do they run away? Do they pretend to see nothing amiss?

Or are they traitors?

Like me?

CHAPTER
TWENTY-THREE

It's too dark to get home through the orchard, so I run along the road. I send Dad a meandering, AddyDay-styled message about how my phone died while at the mock trial practice and how I'll be home in ten minutes.

Dad: I almost called the police.

Me: I'm so dumb. I know you're mad.

Once home, I slow and catch my breath. As I open the front door, it creaks.

"Salem?" Dad calls.

Dad doesn't need to hire gang members to come after me. He has access to me all the time. My chest hurts from so much tightness.

Dad beats me to the door of my room. "Salem, don't avoid me. I told you to be home hours ago." He gives me a once-over. I ran almost three miles after leaving AddyDay's, plus the several before that to get to her house. My ponytail feels awry and whatever make-up I had on has been sweated away.

"You weren't studying," he accuses. "What were you doing?"

I hesitate, unable to think of a quick lie. "Studying."

"Who gave you a ride home?"

I don't answer.

His face clouds with dark suspicion. "Were you with Cordero? Are you dating him?"

Fury erupts inside me. Dad's the one who betrayed me and lied—lied so I don't trust him enough. And I need help now. I need it. And I don't trust Dad to give it to me.

"I'm not dating anyone!" I shout.

Dad feeds off my emotion, becoming more confident in his suspicions, becoming furious, yelling in my face. "Cordero is in the gang who went after your sister. How can you possibly hang out with him?"

"I just said I didn't see him!"

Dad steps away from me, composing himself. His calm words are more threatening than ever. "I consider it my sole job as a parent to make sure you don't go anywhere near Cordero Vasquez. Whatever kind of person you think he is, he has to do what his gang wants. That's how it works."

I don't answer. Cordero won't do whatever his gang wants. He'll take over the entire organization before he'll do that.

"I'm revoking your freedom. I will drop you off at school and pick you up from practice from now on," Dad continues.

I look up. I can't let Dad monitor my every move. I have to meet Cordero at the overpass. "You don't even get home from work that early."

"I'm going to take you to and from any after-school mock trial practices too. And no going near the union events."

"I can't believe you!"

I stomp to my room, furious but relieved somehow too. Dad is worried about me. That's why he doesn't want me to hang out with a gang. It has nothing to do with what I could learn from Cordero about secret grower meetings.

I want to believe myself.

. . .

I wake up the next day expecting police to break through the door and arrest Dad. Instead I hear the sound of his electric razor. So Officer Haynes is corrupt? Or he hasn't found the tape yet?

Dad takes me to school. On campus, my science teacher is in the crowded locker area, announcing that Verona High is on a partial lockdown. I'm told I need to get to class immediately.

"All off-campus passes are suspended for the day, breaks between classes are shortened to two minutes, and lunch will be in the gym," he announces.

Did something happen? Another bomb?

"Salem," AddyDay calls from a few paces away. "How'd it go? Your dad?"

I rush to her, backpack jostling. "I'm fine. What's going on?"

Before she can answer, her friend Marissa pushes between us, headed for the plaza, yelling, "Look, it's a fight!" Onlookers shove so that I can barely see the group of boys throwing punches.

"Go to class!" a campus hall monitor yells into a bullhorn, herding the crowd away.

AddyDay and I struggle to stay together.

"Another shooting," AddyDay tells me as soon as we reach the outdoor quad and aren't pressed by bodies. "Near Benjamin Road. And then, here at school, all these boys were blaming the growers or union about it. That's what the fight's about. It's like the whole town's going crazy."

"Did anyone die in the shooting?"

"I don't know. I checked Twitter, but it just happened. They're saying the shooter was that ex-con guy you were asking about, the clown guy."

I bring my hand to my throat. "El Payaso."

"That's the one who wants to hurt Cordero, isn't it?"

"Get to class!" bullhorn-guy shouts at us.

I dig Cordero's phone out of my backpack and give it to her. "I can't go with you after practice. Dad'll be watching. I'm grounded."

"You said you were fine."

"Well, I'm not dead."

That's more than Carrie can say. Is it more than Cordero can say?

I cover my stomach with my arms. No, he'd never be shot near Benjamin Road. He wouldn't be stupid like that. He wouldn't be.

"Take him food and water, all right?" I say, refusing to believe he's gone—gone the way Carrie is gone. I was in denial when she was killed too. I realize it's not denial if he's not dead, though. The thought confuses me, and I'm not sure what's more delusional, thinking he's dead or thinking he's not.

"I'm sure he's fine," AddyDay calls as we part ways, wide eyes suggesting the opposite.

I'm in a daze. The teachers are on edge. Classes go by, and I read news sites every chance I get. Three people landed in the hospital, including a baby. I consider the possibility that the Último gang is behind the shooting and this is just a random gang act of violence. But random violence is still violence. It still could have hurt Cordero. I reread the same articles over and over. I move to articles about the peach strike, looking for the news that Dad has been taken— abducted by police who have the authority to hold him in jail for murder. I can't want that. But I can't want Haynes to be corrupt. For AddyDay's sake, I don't even want the mayor involved.

With no hope in any option, I feel like I'm trapped in a room getting smaller. Nearly every adult I've interacted with since Saturday night could have made it onto my list of suspects.

During the mock trial class, Mr. White doesn't let anyone talk, lecturing on courtroom procedure instead. I stare at his feathered hair and pleated pants, wondering if I should put him on the list. Slate catches my gaze several times. I should even be wary of him, but I can't be— not when Carrie trusted him. Not when the longest day of school ever finally ends, and I find him waiting for me before cross-country practice starts.

"I'm sorry," Slate says immediately. We're near the doors of the gym, which smells like sweat. The cross-country and girl's tennis teams have both been assigned to stay inside for the entire practice.

"I know you want to know what happened to Carrie." He runs his hand over his bangs. "I just . . . did you listen to the recording?"

I feel so safe around him, knowing Carrie trusted him. But I picture Cordero's narrowed eyes and weigh my words. "Um, my dad . . . wasn't at the peach grower's meeting as long as he thought. He probably just remembered wrong. I turned it in to the police, like you wanted me to. Anonymously."

"I should have listened to it with you. After what happened, after the explosion Saturday . . . just like how Carrie died . . ."

His voice breaks.

"Boys," Coach Johnny calls. "Line up under the hoop."

"That's you," I tell him.

Slate glances at the coach and then back to me. "Salem, you can trust me, yeah?"

"I . . . do," I say.

He's suspended in a final glance at my face—like he's verifying my confidence in him. Then he lines up to sprint across the court.

No matter what, I want to know the evil that took Carrie. But I want to believe it didn't come from someone she loved.

. . .

After endless rounds of sprints and lunges across the gym, Dad picks me up. The drive is quiet. When upset, the Jefferson family exercises its silent treatment like it's a major muscle group. Dad should have been questioned about his broken alibi by now. But I don't want him questioned. Better to have Haynes be crooked than Dad a murderer. What if Haynes is just biding his time before he makes an arrest, though? How long until I can be confident that Dad is just . . . Dad?

"Parental responsibility fulfilled," Dad says once we're home. "Go ahead and rot your brain out with television."

He means it as an olive branch.

"I'll be in my room," I answer.

He sets his briefcase on the table. "The forensic expert is scheduled to come Saturday."

I stop. "This Saturday?"

He nods.

I hesitate, then go to my room and lock the door.

I sit on an ancient desk chair that weighs twenty pounds. Six days until the expert comes. Forty-three minutes until AddyDay is supposed to meet Cordero. Forty-three minutes until I might get some word of whether or not he's alive. Forty-three minutes.

Forty-three minutes.

Forty-three minutes.

Going crazy, I open my laptop and make a timeline of Carrie's whereabouts the week of Juan's death, starting with Wednesday.

Wednesday, May 22

Me	track practice
Dad	???
Carrie	birthday date & witnesses fist fight at Mission Plaza
Slate	birthday date & fist fight w/ Tito at Mission Plaza
Cordero	broke up fist fight at Mission Plaza

I can't think what any of this tells me. I start on the next day.

Thursday, May 23

Me	track practice (got period)
Dad	track practice (to get me), spilled ice cream on shirt
Carrie	talked w/ me on phone while meeting w/ Rick Thornton
Slate	track practice (most likely)
Cordero	???

The following night is when Juan died, between seven and eight. It's even sketchier.

Friday, May 24

Me	track practice, watched Casablanca twice
Dad	left peach meeting early and then ??? (not home)
Carrie	buried Juan's body, went to Mission Plaza
Slate	track practice (most likely)
Cordero	buried Juan's body, took Carrie to Mission Plaza

I put my fingers on the keypad with a sense of foreboding. I don't want to make the last list. The events on the day of Carrie's death.

Saturday, August 10

Me	cross-country summer conditioning
Dad	left home early, said he drove to a business meeting in Reno
Carrie	drove me to school, someone threatened her, she tagged her own car, police came & left, explosion
Slate	cross-country summer conditioning
Cordero	at "gang meeting" with all Primeros

I stare at Carrie's name and the word *explosion*. If I had known what was worrying her, could I have gotten help? My paranoia flares. Got help from whom? Dad's a suspect. Officer Haynes and Mayor Bill Knockwurst would be on the timeline too, except that I know so little about their actions that week there's no point in including them.

At 5:44, my phone rings, flashing AddyDay's picture.

"You're going to meet Cordero now?" I answer. Sixteen minutes until six o'clock.

"He's safe."

The chair creaks as I lean back into it.

"I got here early and he was waiting," AddyDay continues. "He's got his phone."

Sure enough, I get a text from the same number he used last Saturday. I'm hesitant to put Cordero down as a contact in case Dad goes digging through my phone. His response shows up unlabeled.

> Unknown: Benicio is coming Saturday.

Benicio? As in Benicio de la Cruz, president of the farm laborer's union? Maybe we can ask him about the victim, Juan.

"Salem?" AddyDay's voice sounds distant because I'm looking at the screen of my phone.

"I'm here," I say, putting it to my ear.

"Did you know tomatoes are sprayed with pesticide that makes the workers' hands get rashes? That's what Cordero was doing today—picking tomatoes as an unregistered worker at some farm a few towns away. How is that *legal*? Okay, okay." She sounds flustered. "Um, he wants me to focus. I had this idea he wants me to tell you about. Some workers he was talking to got a special invitation for this special union meeting within the Laborer's March Saturday morning."

"Wait, that must have been what Envy was talking about," I say. "She invited me."

"*That's* Envy's secret event? You got invited?" AddyDay says. I can't tell if AddyDay sounds excited or jealous.

"Everyone in the club is talking about it. I've been trying to get invited for days. Marissa and Katelyn are going."

"You'll come with me," I assure her. "I'll tell Envy I'm bringing a friend."

I'll have to ditch Dad's monitoring somehow. He said I couldn't go to any union events.

I pause. "So Cordero's okay? Just a rash on his hands?"

"Do you want to talk to him?"

"What? No." I do want to talk to him, but I feel strange admitting it.

After AddyDay and I hang up, I type a message to him. Texts are better than talking anyway. Texts don't focus all of my attention on his voice, his accent, the temptation of meeting his eyes.

> Me: We heard about the shooting downtown. Are your friends safe?

I have to wait several minutes, but I get an answer.

> Unknown: I don't know.

> Me: Are you okay?

I take the rubber band out of my hair and let my ponytail fall to my shoulders. I'm in Grandma's house, the one I used to visit when I was girl. When my real house burned down, Dad and I had a place to go. Cordero—where's his place?

> Unknown: I'm good.

> Me: Do you have a place to sleep?

What am I doing? Inviting him over?

> Unknown: I am in a truck bed. That's where the workers sleep.

He's obviously working at a place operating outside of the law—a place that doesn't check papers. Cordero isn't eighteen and he's not with a parent, so technically, he's not allowed in the fields even if he's documented, which I don't know. I've never asked anyone before if they're illegal. It'd be like asking if he wore boxers or briefs.

Boxers. It's not my fault I know that. He sags his jeans.

> Me: How many hours will your phone battery last?

I lie down in bed. My muscles cry out in exhaustion after today's sprints, but I don't give in to sleepiness.

> Unknown: 24 hours more or less. I should turn my phone off to conserve it.

> Me: Be careful

I sound lame. I think of what Carrie would say.

> Me: Violence is for the unimaginative.

I'm trying to tease him, I think. Maybe he'll think I'm accusing him of something.

No answer comes. I worry and feel embarrassed as my shoulders relax into the edge of my pillow. My thoughts wander to Juan Herrera, beaten to death. That kind of murder would come from someone who is angry and vengeful—and physically capable of besting Juan. Who fits that description? Dad's not beefy and strong. He's a runner, just like me. Mr. White is even thinner, and short too. Mayor Knockwurst is by far the most likely suspect. He's probably 6'3" and not fat, just big.

I shift on the mattress. At least we have a plan. It's not a great one, and it doesn't give us much time, but it's a plan. Locate President Benicio de la Cruz at the Laborer's March to find out if he has any information about Juan that can help our investigation. Then follow the growers from the mock trial to their secret meeting before the Laborer's Rally ends—preferably before someone attacks it. The bomb threat could be a prank, of course, but I can't treat it like that. Not when Carrie died in an explosion.

It occurs to me that if I sneak out to go to the Laborer's March in Verona on Saturday morning, Dad might not give me a ride to the mock trial in Sacramento later that day. If he figures out I'm snooping around grower secrets, he can keep me away from their secret meeting. Mayor Knockwurst could do the same to AddyDay. And what about Cordero? How is he going to get to Sacramento?

I send Slate a text.

> Me: Dad might be busy Saturday. Are you driving to Sacramento? Could I get a ride with you? And maybe AddyDay too?

I fight my heavy limbs and stand, stretching. Cordero can't hitch a ride with Slate. They hate each other. A quick search through my mock trial paperwork gives me teammate Marissa's number.

> Me: Coordinating rides. Could you take one of the guys to Sacramento Saturday?

I lie down and slip into sleep until my phone vibrates three times.

> Marissa: Do you think it might end up being Slate who needs a ride? Because I ABSOLUTELY will have a spot open.

> Slate : I'm going with Philip. He says there's room for both of you. Hope to see you.

> Unknown: Fine, I'll be imaginative. Just for you, I'll imagine this truck bed is filled with secrets to winning the mock trial.

Cordero did understand I was teasing him. He teased back.

I fall asleep smiling.

CHAPTER
TWENTY-FOUR

I spend the week balanced on frayed nerves, convinced something awful will happen, like that Haynes will arrest Dad or Cordero's lifeless picture will appear in the news.

Every minute outside of school and cross-country practice finds me at Jeremy's house for mock trial run-throughs. At first Dad wanted the practices to be switched to our house so he could monitor me more closely, but I dug in my heels, embarrassed to bring the group to an old farmhouse with bad carpets, few outlets, and poor Wi-Fi. He consented.

Dad and I ignore each other except once when I yelled at him for embarrassing me. He showed up halfway through a mock trial practice in order to verify I was actually there. I can't stop thinking of how a forensic expert will come Saturday, the same day as the mock trial. I can't go to sleep any night until I hear from Cordero.

During the day he works in the fields for cash and information that doesn't come. The rash on his hands is gone now that he's in a broccoli field. I tell him that if Carrie were alive, she'd want the name and address of the grower failing to pass out gloves for sprayed tomatoes. He answers that she used to reimburse him for handing out twenty dollar bills to anyone he thought deserved it. He used the privilege only twice.

I love the idea of Carrie trusting a gang member to do her charitable work. I especially love that he actually did it, choosing a blind Apache Indian from Chihuahua and a Polynesian boy with no shoes.

Cordero says he's worried that he'll be dropped from the mock trial class, so we go over the notes he'll need to write his witness questions. He will play the part of the Cuban conspirator who visited Silvia Odio in 1963. He managed to contact Mr. White on his own and the teacher announced that Cordero's continued absences will affect his grade, but not his teammates'.

Finally, Saturday morning arrives.

I wake up before dawn. The early hour feels calm. I pack the supplies I'll need for the Laborer's March and mock trial. Both today. The forensic expert is also coming today. I pause often to stare out the window. The growers and pickers haven't settled on a wage yet, and it's early September now. The peaches have all dropped. Almost the whole crop, wasted.

Beyond our empty field, the trees of our neighbors blur together in the semi-dark outlines in various shades of dark and light grey. They're just trees. They produce peaches that bring a profit. And someday, new people might die over how everyone is paid.

But I don't want it to be today.

I leave a note on the kitchen counter explaining that I'm safe. Securing my backpack, I dash out the back door. Dad doesn't catch me.

I jog through orchards and hit a chain link fence with wild oak trees beyond. I hop it, passing three tents and several groups of Hispanic adults sitting on camp chairs. The farther I travel, the thicker the crowds become. I hit a grassy field surrounded by gravel parking lots. Children run around waving the purple flags of the union. Trucks and vans are parked haphazardly.

I cross the field and keep going. Envy said to head south into the woods of the state park and there'd be a barn. Finally, I see the bright red building and a swirling mass of people.

I grab my phone. There are no messages from Dad or Slate. Slate is working this morning, and will text me when he's ready to go to the mock trial. I wonder if Dad will text me or hop directly into his car when he figures out I'm missing. I feel guilty, but maybe something else too. Maybe hopeful. If I find out who killed Juan today—and if it's not Dad—then I won't have to suspect him anymore.

I call AddyDay. "I'm here."

"I see you."

I spot her a few tree rows down, motioning me forward.

"Come on," she says when I reach her. "The barn's almost full."

We shuffle inside the huge, dark space, lit by cracks in the wooden walls. Dust and the smell of dry rot fill my nostrils. Between bodies, I see a workbench topped with iron tools that probably haven't seen use for fifty years—heirlooms of a time when small-time landowners picked their own crop.

A short Hispanic man steps onto something—I can't see what—and becomes a head and shoulders taller than everyone else. He's got a round face that's all smiles.

". . . brought you here to train you."

The crowd cheers.

"Let's hear it for Benicio de la Cruz, president of the Farm Workers Union!" a woman in the front says. I recognize her styled bleach-blond hair. Senator Lethco. With her is Rick Thornton with his wild cowlicks.

The cheers become frantic, with whistles and an air horn that makes me cover my ears. Envy and Kimi are in the center of the barn in rapt attention. A half dozen other students are present. I think I see AddyDay's friends, Marissa and Katelyn, back there.

The union president calms everyone using both arms, palms out. "Okay, now you can hear me. Welcome. Welcome. Thank you for coming. Here today, our mission is peace. That is our message."

The barn ripples with excited chatter. AddyDay gets her cell phone out and snaps a picture of Benicio.

"Violence is among us," he says. "It does not come from us, but we must deal with it. We are peaceful. But we do have a weapon when violence happens to us. We have the media."

"Amen," a woman next to me with dark cornrows calls.

"So now I say to you. Bring out those cell phones. That's right. Get your cameras." His voice takes on the timbre of a preacher as the cell phones appear above people's heads. "Now, today. Document what is happening—really happening. The slurs, the man who punches a brother for going on strike, the woman who refuses to see hungry children begging. This is your mission. We will not back down. Come bombs, threats, or death, we won't back down!"

The thunder of the onlookers shakes the wooden floorboards. Dust floats down from the rafters.

"Make it your mission!" he roars. "Find the violence. Expose it. Don't stop until you have pictures, websites, whole newspapers showing the greedy, bloodied hand of the growers. When our nation sees our suffering, it will not turn its back on us."

I watch men and women clap, eating up his emotion.

"The nation will not put up with the violence of the most *murderous* of growers," he continues.

Something about the tone of his voice makes me look up in alarm.

Benicio is looking right at me, eyes narrowed.

"Oh no," AddyDay says as everyone turns to us.

"Do I see someone who wasn't invited to this meeting?" Benicio asks. "Someone who lives on the property Juan Herrera was murdered on? The very dirt used to bury him?"

People gasp as Benicio climbs down from his perch. His shirt is a red and black flannel. It's long-sleeved and buttoned to the collar. Verona High students lean around each other to see, parting for Benicio until he's right in front of me. If he knows who I am, he knows who my sister is. I guess being Carrie's sister isn't enough to make up for living on the property where the body of a union official was unearthed.

Envy steps toward Benicio, anxious. "I invited her."

"Does she know our other plans today?" he whispers in answer. He's old enough to be hard of hearing. I think he thinks he's quieter than he is.

She shakes her head, and he breathes in relief.

"Still," he says so everyone can hear. "This meeting is private. Envy, I'm disappointed."

Kimi steps beside Envy and looks at Benicio in jealous alarm. No one is allowed to pick on Envy but her.

"Salem helped start Students for Strike," Kimi tells him. She points at AddyDay. "It's *this* girl who shouldn't be here."

AddyDay reddens. "You said Salem could bring a friend." She wants so badly to be accepted.

Kimi folds her arms. "We voted you out of the club, remember?"

My shoulders drop in disappointment. I didn't know they'd done that.

AddyDay's two friends step to face her, glaring.

Marissa folds her arms. "I can't believe you came, knowing who your stepdad is."

"No, no!" Jeremy interrupts, threading bodies to get to us. "Let *Addy* tell the union president. You'd love to tell President de la Cruz about where you live, *Addy*? Who your stepdad is?"

"Young lady?" Benicio prompts her.

AddyDay glances at the union president. "Well . . . my mom got married a few years ago and we moved into my stepdad's house. Bill Knockwurst's house."

"The mayor who filed a lawsuit against us?" he booms, louder than necessary. He dons an elaborate frown.

Boos fill the air.

I fist my hand, ready to defend AddyDay. "She has as much right to—"

"No, I don't." AddyDay gives me a significant look and then drops her head like she's sad. "The club didn't invite me—but it *did* invite Salem. She's Carrie Jefferson's sister."

The name sends a ripple through the jeering crowd, silencing it. The expression of the woman next to me changes from angry warrior to reminiscing grandma. Benicio may have known Carrie was my sister, but this woman didn't. Carrie was a hero despite being the daughter of a grower. It's like she's not entirely gone, like a piece of her is lending me her importance and giving me a voice.

Benicio watches AddyDay slip out of the barn. There's a victory in the corner of his lips. He'll never advocate violence but that doesn't mean he can't see it coming, can't use it for his purposes. Carrie was better than that. AddyDay's better than that. She knew I'd get more information if she took the fall for both of us. She's braver than she gives herself credit for.

Inspired, I gather my own courage.

"It's true. Juan Herrera was buried behind my house," I announce. "I came today because I wanted . . . well, I—I wanted to know him, who he was. I lost my sister too, and I just . . . she loved the union so much . . ."

My voice shakes. Dust tickles my nose. Nearby, Rick Thornton listens, nodding. The silence in the barn makes my emotional rawness stand out all the more. I'm grieving, just like they are. It makes me one of them.

"So you want to know about Juan Herrera." Benicio takes me by the shoulder with one hand. He motions for Rick. "Rick, tell her."

Rick looks at him in surprise. The crowd shuffles aside so he can approach.

"Juan grew up troubled," Rick explains to everyone. "I knew him back then. The union gave him a chance. A job."

Benicio nods. "You got Juan that job. How long was he employed with us? You're in charge of our records, right Rick?" His eyes twinkle.

"Oh, now you're making fun of my record-keeping," Rick says with a smile. He addresses the crowd to explain. "I lost the recording of the May grower's meeting. Twice."

"*Twice*?" I say, coloring as the union members laugh. I found that recording and gave it to the police. Here Rick is casually mentioning the tape, obviously not worried about how it verifies many of the grower's alibis and calls into question those of others. When the growers asked him for the recording, I wonder if they even mentioned why they wanted it.

Rick grins. "I left it at the grower's meeting, still going. At the end of the meeting, the mayor stopped the recording and got it back to me. Then I lost it again."

I stare at him in shock.

"The *mayor*?" I ask. "He stopped the tape on May 24? You're sure?"

If the mayor stopped the recording at the end of the meeting, that gives him an alibi for Juan's murder.

Rick nods. "Well, that's what everyone said. Him and Mr. White. Hey, they're not bad on a personal level," Rick says, defending himself from the crowd's grumbling at the mention of the mayor. "We have friends among the growers, remember. Like Carrie. In fact, look at this right here."

Opening up a laptop case, he rifles through it. He pulls out the plaque Carrie got him, calling him the World's Best Union Club Advisor. "I ran into this the other day and, man. It put a smile on my face. Carrie Jefferson ran a club to support the union and she was the daughter of the union. The union helps people. It changes people. It changed Juan. His experience with the union turned him around."

"And then Juan became a victim of a senseless *crime*," Benicio roars, reengaging the crowd. He's so short I can see the top of his gelled black hair. "Why was Juan killed? Why, any of us could have been Juan. But all of us can also be a source of inspiration like Carrie Jefferson."

The mood in the room is electric. Be Carrie Jefferson? Everyone wants that.

They stomp and shout. I have to call AddyDay immediately. I can't believe it. Her stepdad isn't a murderer. But who is? Dad and Officer Haynes are our only remaining suspects.

"For a while, Carrie herself was tempted by lies—the lies of the growers." With his loud voice, Benicio has grabbed the attention of the crowd again. He takes my shoulder. He's about to cry. "She even questioned union officials, concerned someone could take bribes, fussing over voting process details so that every vote for or against the strike would count. Carrie . . . so dedicated to fighting corruption outside the union and even within it."

Any temptation I had to follow Benicio's emotional rollercoaster collapses under the weight of mental calculation. If Carrie thought a union official was taking bribes, she must have had a reason. Who did Carrie think was taking bribes? And why was she worried about the union's voting process?

"Did Carrie suspect *Juan* of taking bribes?" I murmur, realizing my mistake as Benicio's eyes widen.

"You would smear the name of a fallen hero?" Tears stream down Benicio's face, a hand on his chest. He's not mad at my accusation. He's worried my soul is in danger of perishing. "Blame each other, we fall. United, we stand. Unity is the strength of the union. Unity *is* the union. We win by boarding those buses to Sacramento and showing the world we will not be intimidated. We will hold our Laborer's Rally this evening come death! We will fight for fair wages come anything!"

He'll lead his followers straight to the edge of a cliff. If they fall to their death, all the better as long as a camera captures the image.

"I'm taking the first picture of grower violence!" Senator Lethco shouts, holding her cell phone above her head. She races to the barn door.

Amid the cheering, people shove to follow her lead. Someone knocks over the workbench, leading to an eruption of shouts as tools fall. One man picks an old ax off his shoe and slams it in anger onto the floor, broadside. The blade breaks free from the dry-rotted wooden handle.

My phone vibrates. AddyDay's text says she's gone home to get ready for the mock trial and not to worry about her. Meanwhile, I'm supposed to meet Cordero to fill him in on what we learned from the union meeting. There's a message from him as well, a pinged location about a mile from here. We have two hours until we have to leave for the mock trial.

I sprint outside, ready to jog to Cordero and tell him the rumors about union bribery. What did Carrie think was going on? What *was* going on?

CHAPTER TWENTY-FIVE

Backpack jostling, I run through the woods until trees give way to the floodplains of the San Joaquin River. The grass is long and golden brown. This afternoon, the mock trial will start. Soon after, the Laborer's Rally will begin, despite a bomb threat. Peril feels terribly soon—like a literal ticking time bomb.

Off to the side of the country road, Cordero is leaning against the trunk of a shade tree, watching me approach.

A stirring of breeze does nothing to cool my anxiety as he scrutinizes me the way he always does.

The cuts on his arms have healed, as mine have. My heart rate increases as my pace slows. He doesn't react to my arrival, just keeps his head tipped back against the bark, eyes alert. The sixty seconds it takes me to reach him seem to take an hour.

He pushes away from the trunk and faces me. His lips are chapped, but he's managed to shave recently.

"Are you eating enough?" I ask before I can think. Why don't I ease into topics, the way normal people do?

"Yes." A smile plays on his lips. "You looked scared of me."

I make a face and then focus on the news I have for him.

"The mayor has an alibi," I say. "I couldn't believe it. That leaves only Dad or Haynes."

I try to explain what Rick said and how AddyDay was thrown out of the meeting. The people weren't angry, they were motivated. They were true believers.

"It was like church," I say. "Like Juan Herrera's their slain prophet. Rick said Juan was kind of messed up when he was a teen, but straightened out basically when he had the farm union preached to him."

Cordero nods, eyes alert in the face of all the new information. "Yes, this sounds like the union."

"I guess they have to be big-time believers to go on strike. For a group of people who don't eat when they don't work, strikes are no small thing."

"It's better than getting deported," he says.

"True. I just felt like . . . I don't know. Benicio says the right things but . . . I wish I knew what Carrie thought of him."

What I mean is that I wish I knew what she'd tell me if she'd seen him today. She'd probably tell me that she loved him even if he did kick AddyDay out of a meeting. Union officials are dying. What's he supposed to do when a potential spy is in his midst?

"Benicio thinks Juan was just a random victim—wrong place, wrong time," I continue. "But I did learn one thing. He said Carrie suspected a union official of taking bribes. Like she didn't just wonder, she was asking specific questions. Benicio also mentioned she was looking into the union's voting process. If a union official was able to tamper with the vote, he could have made sure no strike ever happened, no matter what union members wanted."

Cordero doesn't answer, thinking.

"Well, what if there *was* a person taking bribes and tampering with votes?" I ask. "Juan Herrera."

Cordero tests the idea aloud. "The growers bribe Juan, who was supposed to throw the vote and keep the strike from happening."

"Exactly. Maybe the deal soured. Maybe he stopped taking their money and told them he didn't want to keep the strike from happening. This gives the killer a specific motive for targeting Juan, but we still don't know who the killer is."

Cordero squints at the field grasses drenched in sunlight. My shoulders drop as I watch his body language. We can follow the growers to their secret meeting, but we won't know who to focus on. Dad's the only grower we have reason to suspect anymore.

I don't want to think about it. I should get ready for the mock trial anyway. I don't have any more reason to stay with Cordero, whom I haven't seen for nearly a week.

"How's . . . your sister? Jimena?" I ask instead of leaving.

He meets my gaze. "I can't visit her. I want to. I wish I could make sure she's . . . better." His hesitation makes it clear that *better* isn't the word he wants.

"Make sure she's healing," I say automatically. Worse, I say it slowly, well-articulated, looking right at him and waiting for confirmation that he understands. I tense at the scowl I know is coming.

I wait a long moment.

"*Que está mejoranda,*" he says. Slowly. Well-articulated. He's teaching me.

"*Que está mejoranda,*" I repeat.

He nods at my pronunciation, pulling his forehead closer to mine, gaze steady. Steady and darkly intense. I'll never be able to hold such a gaze.

I step back, and neither of us says anything. I feel the length of the pause in the pulse of my neck and wrists.

"AddyDay's friend is planning to meet you at the school. Her name is Marissa," I say finally, even though I've already verified this with him. Marissa will be surprised. I have no doubt Cordero will persuade her to let him into her car—probably without half-trying.

"You have the last affidavits for me?" he asks.

"Oh, right." I swing my backpack forward and get out a paper sack full of clothes and typed pages.

He opens the sack with a loud crinkle. The clothes he doesn't care about, but he takes out the papers, folding the bag back down and holding it under his elbow.

"And if I don't understand the questions, I can ask the lawyer to repeat them?" His eyelashes flutter as he scans the page.

I watch him pause and read a chunk of text.

"You really want a good grade."

"Not really. I have no money for college," he says, still reading. "I took the class because Carrie told me to."

"Carrie? Really?"

I love her so fiercely right then. Of course she wanted him to see something outside of his rows of crops to harvest and his violent, gang-infested house at 147 Benjamin Road.

"All that charitable work and Carrie was going to make you a schoolboy too," I say, not sure if I'm allowed to joke about such a thing.

He looks up and hesitates. "Maybe . . . but I was curious. The judge, the police . . . they aren't for us, for those in a gang. She said I was wrong about that."

"Maybe the police aren't perfect, but they go after gang members for a reason most of the time. Some of your gang members are following the killer's orders. I mean, El Payaso and Tito *do* hurt people, and you're trying to protect them."

Cordero shakes his head, expression dead. One mention of turning on his gang, and his moment of sharing is over.

"Come on. You don't think they should go to jail?" I ask.

"Prison is the worst place for them. What do you think made El Payaso so bad? It's up to me to stop El Payaso and Tito, not the police."

"You? How can you be more powerful than the police? Anyway, the killer has hired El Payaso and Tito. You think they're going to stop picking on you if we discover who the killer is? What if we don't have enough evidence to prove the killer is guilty? He'd go free and he'd still be after you. There is a downside to the court system."

"Not all justice is in the courts." Cordero leans to put the notes back into the paper sack, bent as if with grave responsibility.

Memories scroll through my mind like a slideshow on super speed—the flash in his eye the first time I asked him about Carrie, the conflict on his face when Slate and AddyDay talked about soldiers killing for their family.

I back away from him. "*That's* why you're looking for the killer? So you can shoot him?"

"He killed your sister." Cordero's anger is cold and well thought out. He turns away from me. "He's hiring the gang—splitting us up."

That's the plan. That's always been the plan. Find the killer, get rid of him, and get Tito and El Payaso in line. Heck, take over the gang in a blaze of glory at the same time.

Staring into the field, Cordero expression becomes so conflicted I'm not sure he's conscious of revealing his inner battle. Haunting indecision is cut into every sharp feature. I take in the half of his face that I can see, the black of his tattoo and the way he's turned from me, almost in shame. He's not only tortured by the idea of killing someone but by the indecision itself—like hesitancy in the face of moral corruption is some kind of weakness. A luxury that a real *vato* wouldn't allow himself.

"But you . . . you wouldn't . . . you won't," I argue.

Cordero composes himself, turning back to me. "You want the killer to have no punishment?"

"No, I want . . . I don't know—but you can't . . . you can't just kill him. It'd be . . ."

It'd be messy. It'd be a secret. I'd have a secret I'd have to carry to my grave just like Carrie. What about the rooftops I was going to shout from? What about the rage of the rest of the world that was going to match my own? If the killer is shot down, he becomes a person—an entity I'd have to sympathize with. I reject that. I will only hate him.

"People need to know she was murdered," I say. "There needs to be a trial. Your whole idea—everyone knows it's wrong. You know it's wrong. You don't like the way Tito bullies everyone. You broke up a fight between him and Slate the night Carrie came to talk to you and you don't even like Slate."

He stops me. "What do you mean, the night Carrie came to talk to me?"

"When Tito picked a fight with Slate at Mission Plaza."

He shakes his head, confused. "Tito didn't pick a fight with Slate. And Carrie didn't come to talk to me that night. *Slate* came that night to fight *Tito*."

I shake my head. "No, Slate fought Tito because he saw Carrie talking to you."

"That's not what happened," he says, upset—very upset. Slate's name always makes him upset. "Slate was angry. He arrived at Mission Plaza. Carrie was in the car with him. He hopped out and came after Tito. Carrie and I stopped him."

"That's not what happened," I insist, sure there's a misunderstanding. "Slate said—"

"No? That's not what happened?" Cordero leans into me, eyes flashing. "Because I'm in a gang and Slate isn't?"

"Can you just admit there's a reason to be afraid of gang members?" I demand. "You don't act the same around them. You practically threatened me after the drive-by."

"I'll be deported if I'm caught with a gun."

"Yes, and it's the gang that made you *have* one!" So he *is* an illegal.

Conflict is all over his face, but he takes a breath and lifts his chin. "You only understand pride of a gang, not the shame of it. The gang is family."

"You're right. I don't understand you or your gang. Why can't you guys stop hurting each other? Stop working for a murderer? Stop doling out your own version of justice so the streets are a war zone?"

A rustle sounds from the road but Cordero's focus on me doesn't falter. He looks at me, with a vulnerability I rarely see in him. "*You* care what happened to Carrie. *You* understand loyalty. I would die before I left my people."

I want to see defiance sparking in his dark eyes, but I don't. I see moral confidence. I see self-sacrificing commitment.

I see Carrie.

Footsteps crunch behind me and Cordero's gaze shifts. I whirl.

A heavy-set Hispanic man careens toward us through the long grass, his face pulled back into his signature clown expression. El Payaso. He's found Cordero somehow.

"I'll kill you!" El Payaso calls to Cordero.

The black object in his right hand—

It's a gun.

Cordero leaps toward the field. El Payaso changes his momentum, coming toward me now. Screaming, I lurch away too late. El Payaso grabs my wrist, twisting it behind my backpack. I'm bent forward, gasping in pain.

"Let me go!" The pain is unbearable.

El Payaso shoves the barrel of the gun into my neck, and I hear the hammer cock.

CHAPTER TWENTY-SIX

I stop struggling when I hear El Payaso cock the gun. I can't see Cordero. Just the strap of the older gang member's sleeveless tank top an inch from my eye.

"Cordero, you ain't gonna let no chick get killed," El Payaso chokes me with the gun as he spins around, like he's searching.

I hold still, frantic. There's no sound but my labored breaths.

"Let her go!" Cordero's voice is well left of us, approaching rapidly.

El Payaso swings me toward Cordero. I use the momentum to grab a fistful of the man's hair. He drops me.

I land on my tailbone, pain ripping up my spine on impact. I'm screaming, twisting. The gun—Cordero—I can't see anything. El Payaso will kill him right here, right in front of me.

Cordero crashes into El Payaso and the older banger falls on me, pinning my ear to a bed of weeds. The gun tumbles. I roll out from under him and go after it. Dry thatch tickles my throat. El Payaso claws at my face, my hair. Somehow Cordero is at my elbows, lifting me, shouting at me. The gun is in his hand. I'm up.

I'm tearing across the field, Cordero at my side.

El Payaso screams behind us.

"I'll find you!" His words recede quickly.

Cordero breaks toward the river. I keep up easily, long grasses slapping my shins.

Overgrown oaks make our path jagged. At a sudden slope, we splash into the San Joaquin River. I catch my breath, wet to the bottom of my backpack as I fight thigh-deep currents, lazy but insistent.

We climb the opposite bank.

Cordero tucks the gun into a side pocket of his soaked, baggy jeans.

"Is he coming?" I scan the direction from which we came. I was too frightened to look back.

Cordero's chest heaves for air as he looks at me. "He didn't follow."

"He's trying to kill you, not convince you. Kill you," I insist, afraid of everything, even Cordero. I put distance between us. Dark leaves scratch my face.

He pursues me as if to make me feel better. "He is far away. Very far."

Just as he reaches for me, I collide with a dead branch. It catches me under my jaw, splintering from the tree with a crack. Pain cuts into my neck, and something falls onto my cheek from above, small and writhing. I cry out. I swipe my face and bring my hand in front of me. Cordero's chest is at my shoulder blades.

A black widow crawls across my knuckles.

"Oh!" I jump back, pressing more firmly into Cordero.

He reaches around my waist and flicks the spider away. I bring my hand to my face, knocking heads with Cordero who leans to see as well. Black widows are deadly. There's blood on my trembling pinkie finger. But no pain. The blood is from the cut on my neck, not a spider bite.

He grabs my fingers, anxious. "It bit you?"

"I'm fine. I'm fine," I say, turning to him. "I wasn't bitten."

Adrenaline has flooded my system too many times today. I can't stop shaking. I'm dimly aware of Cordero sweeping the wet skin of my neck with both hands, tipping my head back to inspect the underside of my jaw, his pressure holding me steady. I can feel river water snaking from my shorts to my thighs.

"I ran into a branch." I try to pull back from him. He won't let me. "See? It's a cut. See?"

"Is okay," he says, relief in his voice. He straightens and finds my gaze.

There's no release of his hold on me.

Behind Cordero, rays of sunlight speckle brightness onto the oak trees on the far banks. A slight wind sways them. Cordero came back to rescue me from El Payaso and the banger didn't follow us.

I keep thinking about it. How Cordero could have left me with him.

Cordero's fingers are light on my skin, his gaze focused.

"I hate black widows," I find myself saying, confused and not knowing why.

"They're beautiful."

"They're poisonous." If I could calm down. If he would take his hands off my neck.

He doesn't answer. He's close, looking at me with that expression of his that seems so familiar, though I can't read it. Guilty or hesitant. Or vulnerable.

His gaze is slow over my face, intense. More questioning than frantic. He needs me to know what he's doing. He needs my approval. For what, I can't stop to wonder—not when he's impossibly close, not when the hard line of his lips softens so that I know his defenses are gone.

He lowers his dark lashes to look at my mouth.

He's not breathing anymore.

He never moves, I swear, but he's closer. Closer.

Eternity is interrupted as I pull away from him in a stunned search for air, finally understanding his intent. My hands fist over my stomach in insecurity because I can't get the idea out of my mind.

What would it have been like? If he had done it, if he had kissed me?

He turns his back to me. There's a snap of branches past the river.

Footsteps maybe?

Cordero turns and pushes me away from him. "Go."

"What about you?"

"Go!" He darts away through trees toward the freeway. I sprint in the opposite direction.

The river pushes me west. I squish into pockets of sand covered in blackberry vines. Low-hanging willow branches slap my face. When the flowing water blocks me entirely, making the start of an S-curve, I don't check behind me. I splash through it rather than backtrack.

Once up the opposite bank, I'm less than a mile and a half from the Laborer's March and all those camera-wielding union supporters. I head into an orchard and pass a group of Hispanic men. People.

I pause and turn a complete circle, muscles shaking. Why aren't these men at the state park with the Laborer's March?

What if the noise next to Cordero wasn't anything—a falling branch, a fox in a hole? What if it was El Payaso and he catches Cordero? I don't know where Cordero is or what he thinks of me. Does he think I kiss boys just because they look at me too long? That I like him? I *do* like him, but it's not like I admit it or act on it. Should I? How did I have no idea he thought that way about me when I think that way about him constantly?

The more oxygen I gulp down, the more my head clears, but not my emotions. I hate myself for not controlling what I communicate, the way he does. When he's not vulnerable, I mean. When his lips aren't soft like they were as he leaned into me on the riverbank, his gaze unsure and pleading.

I run three strides, stop, and spin again. I smell like mud and I'm all turned around. I'm in an orchard. I feel west of the state park, but as a group of college-aged kids pass near me, moving even farther west, I second-guess myself. That would mean they were headed toward Elena's house and AddyDay's house. I picture Cordero inside Elena's bedroom, the way he looked when he stopped to gaze at me before escaping through her window—bruised, covered in broken glass, less guarded every moment he lingered, with his face just inches from mine. Did he want to kiss me even then?

I refocus on walking but the next thing I know, I'm thinking about the time between today and when Cordero and I kneeled next to each other on Elena's bed. One week.

Is that a long time for a boy to want to kiss a girl?

I continue along the row. I feel ridiculous for not having an answer. For not recognizing that Cordero wanted to kiss me.

For stopping him.

Because . . . because if I had recognized what he was doing I would have stopped him earlier. Or, no, I would have made up my mind first. I would have decided if my attraction meant that I truly cared for him. Before he pressed his fingers into the skin of my neck in his rush to see if I was okay. Before he leaned into me so close that I smelled the river water on his skin and saw from his caution and his longing how very serious, how very irreversible the kiss would be. How can I trust a feeling that takes over so completely? Or is that the very thing I should trust most?

Union supporters come from the east through the trees, chanting, "Right makes might!" A stone's throw ahead, the row of trees opens to a road lined with dozens of idling buses, waiting to take thousands of marching laborers to Sacramento.

In a disorienting paradigm shift, I realize I'm on Louise Avenue, my own street. I made it home. I'm safe now, I guess. If home is safe. I swing my backpack forward and dig for my phone. I've got texts and voicemails from Slate, Dad and AddyDay. Nothing from Cordero.

> Slate: Where should we pick you up?

> Dad: I know you're reading this text. I love you. Please tell me where you are.

> Slate: Earth to Salem.

> AddyDay: Slate says ur not answering. r u okay? Where r u?

> Dad: Where are you?

> AddyDay: Slate's looking for you. He left for ur house, trying to beat the protesters.

I frown. Protesters—at *my* house? What is she talking about?

I text Slate and AddyDay that I'm on my way home and send Cordero a message.

> Me: Where are you? Should I get help?

No answer. More marchers pass me. I spot a pair of bobbing black braids.

"Envy," I call, jogging to her. "What's everybody doing here?"

She purses her lips and looks at the screen of her cell. "I'm getting pictures of grower vandalism."

I lean to see. Her phone displays an image of the ax broken earlier.

I frown. "That's not grower vandalism. That was you guys."

"Could'a been a grower—and it's not like they're getting caught for everything they *are* doing."

"Envy!"

She shakes her head and jogs away.

I watch her leave. Envy is strong and soft—like a 1950s beauty queen. But this strike is changing her. Carrie's strike. It has become a carnival reflection of what Carrie wanted—each side blaming the other, the violence growing more heated, the justification to attack greater.

I contemplate running after her, but footsteps crunch behind me.

"Salem, is that you?" Slate's voice asks.

I spin around. He jogs toward me.

"I was worried," he says.

Slate.

Slate is who I've trusted, not Cordero.

My thoughts mock me in an emotional avalanche. For the first time it occurs to me that Cordero was calling Slate a liar. He said Slate's fight had nothing to do with protecting Carrie, and everything to do with Tito, the gang member who's worked for the killer at least once.

Slate, who I've trusted. Slate, who has lied to me since the beginning.

"Salem—" he says.

"You weren't protecting Carrie that night on your date." I back away from him as the marchers split to walk around us. "You came to Mission Plaza on purpose to fight Tito."

Slate's gaze darts to me, eyes blue as smoke in the distance.

Guilty as the one who started the fire.

CHAPTER TWENTY-SEVEN

I backpedal through a row of trees. Chanting union supporters pay me no attention. I need to be away from Slate.

He pursues me. "Salem."

"You were angry. You attacked a group of Primeros," I say, stumbling on rotting peaches as I go, backpack jostling. Suspicion and fear and the driving need to know what happened to Carrie play against each other.

"It's not my secret," he insists, blue eyes haunted.

"If you're why she died, I'll . . ."

"Anna, she tried to join the gang, yeah?" His expression is twisted by the horror of the memory. "She . . . had trouble making friends when we moved here."

"Anna?" Pausing, I picture Slate's sister and her pretty, heart-shaped face.

"For her gang initiation, Tito wanted her to rob a gas station holding a gun," he says. "She didn't want to be in the gang anymore. She said no. He said yes . . . he attacked her. He hurt her badly. She got away—she came home and only wanted Mom. Carrie knew where Tito's gang hangs out. She drove me to Tito. I hopped out of the car. I just—I beat him up. I wanted to kill him. Other guys from the gang showed up. Carrie parked the car and came to us—Cordero was there. He kept her from getting hurt and broke up the fight—that's when I found out they knew each other, that she'd been hiring him."

Around us, the atmosphere is a party. Marchers ignore Slate and me. Meanwhile my mind edges around the terror of the scene Slate is painting.

Tito, with his wide-set eyes and lust for violence. Every image of him near meek, exquisite little Anna Panakhov is only half-formed before I push it away, sick, wanting anger over fear. Carrie died. I need a face, a name.

"I thought Tito might have come after Carrie to get even with me." Slate's head is bowed. "I even thought the house explosion was set up—like you did. But the police said probably not. After Carrie died, I told them everything."

"*After?*"

Despite my shouting, I think how I've blamed him unfairly. He had nothing to do with Carrie's death.

"There are lists," Slate says. His hair falls into his blue eyes, so unusually light for his ethnic background. "We could be deported if they think we're terrorists. We're careful. No police record, no history of violence."

I don't ask who "they" are. The police. The government. That's why Slate's family is private. They're devout people who don't talk about their beliefs for fear of reprisal.

"When Tito went after Anna, we should have reported it right away," he continues. "But I fought Tito instead. Then I was frightened. He looked bad. Mom didn't want any fight on my file. And Anna—she was terrified. She begged me not to go to the police. She said the gang would call her a snitch and never leave her alone. I promised her I would say nothing. I promised her. "

I can't think of how I'd react in Slate's place. I can't imagine the terror.

"Carrie stayed calm the first night she found out about Anna, but later—the night she called me from Mission Plaza—she was freaked out. One minute she'd demand to go to the police, and Anna would cry, and the next minute Carrie would be confused, like she didn't understand what Anna even had to do with going to the police."

"That's because she wasn't talking about Anna by then," I say softly.

"So . . . what was she afraid of?"

"She was there when Juan was murdered."

"You're sure?"

I nod.

Slate hunches over, a hand to his forehead, eyes pressed shut.

"I miss her so much," he manages to say.

"I—" If I say one word about my longing for Carrie, how I'll never be right without her, I'll cry and never stop.

He pulls me into a hug. We stay that way for a long time.

Finally, he lifts his chin from my head. I'm mesmerized by the way he searches my face, like he's looking for something specific, something always just out of reach.

I know it's not me he sees in my features.

"I'm not Carrie," I say.

My whispered words bring him back from wherever he went, a place far away, a place where Carrie is. A moment with her is what he wants, not this one, not me. My mental image of Slate shifts to dark skin and river water—the intensity of Cordero's gaze. I'm more confused than ever.

"I have to go get ready for the mock trial." I run away, ignoring the gentle plea of his calls.

I plan to go to AddyDay's, which is past my own home. I should dart back into the orchard to avoid Dad, but instead I find myself approaching my *real* home—my old house. The roof over the patio is gone along with huge chunks of the kitchen. What remains is a half a house—one that's eerily familiar. The venetian blinds Carrie and I used to play in are visible in the sliding glass door to Dad's bedroom. The lilac bush sends me its scent.

In the driveway, a white van has accordion tubing running past new police tape and into the garage.

The forensic expert is here.

He's here and it feels like his conclusion might come too late. How could I have thought I'd be able to find Carrie's killer or stop the explosion threatened for today? Following the growers to a secret meeting—what kind of plan is that? The mayor has an alibi now. Dad's the only grower left on the list. I don't know where Cordero is or if I should try to save him somehow.

I'm not secure in my decisions like Cordero is.

Again, I feel the pressure of his fingers against my skin. I feel the tremble as I waited for him to come closer, his eyes black, his expression vulnerable. Like he's not always in control. Like he wasn't conscious of what he was doing at all.

Get out there more, talk, kiss a guy, Carrie told me. And when Cordero tried to kiss me, I stopped him.

I'll never be confident or find her killer. I'll never be strong, the way she said I would be. That dream died when she did.

The pain inside me burns like fire. I run away from the scorched house. I land in a sea of people headed for Grandma's farmhouse next door. A news crew is on the front grass, filming a woman with a handheld microphone. I can hear her loud, clear voice.

". . . the man who owns the orchard behind me," the woman says. "Police say he had money on hand to bribe the murdered union official Juan Herrera."

Police? Bribery?

My mind flashes to the wad of cash in Dad's hand when he took Carrie and me with him to the bank the morning before she died.

I cover my mouth. "No."

Just as I move to go toward the orchard to leave, a guy with a ponytail points his bullhorn at my face. "Look, it's the daughter!"

The volume blasts my ears. I reel away. He follows me. "Better say goodbye. His alibi is busted, kid. Dear old Daddy's a murderer."

Something heavy and squishy slams into the side of my neck. I recoil. Rotten peach-juice soaks into the collar of my running shirt. The peach rebounds onto the grass.

"Look at her!"

"Spoiled rich kid."

Protesters surround me, shouting while I flee. I'm enraged. We're not rich. But I'm ashamed too. We're rich compared to peach pickers. Dad was bribing a union official.

I look back at Grandma's house. Dad is in the driveway, flanked by two officers. His bowed head slaps me harder than any peach could. Without thinking, I veer toward him.

"Dad! Dad!"

When I get close, Officer Haynes cuts off my path to Dad. Two cop cars are parked behind our Prius.

"Calm down," the officer says. "It's just a search warrant."

I dodge him. "Dad?"

Dad reaches for me, standing by the door of the nearest police vehicle. He's not held by the officers or cuffed. The second cop is nearby.

"Salem, are you okay?" Dad grabs my shoulders. "Where were you?"

"They can't arrest you. They can't!" I want to take it back—the grower's tape I handed over. He's just my dad. Why can't the police see he's just my dad? I've lost Carrie already.

"They found the missing tape recording. I left the grower's meeting early on May 24," Dad tells me, as if in shock from the news.

My heart sinks to a new level. He really hadn't remembered.

Someone pushes us. My elbows slam into the cop car side window. Dad stumbles, protectively covering me from a bald man screaming that Dad will pay for his crimes. The man is pulled off of us by Officer Haynes. The second officer controls the crowd, pinning Dad and me against the car's white exterior for a moment. I regain my footing. Dad and I have near privacy amidst the blue of two uniformed policemen and the distraction of a raging man.

I stare up at Dad, my throat dry. "They say you bribed Juan. It was that cash you took out of the bank with Carrie and me, wasn't it?"

Dad fingers my hair, made sticky by peach juice. He must see the yellow strands of fruit dripping down my neck. His face sags.

"I meant it as a donation the first time," Dad says so only I hear him. No anger, no menace. "Years ago. He said it was for a charity for pickers, but I got the hint eventually that he was pocketing the money and possibly tampering with votes to keep the union from going on strike, to keep the money flowing. Juan never showed up for his money this year, but the amount I withdrew matched some records he was keeping. I think Carrie was suspicious. She wanted to know who I was meeting. I'm glad she's not here for this." Choked up, he turns away from me.

My body goes cold under a layer of sweat. Dad was bribing Juan to discourage the union from going on strike, and Carrie found out about it. Dad had nothing to do with any murder.

Officer Haynes takes me by the upper arm. The second officer leads Dad into the police car. He covers his face. The car door slams shut and triumphant cheering bursts from the crowd.

"Do you have any friends nearby?" Haynes shouts to me.

Through tears I look up at his boyish face. Officer Haynes isn't a dirty cop after all. He was simply waiting for the right time to reveal Dad's blown alibi and the idea of bribery. The right way to amplify the impact. The arrival of the Laborer's March in Verona with all its passion. Dad doesn't get a trial by jury—his conviction is here, with the media and the spectators and the perception of his guilt.

I spin away from Officer Haynes in fury.

"Salem, wait," the officer yells.

I escape through the orchard past hundreds of people. I run alongside a bus with open doors, inching forward. I check my phone.

Unknown: I'm okay. I will see you at the mock trial.

My strides get wider, and faster. More determined.

Cordero is alive.

Juan *was* corrupt.

I finally realize that means growers aren't the only ones with motive. What if Benicio de la Cruz found out Juan Herrera was a traitor? Benicio would never go to the media or police with that. Dirt like that would ruin the strike. He'd take care of the problem himself, and if a grower got blamed, all the better. Just today I watched Envy doing exactly the same thing.

The growers' secret meetings. The union's secret plans. Which one is covering up Juan's murder? Which one will result in a bomb today? Which one would have targeted the Taco Shop at Mission Plaza during Senator Lethco's speech? The growers to intimidate the union? Or the union to place the blame on the growers and cry *poor me*?

The growers will be at the mock trial.

Envy and Kimi will be at the mock trial too, armed with their insider knowledge of the union's final secret meeting.

I veer toward the bus. I have to be at the mock trial. I have to follow the growers and the union officials. I'll need help, but I can't go to the police. Officer Haynes may be in the clear, but there's no telling if he'd handcuff me to a peach tree to keep me "safe" and away from the rally.

The bus doors are closing. I hop on just in time. Clueless to my identity, the passengers on board applaud my late arrival while the vehicle picks up speed in earnest. I take a flag handed to me by a squat Hispanic man.

It reads, "Sacramento or Bust."

CHAPTER
TWENTY-EIGHT

The window next to me is glared with sunlight as the bus enters the freeway onramp. My clothes have dried, leaving me grimy and smelly. There are sticky peach guts on my neck.

As we travel, I try to collect my thoughts enough to prep for the mock trial. Digging through my backpack, I make sure I've got everything I packed this morning. I take out the class roster that I'll need to give to the guards at the courthouse. The last page is a copy of a Verona High identification card belonging to Cordero Eduardo Vasquez-Ramirez.

Pausing, I stare at Cordero's sullen expression. Of course that's how he looks—the same as the day I met him. When did I stop seeing him that way? When did my mental image shift, focusing only on his eternal alertness, his intelligence, and the hot-button trigger of his emotional reactions—a kaleidoscope of astonishing variety? The photo at my fingertips is as far from his real character as sand from fresh water.

He knows I'm going to watch him every minute today, obsessed with the riddle of his motive. Will he stick with the gang, no matter what? Find justice in a bullet?

It all comes down to one question.

Who is Cordero really?

The dark expression in his picture is so foreboding, I wonder if even he knows the answer.

My phone vibrates.

AddyDay: C left w Marissa. Says his phone's almost dead. We're almost there.

Me: Your stepdad is cleared. Rick says Bill was still at the peach meeting May 24.

AddyDay: I knew it! I knew it!

I text Dad too.

Me: I'm safe and on my way to Sacramento. I love you.

Dad: Love you too. You'll do great. Don't worry about me.

Don't worry. Impossible words.

I go to the bathroom in the back, behind the seats. I'm lucky I got on one of the nicer buses. I wash my hair in the sink with twenty squirts of foaming soap. The vehicle is bouncy and I hit my elbow on the wall. I use paper towels to coax dried river mud off my legs and peach goo from my neck. I put on the outfit I packed this morning, a sleeveless, yellow blouse and black pencil skirt that hits me above the belly button. AddyDay picked it out.

My luckiest pre-packed items of the day are a brush, hair spray, and all the bobby pins I could want. I backcomb my hair. I sweep it into an updo reminiscent of the 1960s and pin a chic, black pillbox hat over the crown of my head. Makeup takes a while. I catch my reflection in the mirror and don't recognize the troubled, elegant young lady staring back.

By the time I get out, we're in downtown Sacramento. I disembark on three-inch, double-strapped high heels, stepping into a sea of American flags and purple union balloons. Row after row of printed banners stretch the width of a seven-lane street, held by a hundred hands each. Everyone else is clapping in rhythm to chants. A block ahead, the courthouse stands white and majestic. The protesters are headed away from it, toward the capitol building a mile away. Three news helicopters circle blue skies. My damp hair pulls at the base of my neck from all the bobby pins.

Overwhelmed by the smell of exhaust fumes and not at all refreshed from my prep time in the bus bathroom, I cut past rally members, heels clicking. My phone rings, and I answer on the go.

". . . Salem?" AddyDay's voice is faint against the background sounds of air horns and cowbells.

"What?" I yell, pressed by my surroundings. The killer might strike again in just two hours.

"Where are you guys? You only have a few minutes," she exclaims.

"Wait, Cordero's not there?"

I arrive at the base of a grand outdoor staircase leading to the courthouse entrance, and stop, breathless.

Cordero Vasquez stands on the top step, wearing a crisp, buttoned shirt. His open collar is flared in the smooth style of an era fifty years past, partially concealing his gold necklace. Rolled sleeves complete his *West Side Story*–styled suit. AddyDay actually knew what she was doing. His ironed clothes make his dark features shockingly attractive and match the people waiting to enter the courthouse better than my more obviously period outfit. There's nothing common, though, about his measured gaze and the strength of his stillness—a controlled laziness, like a tiger that doesn't need to crouch before it's ready to spring. His tattoo is as fierce as ever.

He's looking at me like he was waiting for my arrival.

My pulse trips—whether in memory of Cordero's breath against my lips, or in anticipation of finding Carrie's killer, I don't know.

"AddyDay, hold on a minute," I say.

Running, Cordero and I meet halfway up the steps, surrounded by interested onlookers. The courthouse is situated in the middle of a wide lawn area dotted with grand willow trees, the area under their canopies shaded with the promise of seclusion.

Two hours since I last saw Cordero. Has it crossed his mind—how I turned from him on the riverbanks?

"They won't let me in," he says, more anxious than I've ever seen him. "Because of the roster—that it's missing."

"I've got the roster," I say as we charge up the steps. I'm mad at Mr. White. He managed to get all the other students in, just not Cordero. "My dad—he was going to bribe Juan Herrera."

He stops. "How did you learn this?"

I turn to face him, even though we're making ourselves later than ever. "The police are probably going to arrest Dad—but it wasn't him . . . I could tell finally. It wasn't Slate either. He fought Tito because . . . Slate's little sister Anna wanted to join your gang but Tito wanted her to rob a gas station with a gun and then . . . then she didn't want to join anymore . . . but . . . he hurt her."

Comprehension lights his eyes. He drops his gaze, voice heavy. "I should have guessed."

Neither of us speaks for a moment. No wonder the other Primeros want Tito out.

I force myself to continue. "Dad said Carrie found out about him bribing someone. She was trying to figure out who was taking the money. Don't you see? The growers aren't the only ones with motive. If Carrie found out about the bribery, someone else from the union could have too, and been really mad. Like the union president, Benicio."

Mental calculation shows in Cordero's features. "Someone hired El Payaso to come after me. If Benicio is the killer, how did he know I was searching for the killer?"

I pause, and then snap my fingers. "Envy and Kimi. They were with Slate that day I texted him about you, remember? They knew I was trying to talk to you about Carrie. If Benicio told them to be on the lookout for anyone close to me trying to dig into Carrie's murder, they could have called Benicio right then."

Cordero goes into action mode. He heads down the stairs toward the Laborer's Rally. "Where is Benicio?"

"No, listen." I pull Cordero back by his arm and let go abruptly, confused and thinking of him tipping my head back to kiss me.

"What?" he demands, facing me.

My phone rings, flashing AddyDay's face at me. Oops, I forgot about her. She must have hung up and called back. But there is no time.

"Listen," I tell Cordero, putting the cell to my ear. "AddyDay?"

"Salem?"

"Benicio is blaming violence on the growers," I tell both of them, continuing where I left off. "Maybe even bombs."

"Salem, the judge just announced if anyone's late, he won't let them in," AddyDay interrupts.

"Judge won't let us in if we're late," I relay to Cordero.

Cordero leans to look at an enormous clock inside the rotunda.

"AddyDay? Are Envy and Kimi at the mock trial?" I ask.

"Yup."

"Envy is the only one I know for sure who is invited to the secret union meeting," I continue speaking into the phone with Cordero's full attention as well. "President Benicio has motive, AddyDay. He could have been mad Juan was taking bribes. But the killer could still be a grower. Here's our plan. AddyDay and Cordero, you two follow the growers after the trial. I'll follow Envy—she'll take me right to Benicio. I can . . . I don't know . . . see if he makes a mistake and reveals something. If nothing else, I can stop him from setting off a bomb if that's really what the killer is threatening." I can't let AddyDay go with the growers by herself. She trusts them too much.

"No," Cordero tells me. "Not alone."

"Slate can come with me." Provided I can convince him.

Cordero scowls, but nods. For the first time I wonder if he's jealous of Slate, thinking the two of us have something between us besides the memory of Carrie. I want to tell him we don't.

"I'm in," AddyDay says.

"We only have three minutes to get to mock trial," Cordero tells me.

I glance at him. "AddyDay, stall the trial."

"What? But Salem—"

"Let's go," Cordero says. Determination shows in the corners of his mouth.

We take the remaining stairs at a run.

A Middle Eastern man in a blue uniform looks over the roster and waves us through the metal detector. Our steps echo inside the grand rotunda, three stories tall and lined on the far side with a curved balcony opening to the main body of the building.

We skip the elevator in favor of stairs. The slap of my high-heels reverberates in the stairwell.

At 3:02, we burst through the doors of the courtroom assigned to Verona High's mock trial.

CHAPTER TWENTY-NINE

I'm prepped for a silent audience and a mock trial already in motion. Instead, hardly a soul spins to see us as the doors fall shut.

Most of the spectators inside the full-capacity courtroom are straining to see Mr. White and the mock trial students in front of the empty judge's desk. Slate is there, leaning over what looks like a digital clock with an eighteen-inch display. A California state flag hangs motionless next to the U.S. standard against the dark mahogany paneling of the back wall. The room smells of varnish and lemony-fresh wood cleaners.

I glance at Cordero—the tension of his lips, his jaw.

"Why did you touch the official time clock?" Mr. White's voice carries all the way across the room as he gestures at the digital numbers, which tick forward from a time of three minutes and twenty-five seconds.

Marissa and Katelyn both fold their arms at Mr. White's question. They've got on pleated skirts and Mary Jane shoes.

"AddyDay said to start the time," Marissa insists. "It's her fault."

AddyDay's near hysterics are perfectly believable as she brings her salmon-colored gloves to her mouth. "I thought it'd be okay to use the timer to practice my witness questions again. What if I go over my time limit? That's a five-point automatic deduction!"

In the benches reserved for the prosecution team, Jeremy lounges in a single-breasted gray suit. McCoy has an unknotted bowtie dangling from his collar. Both boys are laughing.

"How many valley girls does it take to screw up a mock trial?" Jeremy asks.

"Ten bucks says Mr. White has no idea there's a timer on his cell phone," McCoy answers.

I let myself grin at AddyDay's quick thinking. Cordero nudges me forward and I hurry down the aisle, the feel of his knuckles against my skin lingering.

At the judge's desk, Slate punches a few buttons on the side of the clock. The numbers on the clock's display blink, replaced by straight zeros.

"That should reset it," Slate smooths his hair, black and full in a John F. Kennedy sweep across his forehead. He notices Cordero and drops his hand to his side.

AddyDay turns to see what Slate is looking at.

"Finally," she breathes in relief.

Mayor Bill Knockwurst chats with half a dozen men I've seen at grower's meetings. One of them waves at his daughter sitting with the defense team. At a table set up for the defense, Kimi silently analyzes the mayhem from under a sweeping Audrey Hepburn–styled hat. Envy sits next to her, soft black braids covered in a plaid handkerchief pinned under her chin.

"Can everyone *please* take their seats?" Mr. White asks.

Cordero sits at the long prosecution table. As his partner, I'm assigned to the chair next to him. AddyDay is on my other side. Behind us is community leader Rick Thornton, carrying his laptop case. Officer Haynes is absent, probably with Dad at the Verona police station while the real killer is here in Sacramento. Possibly in this room.

Cordero leans into me.

"You have your witness questions?" He's right next to me. My hair sways with his breath.

"Yeah, let me get them."

I'm careful not to react to his presence—careful not to move away from him. I've drifted the opposite way instead, making him closer than ever.

Marissa's shrill voice sounds from the back of the room.

"All rise for the Honorable Judge Steele," she says, performing her assigned role as bailiff.

I stand with the other spectators. Slate comes around the table from the judge's desk, the last person to slip into his spot on the bench behind the growers. He throws a tense glance at Cordero and tries to catch my gaze, as if that will relieve his anxiety. I nod to him, visually pleading with him to trust me. If Slate doesn't follow Envy with me, I'll have to face off with Benicio alone.

A tall man sweeps down the aisle, wearing the flowing black robes of a judge. He's escorted by Marissa and a boy from the defense team, each serving as bailiff.

Judge Steele settles into a plush chair under the flags. Marissa and the male student-bailiff sit along the right wall.

"You may be seated," Marissa calls.

The room shuffles.

"I now call this mock trial to order," Judge Steele announces into a microphone on his desk. His eyebrows are white and bushy.

The primal fear I had in the downtown streets of Sacramento—fear of bodily harm, of pain and death—has dipped. I'm surrounded by the likely killers. No matter the specific location they've chosen for their target, they won't set off an explosion anywhere they could personally get hurt. My sense of security feels hollow and unfair. The protesters outside don't have such reassurances.

"Conspiracy, you have been called to a criminal trial," the judge continues, speaking as if a suspect, Conspiracy, were actually present. "You are accused of misdirecting the people of the United States in the matter of the 1963 assassination of John F. Kennedy. How do you plead?"

Kimi stands. "On behalf of Conspiracy, the defense pleads not guilty, your honor."

Judge Steele nods. "Prosecution, are you ready to present your evidence?"

"Yes, your honor." Jeremy walks to a podium, which faces the judge.

The male bailiff touches a button on top of the official time clock and it starts ticking. Each of the teams will have equal amounts of time to prove their case.

"Your honor, on November 22, 1963, Lee Oswald assassinated the President of the United States." Jeremy's voice reverberates from the speaker system.

"Oswald woke up that morning, wrapped one of his two rifles in a long brown paper bag, took a bus to Dallas, and shot John F. Kennedy from the sixth story of a building. All this he did alone. Without the support or money of any person or organization, powerful or otherwise. And why did he do it? Because he wanted to be someone. Someone history would remember."

Jeremy may be a jerk, but he's our best public speaker.

While he speaks, I write a note to Slate.

Cordero shifts beside me. I think he wants my attention. He doesn't. We both look away. Blushing, I press my elbow to my side to keep it farther from the crease of his sleeve and finish my message.

The day she died, Carrie wanted to go to the police with what she knew about Juan's murder. I think I know part of the story. After the trial ends, will you help me?

I finger the note, wondering how to get it to him.

Jeremy finishes the opening statement and goes to his seat. A redhead from the defense takes the podium. Her rebuttal speech is well written, but has nothing on Jeremy's. When she sits, I lean toward AddyDay.

"Good luck," I whisper.

She nods. Her notes crinkle as she heads for the podium.

"The prosecution would like to call Marina Prusakova Oswald to the stand," she says into the microphone.

Katelyn rises from the bench behind me and goes to the witness stand.

"Marina, you met and married Lee Oswald while in your home country of Russia, correct?" AddyDay asks.

"Yes, I did." Katelyn is a perfect Marina—pretty, easily confused, and embarrassed.

"On September 27 of 1963, your husband Oswald took a trip by bus from Houston to Mexico, didn't he?"

I'm proud. AddyDay has only taken twenty seconds to start setting up the timetable leading to the assassination.

Katelyn shrugs. "That's what he said."

AddyDay approaches the bench. "Your honor, I'd like to submit witness affidavits from two of Oswald's fellow bus passengers as Evidence Numbers One and Two. They verify that on September 27, Oswald began a week-long journey to Mexico—"

A burst of noise interrupts her, like distant explosions. I whirl to face the door and then realize the noise is coming from a floor below me. Slate stands in alarm. Cordero doesn't react with any motion at all. Neither do McCoy and Jeremy.

"Pop rockets?" McCoy says, offended. "I try to sneak a Coke past security and they catch me."

"Life isn't fair," Jeremy agrees.

Slate catches my eye, and I rise to give him my note. Mayor Bill Knockwurst notices me and takes the paper.

"Here, let me help," he says, handing the paper to Slate.

I jerk my hand away from the mayor. Then I remember I don't have to hate him. But who *do* I have to hate?

The judge slaps his gavel.

"I'll read it later," Slate says, tucking the note into his pocket with a glance at the judge.

Disappointed, I face the judge, ignoring Cordero's sideways look.

"We will not bring the disruption of the Laborer's March into my courtroom," the judge announces. "Bailiff, go downstairs and get a report from security. Prosecution, continue."

"I've finished, your honor," AddyDay says while Marissa makes her way to the aisle to head downstairs as bailiff.

"Next attorney?" Judge Steele's white eyebrows are high as he stares at me.

I stand. I stutter as I call Silvia Odio for questioning. Kimi takes her place at the witness stand, smiling as if my nerves are a gift-wrapped box of chocolates.

"Will you—will you please tell the court how you met Lee Oswald?" I say, my voice weak.

"I'm Cuban." Kimi tosses silky black hair behind her shoulder. "My father died, killed in a communist jail. In Dallas, I was visited by two Cuban men and an American they called Oswald."

She continues, claiming that Oswald and two other men wanted to assassinate President Kennedy.

"And this meeting took place in your apartment in Dallas?" I ask. "And then you moved. Your lease on the apartment came up September 30. In fact, you told the FBI that the three men came on Friday, September 27, right?"

The room behind me is silent, watching her. Everyone in the courtroom knows she'll have to depart from her original testimony. AddyDay just submitted two witness affidavits putting Oswald on a bus traveling from Houston to Mexico City on September 27. There's no way he could have been in Dallas on the same day.

Kimi nods curtly. "Yes."

"But you—" I call in a ringing voice.

I cut myself off, feeling my face turn red. Why is she agreeing with me? I glance behind me. People whisper. Cordero stares hard at Kimi, intrigued. He leans into AddyDay to tell her something. She nods and slides him a notebook and pencil.

I turn back to Kimi, still not believing her answer. "You met on September 27?"

Her mouth twitches. I can't read the expression. Victory? The judge leans forward.

"That's what I told the FBI, yes," she answers.

From the aisle, AddyDay slips me a sheet of paper with two words on it. *On purpose.*

I turn to look at Cordero's dark eyes. He can read people. Kimi is tricking me. She's *trying* to make her case seem impossible to believe so that she can hide something and reveal it later—something so big and so surprising that when she uses it at the end of the trial, we won't have time to debate it.

I turn back to Kimi and ask two more times if she moved on September 30. The judge glares at me above folded arms.

"Prosecution, you are on thin ground. Ms. Odio's contract ended on September 30." The judge repeats the phrasing Kimi has said over and over. The contract ended. "You will continue with another line of question—"

I interrupt the judge and turn to Kimi. "Wait, are you saying you didn't actually *move* when your contract ended?"

Kimi's smile disappears. I glance back at Cordero, who nods, his expression confident. The judge's white eyebrows practically come off his face in his displeasure.

"Prosecution, do not ever interrupt me." He turns to Kimi. "Answer her question. Did you move when your contract ended?"

She straightens in the witness seat. "I wanted to move on a weekend. The way I remember it is that I moved out on a Saturday, October 5."

Our entire prosecution rests on the fact that conspiracy has to be untrue because Oswald couldn't have met with Silvia Odio. But what if our team's version of the timing really *is* off? What if Silvia Odio didn't change apartments until after Oswald's visit to Mexico ended? Oswald would have had plenty of time to visit her and plot an assassination. A conspiracy could have existed after all.

The idea rocks me. If I'm off on the timing of Oswald's actions, what if I'm wrong on something infinitely more important?

What if I'm wrong about the timing regarding Juan's death?

"Attorney, your time is up," the judge announces. "We will now take a five minute break."

He slams his gavel.

The teams rise. I hurry to Cordero, mentally reviewing everything I know about Juan's murder. I checked everything, questioned everyone. Hurriedly, I get out my phone and pull up the timeline of Carrie's death, which I emailed to myself. I can't be off on the timing. In between the benches, Mayor Knockwurst shakes hands with Officer Haynes.

I do a double take at seeing the officer. If he's here, where's Dad?

I get out my phone, but there are no notifications. Could he be released from questioning? Or is this terrible news and he's been arrested?

"Salem, that was amazing," AddyDay says, taking my arm.

"Great job," Slate tells me on his way to the defense team's table. He'll talk strategy with them now that their first plan failed. I think I could be proud of myself if I weren't so worried about Dad. When is Slate going to read his note?

Mr. White taps Jeremy's shoulder, nodding at the iPad in his hands. "Put that away."

". . . reports are being circulated about a major announcement from the growers, scheduled to take place soon," a newscaster announces from the speaker in Jeremy's hand.

"I'm not putting anything away," Jeremy answers.

"Yeah, there's supposed to be a bomb at the capitol," McCoy says. He and Katelyn are also watching the news clip.

"Look, it's Benicio," Katelyn says in excitement, pointing past McCoy's shoulder to the screen. "And there's Senator Lethco!"

AddyDay, Cordero, and I look at each other and lean to steal a glance at the iPad.

Benicio is shown hugging a white column inside the rotunda of the courthouse. A rope tied around his waist connects him to the blond senator. Behind them, dozens of people, among them many Students for Strike club members, have tied themselves to each other and the pillars. Tito and a few other gang members are even there.

"I call on the justice system to protect the worker!" Senator Lethco announces via the iPad. "Just like California's legislators do!"

"*Sit-in strike!*" supporters chant.

"*This* is Benicio's secret plan?" I ask.

Kimi turns to me, all animosity from the mock trial gone. She's just Carrie's best friend now and proud of the club they built together. "President Benicio's been planning it for a week. Contacted us in memory of Carrie. Her picture's down there on one of the pillars."

Benicio's secret plan had nothing to do with murder or bombs.

Cordero and AddyDay glance at me.

"Only the growers are left," I whisper.

On the iPad, the announcer's voice plays over the union's chants. "Meanwhile, police might be narrowing in on a suspect in the Juan Herrera murder case."

The pillars disappear. Dad is shown coming up the outside steps of the very courthouse I'm in. Reporters shove microphones at his face. Elena flanks him, face worried and emotional—just the way a proper girlfriend should be.

The reporter continues. "In what may prove to be related news, the house explosion that recently killed suspect Brian Jefferson's daughter Carrie has been found to be caused by sabotage. Carrie had worked closely with the union as a supporter."

Blood drains from my face. It seems every individual in the room reacts, gasping, crying out. Even Jeremy leans to hear better, frowning.

I knew Carrie was murdered. It still hurts. It's still crushing. But . . . but now everyone knows. Like a burden I could never shoulder alone is now being shared.

Cordero steps to protect me from the eyes of our mock trial partners, glancing at me in concern.

"Oh, Salem," AddyDay says.

My phone's screen turns off. Wanting to call Dad, I touch it back on. The screen lights with the email timeline leading to Carrie's death. Before I can do anything, someone calls Cordero's name.

We look over.

"Cordero." Rick Thornton urgently motions for him to come to the aisle. He pulls on his laptop case over his head so the strap crosses his chest. "Mr. White wants me to read through your witness questions with you."

I give Cordero a panicked look. His return gaze is intense. The mock trial's importance fades in comparison to what the news is broadcasting. He nods at me, as if willing me to stay calm.

"Cordero," Rick urges.

"I'll be right back," he tells me. He lets Rick steer him between bystanders and out the side exit near the prosecution table. I feel so vulnerable without him.

As soon as they leave, men hoping to talk to the mayor fill their spot.

"Today's the big day, huh?" one says to Bill.

I stare at the men. Conspirators crafting a bomb plot don't joke about their plans and gather in one body close to the scene of the crime.

Slate comes to me, a hand at my elbow. One look at his face, and I know he read my note. "You found something out about Carrie? I—I'll help."

"Break is over!" the judge announces.

I can't answer Slate. I'm overwhelmed. Benicio's secret plans were innocent. The growers probably aren't orchestrating today's threatened explosion. I could be wrong about everything. And if I *am* wrong about who's involved . . .

Slate frowns, waiting for my answer. The judge raises the gavel with a flick of his wrist. It reaches its zenith and descends in a freefall.

. . . if I'm *not* surrounded by the fanatics willing to blow people up, how do I know I'm far enough from the bomb to be safe?

The gavel hits just as a deep rumble sounds. It's low but immense, swallowing the noise of the gavel.

The floor jumps. It just rises for no reason. One inch, two. A deafening roar sounds from above us. It gives way to a yawning rush of air.

The room's collective gasp becomes a squall of terror.

"The exits!"

"Run!"

Slate and I shoot for the back exit, my hands on AddyDay's shoulders in front of me. We're blocked by McCoy, blocked by growers. Marissa crawls over the table, shrieking.

"Go, go!" I shout. The lights flicker.

The bomb was never meant for the capitol building. It's here. It's inside the courthouse.

Water sprays from overhead sprinklers. My view of the judge's desk refracts, swimming into a set of wavy images. I'm hit suddenly with the whispered memory of happiness. The day I'm reminded of—it was so long ago.

It was before Carrie died.

CHAPTER THIRTY

A spray of sprinklers arced into a rainbow against the sunlight. I was on my way home from the May track meet. I had just got my period and was embarrassed. Dad was on the lawn, getting doused by sprinklers. Trying to avoid them, he tripped and his ice cream cone smashed into his face.

"Guess that's what I get for walking on the grass." He wiped soft serve from his mouth. "Ugh. It's like getting kissed by a snowman."

His phone rang. He wiped his hand on the outside of his pants and looked at the screen.

"It's Carrie," he said.

I found myself smiling, just a little. I got out my phone.

"Carrie always says I should kiss someone," I said. "Maybe a snowman would do. Say cheese."

The thought of Carrie pushing me to kiss a boy made me happy. Carrie wanted me to go after life, not wish it would leave me alone. She thought I was ready for all kinds of experiences.

Just like that, the spring breeze felt warmer and fresher.

Dad's phone rang just as I raised my own phone. "Say cheese."

Despite his protests, I took a picture of Dad as he started talking to Carrie. Laughing, I texted it to her and then emailed it to her and sent it over Snapchat, just to be annoying.

"Three, nine, five, four," Dad said into the phone, rattling off the code for the barn padlock. "Carrie, are you still there? Carrie?" He paused to listen. "No, I went home early from the peach meeting, but then Salem needed me to pick her up from practice. Put the shovel back in the barn when you're done."

PRESENT DAY

The memory of Dad's words sends me crashing back into real time: *I went home early from the peach meeting.*

Overhead sprinklers pour onto the courtroom, which smells of smoke. All around me, people shield their eyes from the spray as they scream and scramble toward the back exit. The happiness of my memory is gone. Carrie is gone. Carrie, who couldn't talk to me on the phone because she was busy discussing union issues. Carrie, who was getting a shovel from the barn, almost certainly to bury a body.

The night I got my period, the night of the peach meeting—

But that's impossible.

Slate and AddyDay surge toward the exit. I stumble ahead with them, fumbling with my phone, blocking it from the sprinklers. I got my period on May 23. The peach meeting was May 24. Those two events can't have happened on the same day. My email app is already open. I search for the picture I sent Carrie—the one of Dad with the ice cream spilled on his dress shirt.

7:54 p.m., May 24.

I cover my mouth.

The recording of Carrie opening a birthday present from Slate must have been time-stamped incorrectly. It wasn't May 22, it was May 23. Which means the next day when Dad picked me up from the track meet wasn't May 23 but May 24.

"*I'm* Dad's alibi," I say.

"What?" AddyDay shouts over the alarms and spraying water.

Smoke burns my eyes and pricks my nostrils with fear. All my dates are off. Carrie didn't discuss union issues with Rick Thornton the day before Juan died, but the *day* Juan died. It means Rick was the other person who left the peach meeting early—the only other person besides Dad who wasn't counted in the second tally. Carrie had discovered Dad that had set up a meeting with the man taking his bribes and knew when it would be—the night Dad was hurrying home for an appointment after picking me up from track practice. Carrie must have called Rick to have someone with her when she found out who the bribe-taker was.

Katelyn cuts between me and a prosecution desk chair, knocking me into AddyDay. She ends up on the floor. My phone tumbles to the carpet, brushing her fingers. She grabs it.

"AddyDay." I pull her by the arm, trembling.

Rick, with his temper, already angry from the argument at the peach meeting. Rick, who led Juan Herrera to "salvation" through the union, only to see him betray the union. Rick, who heard Dad ask if Cordero was the one in his house on the night the mirror fell.

Rick, who sent El Payaso and Tito after Cordero and now—supposedly to practice mock trial questions—has Cordero. Alone.

AddyDay tugs the sash of her silk belt, resisting my efforts to right her.

"I'm stuck!" Her sash is pinned between the chair and the table. She kicks the chair trying to free herself.

"Salem?" Slate yells with a hand on my back.

"You'll help AddyDay?" I yell.

He nods and I change directions, racing toward the side exit Cordero and Rick took. I ricochet from one obstruction to the next.

Rick has Cordero.

Bursting through the courtroom's side exit, I find myself in a hallway with no overhead sprinklers and crammed with

309

dozens of escaping students going right. No one goes left. Which way? Which way did Rick take him?

"Move!" Jeremy slams into me. My ankle gives. The double straps of my shoes cut into my skin.

A furious shout ricochets from around the corner of the hallway to the left.

". . . wasn't trying to kill anyone. The bomb—it went off early!"

I recognize the speaker.

Rick Thornton.

I disrupt the flow, taking an elbow in the ribs. A shout warns that there's no exit the way I'm going. I ignore it, driving my legs forward against the vice of my pencil skirt. My ears strain for any hint of Cordero's voice. Separating from the crowd, I follow a sharp left in the hallway into a wave of heat.

I see Rick, with his back to me forty feet away. His laptop case bobs awkwardly at his side. He's shadowed by a slight haze of smoke. Cordero is on the ground in front of him, kneeling. Rick waves something around—a six-inch knife with a spear point.

"But no!" Rick is screaming. The ceiling above him sags, black and fissured with a treacherous glow. He doesn't seem to notice. "Some girl was trying to get ahold of Benicio saying she had information about Juan—it was *Carrie*. She forced me to kill her for nothing. We were better off without Juan."

Juan. Carrie.

I race forward.

Rick drives the knife forward with a grunt. I expect the blade to dig into Cordero's scalp, but instead Rick carves into an object he's holding in his other hand. Cordero covers his head and leans away from me, as if cringing. I realize the object in Rick's hand is the plaque inscribed with *World's Best Union Club Advisor* that he's been keeping in his laptop case. He marks something on it, finishing with a diagonal up and then down motion that I recognize even though I can't see the face of the plaque. It's an upside down *V*. He's probably carved the *XII* too.

Rick tucks the plaque under his arm when he finishes. "My signature, since Carrie forced it on me. For when a job needs doing."

He aims his knife at Cordero and lunges forward.

Cordero shifts his weight as if to avoid Rick, but then springs backward, slamming into the man's knees. Rick cries in pain. He falls on his side. Cordero snatches the knife from him so quickly there's no struggle. He gets on his feet and turns toward me to lean over Rick.

Cordero points the knife at Rick's chest. "You will never give another order to the gang."

Rick holds absolutely still on his back, palms open at his side. "Please."

"No!" I yell, still ten feet out. The sound of my voice is drowned out by a crack from above us and the screaming of mock trial spectators down the hall.

Cordero registers nothing at my shout. He doesn't see me. Hand clutching the grip of the knife two feet above Rick's face, Cordero's eyes flash the way they do when he's about to act.

The knife shakes.

Cordero's expression steels. This is justice for Carrie's death—a chance to make himself. A real killer. What other choice does he have? It's the path he's been on since he joined the gang.

Only he does have a choice.

Cordero takes a step back, sweat at his temples, the knife still aimed.

I've come to a stop behind Rick. Maybe I say something, maybe I'm just gasping for air. Whatever it is, Cordero's gaze darts to me. Astonishment touches his features. The lights flicker.

Rick scrambles to his knees, turning toward me. He knows someone is behind him, even if he can't see me. From under his shirt he produces a second knife—a switchblade. He hits the release and it springs open.

Cordero's emotion shifts to terror.

"Move!" Cordero yells at me, dashing forward to protect me from Rick.

The hall goes black as the electricity goes out just as Rick spins, lunging at me.

"Cordero!" I can't see Cordero with the lights out. I can only hear Rick's scream of rage, like a wounded bull. I jump back. His shoulder rams into my gut. I fall to the carpet, the wind knocked out of me. I gasp for air. My cheek burns with pain, sliced by the switchblade.

"The union needs people like me!" Rick shouts into the darkness. I see the gleam of the switchblade as he pats the ground like he's searching for something. His voice is so full of shock, I wonder if he knows he cut me—if his brain has processed who I am at all. I can't think what he would be searching for.

I gulp air laced with smoke. The cut on my cheek feels blissfully shallow against my fingertips.

The ceiling groans. Rick finds what he's looking for. He grabs it. His footsteps drum away in the direction from which I came, leaving Cordero and I to fend for ourselves in the burning building.

"Where are you?" Cordero's fingers catch my hair.

Still recovering from Rick's hit, I can only grunt in answer. A wave of smoke drifts over us. I cough. I can't see. I can only touch Cordero's hands as he slides them to my shoulders, each of us going by feel. The cool metal of the long knife skims my skin. He drops it to help me up. It hits the carpet with a soft thud. Cordero didn't kill Rick. He decided.

He's shaking as much as I am, tugging me toward a thin blush of light in the distance. I resist him.

"No exit!" I choke on my words, coming to my feet too slow, too heavy.

A crack sounds, a terrible noise—louder and louder. I look up to dots and dashes of glowing red on the ceiling ten feet ahead, down the hall that is our escape. They're low. They're much lower than the ceiling should be. And the ripping, the cracking. It's immense. Cordero switches the direction of his urging.

A wave of heat slams us to the carpet as a mammoth structure crashes through the ceiling.

Red flame and chunks of construction material fall with a desk into the hallway, landing sideways on the carpet with a thunderclap of noise. It takes the air next to me and collapses forward into the wall ahead of it.

Shielding my face from heat, I scramble up. I can barely feel Cordero's hand. Flames pop and crackle behind us as we run, flying, away from the destruction. I'm driven mad by pockets of decent air that disappear when I try to swallow them.

A curve in the hall ends at a nook. There's a swirl-patterned rug and two straight-backed chairs on either side of a floor-to-ceiling window with no opening mechanism. Cordero hefts a chair and slams it into the glass. The glass is doubled-paned and thick with the importance of courthouse security, despite being on the second floor. Once, twice, he hits it. Filtered sunshine from outside mocks us.

The smoke, the heat. We'll burn. Like Carrie did. Just like Carrie. Even her picture is burning right now, roped to a pillar downstairs.

The window breaks on his third try.

My shoulder presses his as we cough, leaning into bits of cool, clear updraft. Oxygen hits my brain like a drug. I breathe and breathe, not getting enough, not able to believe the relief of it, the clarity that comes from it. Billows of smoke fight us for position, hissing outside around chinks of broken glass.

"We jump!" Cordero stands and grabs the chair again, knocking glass free with violent shattering. Gray smoke is everywhere. I catch a glimpse of a willow tree outside. Thin limbs dangle to the ground far below.

"Here!" I snatch the rug from off the ground and give it to him.

He holds the fabric over jagged glass at the base of the window. I swing my feet outside as he guides me past sharp edges.

"Go!"

At his command, I jump. I grab for a limb and miss.

CHAPTER THIRTY-ONE

I hit the grass with my knees, hands, and forehead in a staccato shock of pain. My skirt rips to mid-thigh. Cordero lands beside me, grunting and pulling me to a stand. We sprint away from heat and smoke, running underneath the willow trees, ever shaded by foliage that brushes the grass. The heel of my strapped shoe embeds in the earth. I trip and don't get up. Dirt and white fertilizer pellets dot my palms and injured cheek. Dropping to the ground, he crawls to me, gasping in exhaustion.

The warmth of his fingers runs up my arm, slips against the silk of my blouse, and touches my lips. The wound on my cheek is bleeding still, but just barely. Hundreds of people are gathered around the courthouse's landscape with their sobbing and their rebounding hugs, controlled by a biological search for comfort. I can't see anything above their calves a stone's throw away. Cordero and I are lying inside a nearly ground-length canopy of tree branches—a beautiful oasis backlit with sunshine, leaving us cut off from the world outside.

"I knew you wouldn't kill Rick," I say. "I knew it."

My hair tangles with blades of grass. The third button of my blouse is open. I can't move to fix it unless I slide my arm under Cordero's, which I don't. His hand has come to a rest against my side. Fire truck alarms wail a short distance away.

"Rick pulled a knife on me. He thought I knew it was him already, because I'd been in his house, searching." Cordero's breathing is heavy, his eyes black and wide. He's still in shock as if reeling from his decision to leave Rick alive.

I'm still gasping for air. "I remembered. I figured it out. Dad was with me. And I think Carrie found out the exact time Dad was planning to hand over his bribe . . . Dad was running late since he ended up giving me a ride. She wanted to confront the guy taking bribes. But not alone. So she called Rick since he worked for the union. He's a true union-believer. He must have been furious with Juan."

Cordero wipes his face, smearing a trail of black across his cheek, his eyes unfocused. "We were in the killer's house. The whole time we cleaned up. Carrie—I wonder if she was in so much shock, she thought I knew he was the killer. Of all the people who would want her to clean up after burying Juan, of course it'd be the killer. Of course she'd be willing to go to his house."

I thread my fingers with his. "When she was ready to turn Rick in to the police, she didn't want give the union bad publicity. She must have contacted Benicio for advice. Rick heard about the meeting. He said so in the hall."

My fists clench. Rick probably rushed to her house. Carrie managed to call police once he arrived, but he forced her to tag her car. Eventually he broke the gas line. He probably watched the news reports of the explosion and thought of how much the media loved it. When the peach strike went into effect and the growers still wouldn't cave on a wage hike for the pickers, he set up one bomb and then another, both in front of cameras, both targeting marks that would put growers in suspicion.

Hesitantly, I bring up my finger and touch the black of Cordero's *V* tattoo, smooth and close—so close I can see the pores of his skin.

"You didn't kill Rick. You're leaving the gang."

His face clouds. He leaves my side and stands.

I rise to follow him. Bruising pounds every inch of my body. I make him face me.

He looks at me through dark lashes with the hard reality of a truth I don't want to understand.

"You have to leave them," I cry. "El Payaso said he'd kill you."

"You're like Carrie, always against the gang. But you don't know the drive-bys, the violence. When we bind together, we're strong. I'll convince Tito and El Payaso to go against Rick now that I know who he is. He's not so tough."

"*What?* Rick's going to jail."

Cordero shakes his head. "We have no evidence."

I step back from him, horrified. "We have your testimony and mine. And Juan's car keys, which prove you were there the night he died—you're not just making the whole thing up."

Following me, Cordero grips my upper arm. I feel a tremble in his fingers. "You can never tell anyone I was there. Or it will be prison for me, for Juan's murder. They'll think I set the explosion in the courthouse too. The knife inside has my fingerprints." He nods toward the window we escaped from.

"We have to. We have to go to the police."

"No police."

"A lenient judge," I argue. "You'll give him Juan's car keys and tell your whole story. He'll know you had no choice—"

"I will never let the police find the keys." Cordero's scowl utterly rejects my proposal. He's incapable of hoping for support from an authority figure.

"What do we do then? Wait for Rick to kill us? How can you possibly think it's wrong to leave a gang?"

"I *need* the gang," he insists. "*We* need it. With the gang, we'll force Rick not to hurt me. Not to hurt you." He doesn't trust his own plan. He hasn't had time to think it through. Tito and El Payaso won't help an outsider like me.

I position my face in front of his. "I'm going to the police with or without those keys you have. If you won't testify with me, maybe Rick will get away with murder. Maybe he'll figure out a way to kill me too. But I'll tell you one thing—you and I will be enemies. Forever."

The truth of my words hits us both.

Cordero's fingers tense at my arm. Neither of us moves.

His face is heartbreaking, pleading, sorrowful, frightened. His black eyes are close and fierce. "I want Rick to be caught. I do. But I can't go to the police with those keys."

The noise of thousands of people outside the canopy seems close suddenly. Chants, sobs, police sirens.

Cordero and I hesitate. Both of us need to control the other. Just like when we first met. Only it's nothing like before. It's agony.

"You're wrong that the gang is bad," he says.

"I'm right. I never trust anything I feel, and I still know I'm right."

I never trust anything I feel.

It's just what Carrie tried to tell me all those years ago, when she said someday I'd find out who I was. She said I'd become strong. I spent years doubting what I felt unless Carrie approved of it, but somehow she knew I'd learn to trust myself. All the things she tried to teach me, all the things she told me to do. I talk. I get out there more. And as for kissing a guy—

Without permission, my gaze rises to Cordero as he stares through the branches of the trees, his lips pressed together in grim contemplation. A life on 147 Benjamin Road. Forever.

I know why I was afraid to trust him at first—because I didn't trust *myself.* I didn't trust I could evaluate his morality when every glance, every tweak of his expression, made me emotional. Made me defenseless and filled me with longing.

His fingers are barely touching the skin of my arm.

I realize just how far our lifestyles are from each other. Just how different we really are.

He looks down at me and I'm shocked at my own impulse, like Carrie's right here, egging me on. *You're going to grab a guy and plant one on him?*

He frowns at my change in emotions, unable to probe them.

Leaves on the edge of the canopy sway against my shoulder blades as I stare at the dark line of his lips, pausing because I know it's now or never.

Carrie wanted me to be confident. She wanted me to go after what I wanted.

Heart pounding, I step to him and close my eyes, going by feel. My lips hit him on the crease between his chin and mouth.

I drop down from the balls of my feet and turn toward curtains of tree limbs, my face blazing.

His fingers close around my arm, spinning me to him.

He's so close and I'm shaking against the anchor of his hands on both sides of my jaw, his grip warm and light, his mouth the same. I clutch his wrist, and his lips pull away just as they meet mine, hovering. His whole body is tense because he doesn't want to hesitate and my shallow breaths are on him and then we're together, pressed tight, lips touching.

I have no thought in my head. I have nothing but the feel of his hands on my skin, and the fire of his pulse under my fingertips, and disorienting pleasure so I don't know how I'm standing. I have Cordero's image from inside the courthouse. He's looked down the blade of a knife from the side I never thought to contemplate. He made his decision. Just like I'm making mine. I'm what Carrie wanted me to be. I'm choosing what I want.

Only . . .

I drop from my toes.

I can't choose what he is or be with him, watching the compromises he'll have to make, the ones he's already made. I can't choose that.

He leans to follow my mouth with his. His thoughts are gone.

"Good-bye," I say.

Breaking from his embrace is shocking. It's jumping into ice water. It's the scratch of twigs on my face as I sprint through branches of the willow tree. I need to find Dad and tell him everything before the police don't just question him, but arrest him. Before Rick finds me.

Before Cordero stops me.

CHAPTER
THIRTY-TWO

A breeze stirs, laced with smoke and the first hint of autumn.

I dash through trees away from Cordero on bare feet, my high heels in tow. I think of the people I know who were near the blast. AddyDay. Slate. Dad. I wonder for the first time who is hurt. Who is dead. How many more will die if I don't hand Rick over to the police before his rage strikes again? I tell myself the police will force Cordero to turn over the keys, no matter how he protests. I'm only a little ashamed of my plan. He'll become a witness against Rick. If his gang turns on him for working with the authorities, then he'll have to leave them. It's the choice he should be making.

I push my legs to go faster.

Breaking from the final canopy into sunlight, I land smack in the middle of a stream of adults and teens spilling from a courthouse side exit. President Benicio is there. A girl with a nose ring crawls on the grass, her face streaked with soot and tears. A boy stumbles next to me.

I'm disoriented by the chaos. Nearby, a solid mass of rally-goers fills the wide lawn, held back from the courthouse by police tape. Helicopters buzz overhead. The loudest noise is coming from two audio speakers competing for attention next to the exit.

"That's why I am postponing the press conference to announce my bid for the U.S. senate seat," one of the amplifiers booms in a familiar male voice. It's Mayor Bill Knockwurst. "I am grateful my family and supporters are accounted for, but right now, all focus needs to be on saving those who are still missing."

I pause. Bill Knockwurst's secret counterattack—he's running for senator. AddyDay was right that he wasn't doing anything wrong. Not only that, Bill said she's safe.

". . . just getting word now that Senator Lethco is injured," the other speaker declares in the practiced voice of a newscaster. "She and Union President Benicio participated in a sit-in strike with a dozen teens from Verona High's Students for Strike Club, tying themselves to pillars inside the courthouse. They nearly knotted themselves to their deaths. Police say all have escaped, lucky to be alive."

The girl with the nose ring leans forward in a coughing fit. She's one of the students who were trapped and nearly killed.

I react without thinking. I touch her arm and ask if she's okay. She rises, using my arms as support. Green nylon rope bracelets her wrists.

"We got out," she sobs.

Traces of heat and smoke come in waves from the direction of the courthouse. A fireman emerges from the trees Cordero and I had been under, escorting a guy who is doubled over. It's Tito. I guess he escaped with the other protesters. He staggers, disoriented and crying. My insides swirl with sympathy—but he hurt Anna. How can there be forgiveness for that?

Two paramedics with a stretcher appear next to me.

"Sit down," one yells at the girl with me. He directs her onto a stretcher. "Head forward."

The man puts an oxygen mask over her. He runs the stretcher away and another man turns to me.

"You can walk?" he asks. "Are you bleeding anywhere besides your face?"

"I have to report a crime."

"You're in shock." The paramedic forces me to sit on a second stretcher, attaching the same sort of face mask to me that he put on the girl. The oxygen smells bitter and comes out with a steady whistle.

I tear off the mask, but the paramedic is already wheeling me away from the courthouse and toward the crowd. There are cops all over the place and a sea of rescue vehicles. Someone calls to me from behind the police tape.

"Salem! Over here! Salem!"

"Dad!" I answer, jumping from the gurney.

"You're not released yet!" the paramedic shouts after me.

No one stops me from darting under the tape and running to Dad. I pass Mr. White. He waves at me and marks something down on a clipboard in relief, like he's keeping track of which mock trial students are still missing.

"Salem! Oh, your face. Oh, Salem." Dad hugs me, shaking. Elena and AddyDay are there, smiling and crying.

"Dad, listen, Dad—"

"We know. We know." Dad brings his hand from my waist. He's carrying a phone—my phone. My phone that AddyDay grabbed when she was pinned on the floor. My email is still pictured on the screen. "You found an alibi for me."

"It's just amazing," Elena says, choked up.

"What?" I cry.

"I already showed it to police," Dad says and then hesitates. He looks like his heart is broken. "Salem, honey, listen. I . . . they found out about Carrie. The pipes were smashed—"

"I heard. It's okay. I'm okay."

He looks to make sure I really am and then hugs me. "We'll get through this."

I hug him back fiercely. He needs me more than I need him for this. I already knew Carrie was killed. He's getting hit with it for the first time.

"Guys, guys!" AddyDay starts jumping up and down. "Mr. White just announced everyone from the mock trial is safe."

Students cheer and hug. AddyDay's two friends, Marissa and Katelyn, are nearby, telling me how glad they are that I'm all right. I should be yelling about Rick's guilt, but instead I search the crowd. Mr. White said everyone was here. That means Cordero's been spotted. He came out from under the willow tree. I scan the area around me. I don't see him.

Slate and Officer Haynes walk to us.

Officer Haynes addresses Dad, all trace of his former animosity gone. "I've got the email address I want you to forward your alibi picture to. We'll have a press conference when you're released as a formal suspect in Juan's murder. We will start investigating Carrie's case immediately." He nods at me in respect.

I lower my head as Dad squeezes my hand. The officer keeps talking to Dad. When Slate motions to me, I move away from them.

"Salem." His smile is more bittersweet than happy. "You were right. You never gave up. Carrie would be proud."

My chest feels tight, despite the ease of settling next to him. Elena and AddyDay hug each other, giving Slate and me some privacy.

"All of this has got me thinking," he says quietly. "I'm going to talk to my sister again about bringing charges against Tito."

"I hope . . . things get better for her."

"Friends?" Slate's eyes are free from the intensity he reserved for Carrie and her memory, but they're blue and clear and kind all the same. Quiet with the pleasure of hope.

"Friends," I answer. Part of the ache from today's events lightens inside me.

AddyDay interrupts us. "And Salem, guess what? My stepdad is running for senator—that was his secret. He's talking to reporters and everything. He's the one who said I should give your phone to your dad. I figured out right away that the photo on it was his alibi. I mean, there your dad was on Verona High campus with ice cream all over his face and the timestamp was 7:50 p.m. May 24."

"You should have seen it," our teammate Philip brags. There's a small crowd of mock trial members gathered around to listen. "Jeremy tried to stop AddyDay. He said he didn't want her helping a murderer. So she got in his face and told him your dad wasn't a murderer and she could prove it."

"In front of news cameras," Marissa says.

"In front of the whole class," Katelyn adds.

"You stood up to *Jeremy*?" I ask in shock.

AddyDay frowns, confused. "Don't you think it's about time?"

"AddyDay!" I cry. Everyone else laughs, even Dad and Elena, while AddyDay basks in the praise.

All around me, people are smiling and grateful to be safe. Dad is sad about Carrie. But I'm the only one plotting and thinking, knowing a killer is possibly still on the loose. Where *is* Rick?

"See? Jeremy's super mad," Philip says, gesturing.

I turn. Behind me, news crews have gathered near the police tape. Jeremy sulks nearby. McCoy waves to the cameras, blocking my view of whatever is being filmed.

Philip continues. "McCoy's trying to get on TV with the guy who rescued all those students roped to the pillars."

McCoy moves, revealing Rick Thornton surrounded by microphones.

My gut hits the grass under my bare feet.

I stumble backward, expecting the murderer to come after me. But Rick isn't looking at me. He's looking at two Hispanic boys at his side.

Tito and Cordero.

Cordero stands in front of Rick, his palm extended for a handshake. The suit pants and button shirt Cordero wears are overshadowed by Cordero himself. Cordero, with his loops of gold necklaces, his *V* tattoo and the line of black facial hair at his jaw. Cordero is a banger, plain and simple. He's offering to shake hands with the day's hero while the nation watches.

The mock trial members stop talking as they watch how Rick is unable to accept the offered hand. His eyes are glazed in shock and dread and fury, blond hair tumbling in the slight breeze. His switchblade is out of sight—perhaps tucked away on his person. It's the weapon he scratched into my cheek, still bitten with pain. It's the tool he probably used to save participants of the sit-in strike as they screamed for help. Because I believe it—that he was the one who rescued them. I believe it completely. When he's in a rage, he kills. When he's inspired by sympathy, he's a hero. He's as fickle as the knife he wields. Under different circumstances, he could just as easily have taken a bullet for Carrie as murder her.

Fury hits me fast. Hard.

I run toward the cameras. The world is going to know who took Carrie from me.

Dad and the students call after me. I focus on my goal. Eyes on Cordero, Rick's face is twisted with hatred. He still hasn't taken the teen's hand. Rick knows Cordero could call him out on two murders.

Just a few yards away from Cordero and Rick, I collide with an officer, who steadies me with one hand.

"Watch it." The officer's other hand holds the arm of a man sitting on a gurney. The man is Benicio de la Cruz, president of the union. A second officer holds his other arm.

Benicio has an oxygen mask around his neck. He speaks in a slow, heavy voice while the second officer takes notes. ". . . had a courthouse security guard help us. We were only supposed to pass bags of rope around security. If one of the bags had explosives in it, I . . . I'm . . . I'm so sorry." Fat tears roll down his cheeks. "I didn't know. I promise."

Meanwhile, under the eye of the news cameras, Rick lifts his hand to shake Cordero's. He pauses before coming into contact with the gang member. I push toward him through the crowd, passing cameras and bystanders. Cordero notices me. His expression becomes alarmed. He shakes his head. Rick's face is still enraged, still focused on Cordero.

The crowd seems to hold its breath.

Rick finally masters his anger. "These two boys were up on the second floor with me, both of them." He grabs Cordero's palm in a hearty shake and reaches for Tito's shoulder. "The three of us barely got out." He pulls each into a hug, voice emotional. People cheer. Cameras are rolling.

Cordero's gaze locks on mine. Our lips are mutually parted, our eyes wide, mirroring each other's shock. I finally get through the crowd to the inner circle where Cordero and Rick are. Rick's face is hidden behind Cordero's shoulder.

Rick thinks *Tito* was the person in the hallway with Cordero. That's what he just said. He said that two boys were on the second floor with him—two *boys*. Rick doesn't know at all who he attacked after Cordero got the knife from him. He doesn't know it was me. I'm standing practically right next to him, and he's not even bothering to notice me.

It means Rick has no reason to come after me. Keep my mouth shut, and he'll never know I saw him try to kill Cordero.

It means I'm safe. It means Carrie's killer could get away with murder and I could live out my days without the killer ever knowing I know.

Dad, Elena, and AddyDay have nearly caught up, calling to me from behind Benicio and the two police officers.

"Salem, what are you doing?" Dad calls, worried.

No way can I keep my mouth shut. It doesn't matter if I'm safe. Rick could kill someone else.

Carrie needs justice.

"Rick Thornton!" I knock into two microphones, pushing to stand right in front of him.

"Salem." Cordero grabs my arm. His iron gaze orders me to quit talking.

"Salem?" Rick's brows rise in surprise.

I can't believe he doesn't know I saw him try to kill Cordero. I can't believe I would have fallen for his good-guy routine if I hadn't.

Reporters stick microphones under my nose. This is it. I'll accuse Rick right now. It doesn't matter that I have no evidence and that the only witness who can back up my story is a gang member who will refuse to say a word. So what if I look crazy?

But for once it's not my emotions screaming that I can't look crazy, it's my brain. I can't look crazy or no one will believe me. Rick will go home and play the hero. And I can forget proving Rick's guilt in my spare time. I won't have spare time once he gets rid of me.

I notice a strap resting diagonally across Rick's chest. It's black. It belongs to his laptop case.

I'm hit with a series of realizations that come so fast, I see only a string of images. Rick, carving his murder-signature on the plaque Carrie gave him. Rick, dropping the plaque when Cordero tackled him. Rick in a haze of smoke, searching the ground for something while Cordero and I tried to escape from him.

I launch myself forward and hug Rick. I wrap my arms around him and dig both hands into the laptop case behind his back. The crowd cheers.

"There, there." Rick pats my back. "You okay? These kids."

I feel smooth wood at my fingertips. I start shaking. It's here. The plaque with the murder signature is here. Rick must have grabbed the plaque after Cordero got away from him.

Rick chuckles, sounding uncomfortable. "All right now. Let's get you to your dad." He tries to pull away from me, craning his neck to see what I'm doing behind him.

I try to lift the plaque and cut my index finger, crying out. His switchblade is in there too, still open. The plaque slips farther down into the bag.

At my cry, Cordero moves to meet my gaze above the killer's shoulder.

I angle myself to reach farther into the case with my right hand. Blood makes my fingers slick as I push aside a mini laptop to get to the plaque. "Help. Please," I plead with Cordero.

Cordero is motionless, yet intense, looking at me with black eyes made fierce with understanding. "The symbol."

In a flash of decision, Cordero supports Rick's laptop case from underneath while his opposite hand joins mine in searching, never more warm and welcome.

Rick pushes me away in confusion. "What are you doing?" He turns, yanking my arm, which is still in his laptop case. Cordero is jostled as well.

Rick's face is now angled to see Cordero, rather than me. There's a pause. Then the man's motions become strong and forceful, shoving us away from him.

"Hey, stop." His cries are loud, like we're a pair of poisonous snakes. "Stop it! Get them away from me!"

A reporter grabs my arm. One of the policemen near Benicio's gurney comes toward me, shouting for me to settle down. Rick gets away from me and Cordero, taking his laptop case with him. I come out empty-handed. Cordero has seized the switchblade.

"Rick has a knife!" Cordero shouts, holding it above his head.

Someone screams. My view of Dad and AddyDay is blocked by Officer Haynes, cutting in front of them at a run. He looks right at me, alert and questioning. He shouts for officers to follow him.

In front of me, Rick swings his laptop case around to be at his stomach. His face is cherry-red. He speaks to first one camera and then another. "Of course I have a knife. I saved the people at the sit-in strike. I cut them free. That knife did good."

A man from the crowd touches Rick's shoulder, thanking him. I'm jostled by a reporter trying to get the scene on camera. In the background, Benicio is shouting. He struggles to stand from his gurney, his tan face fierce with emotion. I can barely make out his words. ". . . it's him. *Rick*. He's got a knife. He got a knife through courthouse security. He could have gotten explosives through security too. It's my fault."

I step in front of Rick, who's still facing the man thanking him. I make my voice loud and distinct. "You used a knife to cut a symbol into Juan Herrera's shoe after you killed him."

At my accusation, the sounds of shuffling and protests break out. Hundreds of people push to see and hear better. Microphones appear.

Mouth ajar, Rick shakes his head vigorously. "You're insane." He hugs the laptop case to himself, staring at me like a deer caught in the headlights.

"You killed Carrie too." My loud voice gets thick with emotion. A dozen microphones are aimed to catch my words, some within two inches of my mouth, some several yards away. "You tried to kill Cordero and me, and you have a plaque in your bag right there with a symbol cut into it—a Roman numeral twelve crossed by an upside down *V*, the symbol found on Juan's shoe." I nod at his laptop case.

Rick turns tail and runs.

Shrieking, people dart to get out of his path. With determined faces, a camerawoman and a male reporter directly behind Rick come after him, blocking his way through the tight circle of reporters. Rick elbows the woman and leaps to pass between her and an ambulance worker. A camera falls off a tripod onto the grass with a thud. Officer Haynes dashes from around the ambulance worker and tackles Rick. The laptop case is tipped upside down. The plaque slides out, landing face down on the grass.

I dart past the camerawoman and grab the plaque, bringing it directly in front of a camera resting on top of a man's shoulder.

"Look? See?" I trace the thin grooves of the knife with my uninjured index finger. I lean into the nearest microphone. "A Roman numeral twelve, to make it look like Juan was killed by Primeros. And an upside down *V* to warn of old power—the power of the people."

Cordero comes to my elbow, tall and calm. He announces to all the people watching. "Rick Thornton cut that symbol. I watched him."

Shaking with every emotion possible, I move to make room for officers racing past us, rushing in from all directions. They surround Officer Haynes as he cuffs Rick, who is lying on the grass with a tuft of rope stuck in his hair.

"I didn't kill anyone," he shouts, no longer physically struggling. "I . . . I am for the union! United we stand!"

Camera operators film the officers reading Rick his rights. Reporters shout questions to Cordero and me. We've moved closer together. His arm comes around me.

"Will you testify?" one yells to me.

"If police help protect Cordero." I look at him.

He turns to face me, sliding his other hand behind my back. I let my eyes take in his *V* tattoo and closely cropped hair. The crowd around us disappears. We're in a moment as intimate as anything under the willow tree.

My breath hitches with hope that borders on desperation. "You'll leave."

He nods slowly, his eyes one-part fearful and one-part hopeful. "I'll leave."

I smile with my whole body, pressing close to him. His gaze sweeps my mouth. We're on the edge of a pool, about to fall in. He pulls my waist to his and kisses me.

"Where are you? Salem?" Dad voice sounds frantic, approaching from within the crowd.

I lower my face from Cordero's.

Dad comes to my side next to Cordero, who still holds me close. Nearby, AddyDay covers her mouth while Elena tries not to smile at Cordero kissing me. I realize I don't have to figure out a way to feel comfortable around her anymore. She stood beside Dad when he faced murder accusations and made herself part of the family without my help.

Cordero moves away to let Dad hug me, clearing his face of all emotion except self-respect, like he's worthy of kissing anyone who wants to kiss him back. Like he has no time for people who want to treat him as just another gang member. He's never had time for them.

"Cordero," Dad says, addressing him with a nod.

"Mr. Jefferson." In spite of the continuing drama just a few yards away from us, Cordero turns back to me. "I should get to Marissa. She's my ride home."

Dad shakes his head. "Why don't you catch a ride back to Verona with us instead?"

Dad acts like his offer is no big deal, but Elena and my friends are amazed. Cordero hesitates, maybe sensing a trap. But I know better. Taking sides and refusing to compromise has made Dad lose too much already. The other growers—spread throughout the crowd, hugging union members and family—seem to feel the same way. For the first time, I sense a hope for negotiation regarding the wage increase and an end to the peach strike.

"There's plenty of room in our car," I assure Cordero. "Why don't you come?"

He relaxes into a smile, sharing a look with me. "Sure."

Elena and AddyDay beam at each other. Dad puts his arm around my shoulders. I realize Dad is proud of me for talking so easily with Cordero. I think he's wanted me to be confident around others for a long time. He's happy for me.

After police assure us they can get more details later, the five of us leave for the car, with Dad and Cordero on either side of me. Strangers, growers, classmates—dozens of people stop to thank Cordero and me. They cheer for us. Some of them, like Mayor Knockwurst, specifically assure us that Cordero won't be forgotten, no matter his background. I sneak a final glance behind me at Rick's bowed head and think of Carrie. She did it. She fought for a cause she believed in and brought a killer to justice, losing her life in the process. I wasn't the strong one and neither was she.

We were both strong.

Author's Note

According to the Journal of Adolescent Health, 400,000 teens will join a gang every single year. These youth are disproportionately male, black or Hispanic, from single-parent households, and from families living below the poverty level or already affiliated with a gang. The public has been led to believe that once someone joins a gang, that person cannot leave the gang, which is patently false. The truth is that nearly 400,000 teens leave a gang every year, almost as many as join. Gangs have to recruit constantly. They promise the good life. They do not deliver. Approximately one in four juvenile gang members will live in a correctional facility by the time they are eighteen years old. Gang members are significantly more likely than the general population to become victims of violent crime, including murder. Please reach out with kindness to anyone trying to leave a gang. If you or someone you know is at risk of joining or staying with a gang, please visit www. nationalgangcenter.gov. A better life is out there.

Discussion Questions

1. After Carrie dies, Salem feels like she has no social identity. Why is it important for teens to have their own identity? Do adults understand this?

2. Carrie believed her concern for the union and farm workers made her choice to get involved with a gang "right." Do you agree? How far is too far when you think your government supports repression?

3. Cordero doesn't report a crime he witnessed because, like some people involved in the #BlackLivesMatter movement, he believes the American justice system will be unfair to him. Is this a belief you feel you understand? What advice would you give to someone who believes this?

4. AddyDay suffers from emotional bullying. It's easy to blame Jeremy for this, but most of the students in the school also hold some responsibility, even Salem. What can we do for the AddyDay's in our life? Do you think you always know who they are?

5. Salem and her dad have a strained relationship. Do you think this is because their personalities are very different or too similar?

6. Salem distrusts Cordero the moment she becomes aware of his ethnicity and affiliation with a gang. Does that make her prejudiced? How can we avoid someone who seems dangerous while still accepting and loving those who are different?

7. Crop-pickers want more pay. Growers want more profits. People who eat—like you and me—want cheap food. This fight for resources has left our country with racial, illegal-immigration and poverty issues that often breed crime and gangs. Are these problems that can be solved? How do you grow up as a laborer, a grower, or even an eater, and keep from mistrusting the other "sides?"

Acknowledgments

Publishing a book is more journey than event. As a debut author, I owe huge debts of gratitude the many hands who support this work, some for more than a decade.

First, a tremendous thanks to my editor, Hali Bird, for seeing potential in me and to my author liaison Jessica Romrell for feeling my feelings. To the rest of the team at Cedar Fort—Priscilla Chaves, Vikki Downs, Devin, and others—you rock! Quick shout out too to my former agent, Josh Getzler, who doesn't work in YA anymore, but made *Shatter* what it is.

Long before a publishing contract, I had the Wasatch Mountain Fiction Writers—Kathi Oram Peterson, Maureen L. Mills, Dorothy Canada, Char Raddon, Roseann Woodward, Ann Chamberlin, and Brenda Bensch. Kathleen Dougherty, no content editor outshines you. I also want to thank Sarah Beard, Caryn Caldwell, Rebecca Scott, Juliana Ali, Sabine Berlin, Janelle Youngstrom, and Shari Cylinder. Because girl parties.

Eric James Stone, I miss our original B&N writers' group—Spencer Ellsworth, Carlajo Webb, Becca Fitzpatrick, Jade Weedop, Faith Hofer and others. May

Buffy the Vampire Slayer and Caleb Warnock tie us together forever.

Heather Clark is the best best friend and not a bad writing webinar co-host either.

At the beginning of this journey, I was terrified to pipe up on social media circles. J. Scott Savage pushed me to post news about my writing webinars, attended by James Duckett and his many (many) friends. Jenny Proctor and Melanie Jacobson said, yes, I could to host a random dance party at the LDStorymakers Conference and put me on the committee. Nichole Giles and Michael Bacera kept my ideas for the newly reformed Storymakers Tribe sane. All media following I have, I owe the tribe. You are family!

Jolene Perry and Emily Wheeler, you came to the rescue with endorsements for *Shatter*. Thank you. Karen Gifford, I'm proud to have a sister who will always be more famous and attractive than I am. Thanks for lending me The Food Charlatan's media reach.

Hannah Price, Linda Trionfo, Kaylie Walker, Eliza Hinton, KJ, Kimber Young, and Emily Nelson—you were my first readers! Thanks for encouraging me to try for a publisher.

My success in this dream of writing stories ultimately rests with new readers. I'm in awe you would take the time to read something I care so much about. I have a survey at www.nikkitrionfo.com/Shatter for feedback and encouragement. Encouragement fuels the stories burning inside me. I can't thank you enough!

The seed of this story was planted exploring my grandparents' almond orchard, blooming in my early adult years as I studied Spanish, taught English-language-learners and lived for a time in Puerto Rico. Class-tension and culture-duels laced my childhood. *Shatter* let me re-examine with an adult lens the hardened teens I used to crush on, sneer at, and play with. This novel represents both my deepest fears and greatest hope.

Finally, my family celebrates with me even when I feed them frozen sausage croissant biscuits. Mike, bless your heart. Mom, Dad, Eric, Laura, Sandi, Nate—thanks for being interested in my stories back when that constituted charity. And to my little ones who are as excited as I am about venturing into the jungle of art and marketing, I say live your real life and dream your wildest dreams. When one trips you, the other holds your hand.

About the Author

A genuine California girl, Nikki bought snow boots to attend Brigham Young University because she had no idea what a plow was. She went on to teach middle school chemistry and physics to teenagers. When she and her computer-code-writing husband found themselves without kids for several years, she took a writing class to "find something to do." Proving its sense of humor, life sent them five children. She now stays home in Riverton, Utah, corralling the crazy to the tune of hip hop background music.

A committed party girl, Nikki serves as the social coordinator of LDStorymakers Conference and chair of Storymakers Tribe. Her teen murder mystery, *Shatter*, won grand prize in LDStorymakers' First Chapter Contest and first place in LUW's YA Manuscript Category. *Under a*

New York Skyline features four of the hippest, sweetest teen romance novellas evah!

If you want to read more by Nikki, she sends out free short-story romances occasionally, because romance. No explanation needed. Reach out to her on Facebook at Nikki Trionfo or sign up for her newsletter at www.nikkitrionfo. com.

Besides writing, Nikki enjoys throwing parties, playing the piano, attending dance-step classes at the gym, and swapping mom horror stories. If you run into her, she gets down. Truly.

Scan to visit

www.nikkitrionfo.com